STELLA WHITELAW'S
CATS' TALES

A TREASURY

Also by Stella Whitelaw

CAT STORIES
MORE CAT STORIES
TRUE CAT STORIES

STELLA WHITELAW'S
CATS' TALES

A TREASURY

MILDMAY BOOKS

LONDON

Mildmay Books Limited
Glen House
200 Tottenham Court Road
London W1P 9LA

This edition 1987
© Stella Whitelaw

These stories were first published in book form by
Hamlyn Paperbacks and Arrow Books Limited.

Designed and illustrated by Pauline Bayne
Typeset by Input Typesetting Limited, London

Printed in Great-Britain by Redwood Burn Limited,
Trowbridge, Wiltshire

British Library Cataloguing in Publication Data
Whitelaw, Stella
    Stella Whitelaw's cats' tales – a
    treasury.
    I. Title
    823'.914[F]   PR6073.H57/
    ISBN 1–869945–14–X

Contents

The One-Eyed Angel *7*

Splodge and Tab *14*

The Cat that Could Fly *21*

Travels with Inky Packer *32*

This Man is Mine *38*

The Uninvited Guest *44*

The Clown *51*

White Tiger *57*

The Cat from Next Door *63*

Curtain Call *69*

Cat Knievel *77*

Cloud Eight *83*

Black Tom *87*

Independence Brown *96*

An Absolute Bargain *104*

Lucky's Story *112*

Scraps *120*

A Thoroughly Bad Lot *128*

Felis Domesticus Surrentum *135*

Nirvana *156*

The Vanishing Act *159*

The Window-Dresser *167*

Chimneys *175*

The Terrible Three *186*

The Highland Hunter *193*

Flat Cat *199*

Top Cat *208*

Xinia and the Witch *216*

'Splodge and Tab', 'The Uninvited Guest', 'The White Tiger', 'Cat Knievel', 'Cloud Eight', 'Lucky's Story', 'Scraps', 'Nirvana', 'The Highland Hunter', 'Flat Cat' and 'Top Cat' are all true stories. Black Tom was a real cat, so was Inky Packer and both cats in 'A Thoroughly Bad Lot'.

The One-Eyed Angel

There had been a very heavy frost the morning they found Rags, and a bitter wind with a piercing drive came from the east. The windows were thick white with frost rime and Lynne could hardly see out of them. Philip pulled on a sheepskin coat, intending to de-ice the car windows, but on stepping outside almost fell over a small huddled mound.

'Found this on the path,' said Philip, carrying the inert bundle into the kitchen. 'It's half frozen to death.'

Lynne came over with Philip's breakfast mug of coffee. She was only half awake. 'Good heavens,' she said. 'What is it?'

It was, in fact, the ugliest cat they had ever seen, with a face that was a cross between a bear and a seal, and short stubbly fur that resembled a freckled doormat. The cat looked even worse at that moment because he was covered in mud and one eye was closed with blood.

'Probably a hit-and-run casualty,' said Philip. 'The roads were pretty treacherous last night.'

'He must have dragged himself into our garden. He's badly hurt. I'd better take him to the vet's.' She began to bathe the damaged eye with plain warm water. 'He does look a rag-bag. I think I'll call him Rags. Whatever happened to you, poor Rags?'

Rags growled. He didn't know. He couldn't remember a damned thing. His bones ached, his head ached, his eye hurt, he was tired and hungry and he hadn't the slightest idea how he came to be in this rather small kitchen being tended by a slip of a girl with gentle hands and shy face.

He staggered about in a dazed fashion, then took off roughly in the direction of a saucer of warm milk. Lynne watched him closely. The cat did not seem at all right.

'I think he's got concussion,' she said.

Rags drank the warm milk, hardly stopping to breathe. Then, stumbling over his long rope-like tail, he suddenly went to sleep in a heap on the kitchen floor.

'Definitely concussion,' said Lynne, seeing her brother off to work at the door. Shivering as the chill air struck through her thin dressing-gown, she waved goodbye but Philip was not watching. She turned back indoors and viewed the day's routine chores with resignation.

Lynne kept house for her bachelor brother, a kind, vague man who was fifteen years her senior. She had been studying textile design at art school in London when their mother died quite suddenly from a heart attack. Philip had been hopelessly lost and quite unable to cope, muddling along on cold baked beans and putting on damp shirts. So Lynne had come home to look after her big brother. At first it had only been a temporary measure – until he got a suitable housekeeper, Philip reassured her. But two years had gone by and a 'nice, capable woman' had not materialized. And Philip had stopped advertising.

'Now I suppose I've got another lame duck to look after,' said Lynne, stroking the ugly cat behind his ear. He made a low, growling sound. It might have been a purr. Whatever it was, the sound made Lynne feel less alone. 'That's better,' she said.

She took the injured cat regularly to the vet's. The bruises and stiff joints soon healed, but the eye was permanently damaged and never opened properly again. Rags had a very rakish air.

'Can a cat have concussion?' Lynne asked the vet.

'Quite possibly,' said Mr Browning, who was very hygienic and efficient in a white coat. 'If they get hit on the head, the injury is the same as in humans.'

'Sometimes I think Rags has got amnesia,' said Lynne. 'His behaviour seems positively uncatlike. He doesn't seem to remember that he's a cat.'

'Of course he's a cat!' laughed Mr Browning, rubbing the stubbly fur with brisk affection. He hadn't time to go into anything as fanciful as feline amnesia. 'I don't think you need bring Rags again unless you're worried about anything.'

'I'm worried about his amnesia,' said Lynne with a determined thrust of her small chin.

'It'll just take time,' he said, showing them out of the door. 'Next please.'

'I'm sure you don't know you're a cat,' said Lynne to Rags through the wickerwork of the cat basket as she carried him home. 'I've been watching you, and you don't behave like one at all.'

Rags arr-owed his strange miaow. He didn't have a clue what he was. It was very disturbing and puzzled him a lot. Now that he had almost recovered from the accident, he was reasonably sure he was not a lame duck. He often wandered about the garden, jumping off the rockery with his paws splayed out straight in case he was a bird. But the squabbling black crows told him where to get off. It was quite unpleasant.

On either side of Philip's house lived a dog. One was a fat white woolly dog with hair all over its face, who lay on the front doorstep in perpetual exhaustion, his tongue hanging out and panting. On the other side lived a mad mongrel puppy forever chasing its own tail and grinning mischievously.

Rags spent one entire week being the woolly dog, flat out and panting with exhaustion; then the next week being the puppy, chasing his own tail in ever increasing giddy circles.

'Don't be so stupid, Rags,' Lynne scolded him. 'You're not a silly dog so stop acting like one. Come and have some supper. I've done you some lovely minced rabbit.'

'I suppose I've got minced rabbit as well,' said Philip. 'You make more fuss of that cat than you do me.'

'You've got rabbit pie,' said Lynne, hiding a smile. 'Rags only got the scraps.'

'Perhaps he'd like to come and sit at the table,' Philip suggested with a hint of sarcasm.

Rags sat quietly on the window-sill, looking out into the garden with his one eye. If he wasn't a bird, or a dog, or a lame duck, then what was he? He watched the rivulets of rain running down the window-pane and knew instinctively they weren't worth chasing.

'You used to like drawing,' said Philip over supper. 'Why don't you enrol at an evening class? You ought to get out more. Or you could do cooking or needlework . . . there's lots to choose from. You've been looking a bit peaky lately.'

Lynne grasped at Philip's suggestion like a drowning sailor for a straw. 'Yes, I'd like that,' she breathed. 'But not cooking.' She spent the evening hunting out her old brushes and paints. The tubes of oil paint had hardened and were useless. She would have to buy some more. She found some broken charcoal and pastels, and a pad of art paper. She touched the texture of the paper with loving fingertips . . . she could almost feel a picture growing.

How the wind howled for her and the rain cried the first evening Lynne went to her class. The group of aspiring artists gathered round a cage in which there was a gorgeously plumed parrot. He side-stepped on his bar, regarding them doubtfully as they took up their brushes. 'Gertcher,' he remarked gloomily.

Lynne caught his beady look as he peered over his shoulder. It was not textile designing but it was good to feel a brush in her hands again, and to experience that single-minded concentration. Thoughts of food and cleaning vanished.

'Oh, I have enjoyed this evening,' said Lynne, arriving home wind-swept and wet. She carefully unwrapped the ran-spattered polythene sheeting from her picture. 'There you are . . . what do you think of it?'

'Not exactly a Rembrandt,' said Philip, glancing up from his paper. 'Perhaps a touch of the Dali's. Couldn't they afford a real model?'

'It wasn't stuffed!' Lynne protested. 'Look, even Rags can see it's not a stuffed parrot.'

She propped the picture against the wall, and hearing his name mentioned, Rags ambled over to look at it. Perhaps they were telling him what he was – a stuffed parrot. He certainly had a long tail like the parrot and he could look over his shoulder with a beady eye . . . but this creature seemed to be inside a cage thing. Rags scratched his ear and stretched. He began to wander round the house looking for a possible cage thing.

'I don't know what's got into Rags,' said Lynne with some exasperation when Philip came home from work the next day. 'He spent the entire day sitting in my wire vegetable rack with his head crooked over his shoulder.'

'Positively unhygienic,' said Philip.

'Do you think he's paralyzed?' Lynne asked anxiously.

'Probably peckish for an odd carrot to help him see in the dark,' said Philip, tipping the cat into the garden. Rags fled. He was fed up being a parrot. His neck felt permanently out of joint.

Rags strolled through the grass, his long tail thrashing the slender blades. The sky was dark and rolling murkily. Something was going to happen, he knew, his whiskers twitching. Minutes later flakes of white landed coldly on his fur and melted. Rags shook himself free of them and growled. He trod gingerly on the falling snow and hurried towards the lights of the house, but they had closed the curtains and switched on the television and did not hear his howls of indignation.

When Lynne eventually found him, huddled up on the doorstep, Rags was covered in snow. His one eye glared at her . . .

'Oh my goodness,' she laughed. 'What have we got here? A polar bear, to be sure.'

Rags growled at the white flakes on his nose.

'Poor bear,' she said, bundling him up in a warm, sweet-smelling towel. 'I'll give you a lovely rub-down.'

Rags liked the rub-down. Perhaps being a bear would not be so bad. And it was quite fun leaping about in the snow when you got used to wet paws. But he knew nothing about the snow thawing and one morning when he was being a flying bear, he went right through the thin ice on the fish-pond and landed up to his neck in algae. He came indoors and sat on the kitchen floor, eyeing Lynne defiantly and dripping green everywhere.

'I don't care what you think,' said Lynne, tying a plastic apron round her waist. 'But you will have to have a bath.' She tested the water with her elbow and grasped the cat firmly with gloved hands.

Rags thrashed and spat. He did not exactly bite her, but he put up a hell of a good fight. She got soaked. The walls were streaming, the floor became a skating rink. As fast as Rags scrambled out of the sink, so Lynne put him back in. His wet fur clung to his skinny body and he looked worse than a drowned rat . . .

'Okay, time's up,' said Lynne, drying him briskly on her lap. She flicked strands of wet hair out of her eyes. 'At least you smell better now.'

While Lynne was mopping up the kitchen floor, Rags stalked into the sitting-room to lick down his disarranged fur. He sat in front of the flickering television, seething with rage and not talking to anyone.

The matinée film was starting. On the small screen appeared the head of a magnificent animal, a wonderful mane of golden hair falling to its shoulders, its powerful jaws yawning . . .

It roared, and Rags jumped back. The lion roared again, and Rags was transfixed with adoration. He had never seen anything so superior and awe-inspiring. A small growl began in his own throat, growing, gathering volume until it became a miniature roar.

'Oh dear, I have upset him,' said Lynne, still on her knees in the kitchen. She had planned to have the film on while she did the ironing. It made the task less boring.

Rags practised his roar for several days, then he took to sitting on top of the television set, roaring in all directions. He looked happier than he'd ever looked before.

'Can't you shut that cat up?' said Philip. 'I want to watch Panorama, and I can't hear a damned word with that cat bellowing all the time.'

'He thinks he's the MGM lion,' said Lynne, who was quite quick on the uptake. 'Don't disillusion him . . .'

Rags eventually settled down into being a kind of parroty bear with lion overtones. Occasionally he lapsed into chasing his own tail or leaping off the rockery. He decided not to worry about his identity any more.

There came overnight a blessed change in the weather, and a south-west wind warmed the rain clouds. Before you could say cuckoo, the birds were all madly building nests and gardeners got their annual dose of planting fever. In no time at all it was the summer flower show, and the organizer, Mrs Weston, was charming everyone into taking part.

'You will enter something, won't you?' she said, stopping Lynne outside the shops. Mrs Weston was a bustling and energetic widow, with a sweet, winsome smile that made it difficult to refuse.

'Well, all right,' said Lynne reluctantly. 'But I don't grow anything special, and my jams never set.'

'I'm sure you'll find something,' Mrs Weston smiled. 'It's taking part that's important, not whether you'll win a prize. Here's an entrance form. I look forward to seeing you on Saturday, my dear.'

Lynne read down the list of classes: roses, sweet peas, dahlias, preserves, vegetables, dried flowers, miniature arrangements, handicrafts . . . There was nothing she could really enter. Then she saw the last class in the children's section: the best-loved family pet. There was no alternative. She would have to enter Rags.

Rags did not take kindly to being put into his wicker basket on a hot Saturday afternoon and carried to a fenced-off area of the crowded park. Lynne stood in a line with the small owners of the white woolly dog, and the parrot, and various rabbits and hamsters.

'You're a bit old,' said the organizer dubiously. It was Mr Browning, the vet, who did not quite recognize her.

'It's my little brother's,' said Lynne. 'He's too shy to come.' Rags roared noisily in agreement.

'Well, I dunno . . .' said Mr Browning. 'I'll have to ask Mrs Weston.'

Mrs Weston did not mind bending the rules a little bit, just so long as everyone came. And of course, Rags won first prize. After all, who could resist a one-eyed cat with fur like a doormat who thought he was the MGM lion? There was much youthful waving and cheering, and Rags was presented with a yellow rosette.

Lynne hurried home to get Philip's tea. There would be time to make some scones and some rock cakes. She was washing lettuce and radishes when someone stepped lightly down the garden path and rang the doorbell.

'I'll answer it,' said Philip, coming in from the garden.

'You forgot your cat's rosette,' said Mrs Weston. 'For the best-loved family pet.' She held out the ribbon.

'Oh?' said Philip.

'And are you Lynne's little brother? The one that is so shy?' asked Mrs Weston, with the suspicion of a twinkle in her very pretty blue eyes. Philip stared down at her.

'I beg your pardon?' he said.

Rags finished his celebration supper of chopped liver and then chewed thoughtfully on his yellow rosette. The best-loved family pet. Was that what he really was? What a mouthful . . .

Rags had almost got used to the idea, when one rustling and fragrant autumnal day Philip came home and took Lynne gently aside. 'I've got something serious to tell you,' he said, his kind face looked troubled. Lynne stopped laying the supper table.

A little while later, without even having his supper, Philip went out, and whatever it was he had told his sister, Lynne looked far from troubled. She came dancing into the kitchen and scooped Rags joyfully up into her arms.

'He's going to marry Angela Weston,' she sang happily, her eyes bright and sparkling. 'She's only two years older than him and they've fallen in love! Oh Rags, isn't that marvellous. Now I can go back to art school and start living my life again . . .'

She gave the cat a big, contented hug. 'And it's all thanks to you,' she smiled. 'Rags, you're an angel!'

Rags licked her chin and began to purr. An angel . . . Yes, he'd settle for that. It suited him.

Splodge and Tab

The strongly marked grey and black tabby was the wildest cat for miles around. No one could catch him or touch him. He prowled the neat Surrey gardens as if remembering the days when it was a primeval forest and ferals roamed in packs; or perhaps his ancestral memory went back to the century when huntsmen flew along the ridge of the North Downs led by their cruel king, a heavy man whipping his steaming horse.

Battles had been fought where there are now leafy suburban gardens, and a medieval cannon-ball had been unearthed near where the tabby sat, so still, like a statue, watching the family going about its tidy, methodical ways.

He did not know if he envied them, but something drew him to the family. It was more than curiosity. He was not starving. There were mice enough on the farm where he hung out. He needed this family but he was not sure why.

They tried to approach him but immediately his upper lip curled back in a ferocious snarl, a deep hiss coming from his throat. Then he was off like an arrow into the safety of the bushes. He watched from his hiding place as they searched for him, making soothing noises.

'Puss, puss, puss. Where are you?'

He stayed hidden. Eventually they gave up and went back indoors, but the woman returned with a saucer of milk, which she put down. He did not touch it.

She did not give up easily. She gave him a name.

'Tab, Tab, Tab,' she called now. But he made no move towards her. He came and sat and watched. If anyone came too near, he hissed, fangs bared.

She began to leave food. He had never smelt anything like it before. He could feel his resistance slipping as his salivary glands began to work and his stomach churned. How did she find such delicious food? There was none of it around the farm, only mice, dormice and moles. Sometimes he caught a squirrel, but their fur was so rough and harsh in his mouth. Once he had chased and pounced on a rabbit in the field behind the church . . . now that had been a feast. Perhaps this woman had been into the field chasing a rabbit . . .

He waited until she returned indoors, shutting the back door. She was watching from the kitchen window so he did not move. It was hours before he crept forward in the growing darkness and tentatively sniffed at the new food. It was good. He gulped it down and fled.

'Tab, here's your supper.'

She was there again the next evening with a saucer of food. It was not fair. Tab could not resist. But he did wait until all the humans had disappeared before he ate. This food was so much nicer than mice and so much easier to get. A plan formed in his mind.

One day he came to sit in the garden and watch, and he was not alone. He had brought another feral with him, a small black cat. She was a thin creature but her stomach was swollen with pregnancy.

It is thought that ferals always fight over food, but Tab allowed the black cat to feed first from the dish that had been left out. Then he finished off the remains. The female cat was too heavy to hunt now. Someone had to take care of her, so he had brought her to the family.

'Do you think it's his mate, or his sister?' they whispered. 'She's as wild as he is.'

'Perhaps they are just good friends.'

'I'll find a box and put it outside in the covered way. It's getting cold at nights,' said the woman. 'She may have her kittens here.'

Titch produced four kittens in the box . . . two grey, one black and a tabby. Tab grew more handsome in appearance despite his ragged cauliflower ear. The black markings were dense on his brown ground coat, the rings narrow and numerous; and his round face was fiercely protective. But he was affectionate towards the kittens and could be seen washing them occasionally.

Titch was a good mother, though she was even wilder than Tab. She reared her kittens well. But the road was a hazard she did not understand. As her kittens grew more independent she often left them to escape to the fields. It meant crossing the road. One day she did not make it.

Tab remained, thrown by the death of the female feral. He stood guardian over the kittens, disturbed to find that they were also disappearing from the box. They were being found good homes, civilized homes in houses with doors and windows and rules for cats. He did not know whether this was a good thing; it was not something he wanted for himself. He wanted freedom and life in the wild. But other cats seemed to like it and even thrived on domesticity. He had seen them cleaning their paws on doorsteps in the sunshine.

One of the grey kittens was a pretty long-haired fluffy creature with a fawn splodge on the side of its neck. The woman seemed to favour this kitten, picking it up and talking to it.

'Come along, Splodge,' she said. 'You're going to live with us. I think you'll like it.'

The kitten was quite happy with the idea. She liked the woman and the family of four children, and she took to living in the house with a natural grace.

Tab wandered back to the fields around the farm and thought about this new development. Would the woman still put out those delicious saucers of food now that she had her own cat? Perhaps he would be back to catching mice and more mice. He roamed the North Downs wondering if the woman was catching rabbits for the grey kitten.

But he could not keep away. He came back and sat in their garden to watch the strange business of training the kitten. It required a lot of putting out and bringing in, and calling.

'Splodge, Splodge, Splodge . . . kitty, kitty, kitty.'

The woman pretended not to notice Tab though she was well aware that the feral was watching, almost camouflaged by the leafy shadows and ferns sprouting from the next door rockery. She was teaching the kitten to dig in the soft dry earth. Splodge was wriggling and rolling over in the dust on the garden path.

As they went indoors together, the woman looked over her shoulder, directly to where Tab sat immobile in the shadows.

'Hello, Tab,' she said. 'I'll put your supper out in a minute.'

He snarled and hissed though she was nowhere near him.

No one knew that Tab's eyesight was not as good as it used to be. He thought perhaps the world had gone hazy and that it was an atmospheric change due to the weather. He had always been able to roam and climb as vigorously and fearlessly as any feral; nothing was too high or too difficult.

There was a willow tree in the next door garden. He had climbed it many times. Sometimes he had climbed to the topmost branches so that he could see into the upper windows, watching the family at their curious activities.

This day he climbed to the top of the willow, leaping with ease from branch to branch, scattering the twittery birds and hovering bumblebees with a lash of his tail. Perhaps today they would be gardening or washing the car; or the boys would be kicking a football around in some game in which he longed to join.

As he watched, he slowly noticed that this atmospheric change in the weather which was affecting his eyes seemed much worse today. He could hardly see what was going on below. Then he realized that he could not see the other branches of the tree either; that it was all a confused pattern of changing shapes and shadows that bore no relation to the tree which he had climbed.

He waited, hoping that the mist would clear. He sent silent distress signals into the air waves. But who would hear him? He had no friends.

Splodge was by now almost fully grown, a beautiful cat with a long silky grey and fawn coat and big amber eyes. She summed up the situation at once, and climbed the tree with the agility of youth. She came to within a few feet of the feral cat and miaowed.

Tab turned his head towards the noise. He vaguely saw the young cat, recognized its smell. It was one of those kittens, the one that went to live in the house. He had observed its antics as it was put out and called in. But it was the kitten of the black feral and therefore not alien.

Splodge miaowed again and moved along the branch so that the long swaying leaves made a noise. Tab realized that here was an opportunity to descend, even if only to one branch lower. He jumped.

The family watched from a window. They were amazed, calling to each other to come and watch.

'Just look at this. Splodge is helping old Tab get down the tree. I've never seen anything like it. Look, she's actually guiding him . . .'

It was true. Branch by branch, with infinite patience, the young cat was showing the feral where to jump, guiding him down a safe route through the swaying and rustling tree. Splodge jumped to the ground and looked back. Tab followed, feeling the earth beneath his paws with a wave of relief. The two cats looked at each other, and then with one bound Tab disappeared into the bushes and ran home to the farm.

The family made a great fuss of Splodge,' with much stroking and patting and a saucer of cream from the top of the milk. She was a heroine.

'Clever Splodge. Well done, Splodge.'

'Old Tab didn't seem very grateful.'

'How can you tell if a cat is grateful?'

They wondered if Tab would now seek different pastures, but after a few days he turned up again. Still watching and waiting and eating whatever was left out for him when everyone had gone.

If there was a rapport between the two cats, it was unspoken. There was no obvious comradeship. But there was a degree of communication indiscernible to humans.

The woman was quietly ironing one afternoon by the window that looked onto the back garden. There was no one else about and she was making very little noise. Through the glass serving partition into the kitchen, she had a good view of the back door.

Splodge came in through the open door, hesitated and looked back. To her amazement, the woman then saw the striped front paws and flat nose of the wild feral. He peered into the kitchen as if into another world.

She expected him to immediately turn tail and race back into the garden, but Tab's long white whiskers were twitching with all the new smells, and curiosity overcame his fear. Splodge moved a few paces over the polished lino and looked back again. Tab followed slowly until the whole length of his body was over the step. But that was as far as he was going.

The woman held her breath. Splodge had achieved the introduction where they had all failed. The wild cat was actually in the kitchen.

Tab looked around with wide-eyed wonder at all the strange things – cupboards and kettles, sinks and saucepans. He had never seen such objects and had no idea what people wanted them for.

Splodge moved a few more steps and looked back as if to say, 'come on'. Tab followed Splodge into the sitting room, amazed by the softness of the carpet under his paws and the warmth from the fire. He saw the woman outlined against the window, but it was as if she was just another object. He was walking through a wonderland, treading carefully, unsure of everything, tense, but following Splodge like an open-mouthed tourist through a palace.

Splodge took Tab on a complete tour of the house. They went upstairs, into every bedroom, even the bathroom. There was not one nook or cranny that Tab did not peer into. It was the most amazing adventure of his life. He could not believe all that he saw.

But it was also quite overwhelming. There was so much that he did not understand, so many things that puzzled him. He looked at Splodge regretfully. This could never be his world. His life was the open fields, the wild and wet woods, the stream that threaded through the gardens, and the echoing barns around the farm. He could not stand four walls.

He finished the tour politely enough. No panic or mad rush to escape outside. He left as quietly as he had entered. Splodge sat down and began to wash her long pinky-tinged fur. She had done her best. She had been a good hostess, shown the visitor around, and when he wanted to leave, she had let him go.

The woman was speechless. She had never seen anything quite so moving between two animals . . . first the intelligent rescue from the tree, and now the guided tour of the house.

She held the beautiful, purring grey cat in her arms, thinking how strange it was that in a world full of bitter fighting and global tragedies, two cats, one wild and one domestic, could actually show some concern for the other.

Then Splodge disappeared. At first they thought that she was just being wilful and staying out all night. But night turned into the next day and she did not appear. Day one grew into day two and the woman was sick with worry. There was a busy blind junction at the end of the road and she remembered little Titch. A stream of lorries came from the chalk pits that were being dug out of the North Downs. And not far away, behind an embankment, the new motorway thundered with vehicles day and night.

Days turned into weeks, then a month. Tab still came to their garden. He saw their distress, but how could he tell them anything? He was only a cat. He was powerless. He could not take the place of Splodge. He could only try with his continuing presence to give them some comfort, little as it was.

The woman continued to put out food for Tab in the cold and frosty December days.

'Here you are, Tab,' she called out, but her voice was without joy.

It was five weeks since Splodge had disappeared and it was Christmas Eve. Although they had searched around and asked neighbours and given the police a description, there was no news and they had given up hope. They could only cross their fingers that death had been kind and that she had not been stolen for her beautifully coloured coat.

School had broken up and the younger son was in the kitchen. He was looking out of the window, thinking of what he had yet to do for Christmas, when a grey shadow crossed his vision. A cat was strolling nonchalantly up the garden path, its long tail sweeping the stones.

'Mum, Mum,' he called out. 'Come here! There's Splodge, I'm sure. She's coming up the garden.'

The woman had never taken the stairs so quickly. She flew down them, her heart in her mouth. Could it be . . . could it be their Splodge, or was it just some other cat that looked like her in the gathering gloom?

Her son opened the kitchen door and the grey cat sauntered in, slightly overdoing the casual act. She went over to her chair, jumped up onto it and sat down as if nothing had happened.

It was Splodge, thinner, a little bedraggled, her lovely grey and fawn fur dirty and tangled; but it was the best Christmas present the family had ever had.

Tab sat outside in the garden, the frosty stars bright in the December sky. He had watched the cameo of the return and was satisfied that the family were reunited.

Only Splodge and Tab knew where the grey cat had been all that time. Perhaps Tab had taken Splodge on a tour of his world, through the acres of fields and woods. Perhaps Splodge had felt the stirring of her ancestors' blood and tasted the delights of freedom. Perhaps she had forgotten about the family in the heady joy of running wild.

It may have been the cold that drove her back to her chair and the fireside. The diet of mice could have palled and become hard to find. Perhaps she longed for a dish of chicken or liver.

Or perhaps Tab had brought her back. No one knows and no one would ever know.

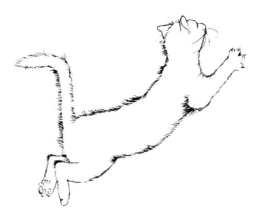

The Cat that Could Fly

It began on a curiously still morning when not a leaf stirred and even the butterflies seemed to hover over the flowers without moving. The dead elm stretched its ashen branches skywards waiting for the chop that was a long time in coming. A mile up, a chartered TriStar ferried yawning early-starters to a package holiday on Majorca, its gentle hum followed by vapour trails in the sky.

Leopold trod the dew-hung clover with delicate paws. He was a big ginger and white cat with a wide, surprised face and fluffed cheeks. His eyes were very green and brilliant, which added to his startled look. He lived an uncomplicated life: he ate and slept; he caught the occasional bird or shrew just to keep his hand in.

The family that he lived with were what Leopold called sleek. They had everything – two cars, two colour television sets, a video recorder, wall-to-wall stereos, a deep-freeze that could take a whale, every domestic appliance on the market – and yet they were as mean as a cross-eyed snake. They bought him unbranded cat food, a mish-mash of wet cereal and unmentionable animal parts; he never got a taste of fresh liver or fish. They drank the cheapest coffee, bought broken biscuits, and cut all the tenpence-off coupons out of the paper. They were sleek all right.

They were sleek on affection too. If Leopold jumped onto a vacant lap, he was hastily brushed off.

'Gerroff my suit! I don't want your hairs all over me. Shoo. Shoo,' said the sleek man impatiently.

The sleek woman was as bad. Her clothes were also uncatable. The one person who liked Leopold was the daughter, Dana, but she was preoccupied with exams and boy-friends, and the only time Leopold saw her was when she came in late from a disco and they shared the cosy quietness of a 2 a.m. kitchen.

As Leopold took his early-morning stroll down the garden, he heard a faint chirp-chirp. The sound made his stomach contract. He was hungry. Last night's supper was best forgotten, and they would not give him breakfast until he had been outside for at least an hour. Leopold did not understand these rules. It was another of their odd ways. He noticed that they ate broken biscuits whenever they felt like it.

Leopold crept up on the sound. It was a baby thrush, softly speckled brown and white, a big fluffy helpless creature, looking straight at Leopold with bright, trusting eyes. It staggered a few inches and fell forward onto its plump breast. Leopold's surprised expression sharpened with delight. This was obviously some sort of game. He patted the soft feathers with a tentative paw. The bird chirped encouragingly and hopped another few inches. A few trees away, the mother bird heard her baby's call but was not alarmed. It had to learn to fly by itself.

Suddenly Leopold pounced. The baby's neck hung limp between his jaws. Leopold growled, a low rumbling jungle sound echoing back from his wild ancestors. He paraded his victim, the feathers stuck out round his mouth like an air force moustache. He crunched the tiny body thoughtfully, getting blood on the short white fur under his nose.

The mother bird went crazy. She flew from branch to branch in distress. She swooped over the ginger cat and what was left of her baby, her cries loud and distraught. But it was too late. There was nothing she could do. She took one last look at the big cat and flew blindly into the empty air, not caring where she went.

There was a great oak which Leopold liked to climb. He never went very far because he knew his limits. But today the baby bird lay heavily on his stomach, and Leopold climbed higher, hoping to leave the uncomfortable feeling behind. The thick tangled branches gave no hint of how high he was climbing. He went on, up and up, leaping from one claw-hold to the next. Because there was no wind, the branches barely moved, again giving Leopold an unfounded sense of security. When a broken branch revealed a glimpse of the land below, Leopold was quite amazed. He could see the tops of other trees, padded with green like cushions beneath him. The garden of his house was a smudge of blurred colours. In the distance was the church spire, almost eye-level. A helicopter whirled into sight, coming straight towards the oak, its rotor blades clattering discordantly.

Leopold leaped back. He forgot he was on a branch, up a tree. He took off backwards, falling head between heels, somersaulting through a cascade of leaves and broken twigs, the wind rushing through his whiskers, flashes of sky and earth alternating as he hurtled towards the ground.

He spread his paws helplessly in a gesture of supplication to the great cat god in the sky. He closed his eyes tightly. He did not want to see what was coming to him.

Leopold first became aware of a change when the swift rushing wind in his ears slowed to the merest whisper. He was still falling, but no longer that shattering, pummelling plunge earthwards. He seemed to be drifting. Perhaps he had died.

He opened one eye the merest slit. He saw the Japanese maple, a beech hedge and, below him, a bed of button dahlias, prim and tight-headed. He landed right in the middle of the flowers and shook himself.

'Gerroff my dahlias!' the sleek woman yelled from a bedroom window.

Leopold extracted himself from the damaged flowers with dignity and walked away, a curled yellow petal behind one ear like a Hawaiian hula dancer. He had too much to think about to be worried by appearances.

After breakfast he sat looking at the oak tree. It did look very high. What had happened to him? How could he have fallen all that way and survived? He knew that cats could fall from the roof of a house and land unhurt on four paws, but that tree was at least three houses high, or so it seemed to Leopold. Eventually he wandered into the wood, to the far end where it was secluded and the blackened stump of a tree struck by lightning stood lonely and unloved.

He climbed the black stump, sniffing the lingering smell of sulphur. He sat in the fork and looked down on the carpet of pine-needles below. It was about eight feet high. He could either scramble down the charred bark, or he could jump.

He jumped. He expected to land on the bed of needles in about one and a half seconds flat. But strangely he seemed to float. It took four seconds to land. It was puzzling.

He thought about it for a time, then decided to climb the stump again. He jumped off from the fork. This time it took six seconds and he landed some yards away on dry bracken.

Leopold was beginning to enjoy himself. After all, what harm was there if he wanted to spend the afternoon jumping off an old tree? What the hell! He climbed again, rapidly, like a red arrow. He jumped again, quite merrily, paws spread, wondering where he would land.

Suddenly he saw a clump of nettles right below him. Despite his thick fur, he knew all about nettles. His pink nose was particularly vulnerable. He stretched wide his paws in horror and sailed over the top of the clump. Without thinking, he lifted both his right legs and wheeled away in a shallow curve towards an open patch of ground.

When he returned that evening, the family scolded him and said he was too late for supper! They sat round the television, dunking broken biscuits into watery coffee. Leopold licked at the dried bits still stuck on his breakfast saucer. His drinking-bowl had not been changed and the water was practically growing algae. He jumped on the draining-board and stretched his neck towards a dripping tap.

'Gerroff the draining-board, you wicked cat,' the woman shouted. Leopold obligingly removed himself. For a split second, as he jumped, he almost spread his paws but an inner caution stopped him, and he landed awkwardly, unbalanced.

'Now don't do that again! I won't allow it.'

He sat on the front steps in the dark until Dana came home from her date. She was sniffing into a twisted scrap of handkerchief and her mascara had run into panda smudges. She made herself a mug of milky cocoa and poured a large saucerful for Leopold. She knew where her father kept a hidden packet of chocolate biscuits and she helped herself, spreading out the remainder so that he would not notice the difference.

'Of course, I can never tell them about Roger,' she said to the cat, stroking his ears. 'They wouldn't understand about him not having any money, or a job. They'd never understand.'

Leopold daintily mopped up the fallen crumbs. No, they would never understand. The next morning, he was at the door, waiting to be let out, and streaked through the moment there was a crack. He spent all day practising, graduating from tree to taller tree. It was exhilarating. By mid-afternoon, he acknowledged what he had been wondering about ever since his miraculous escape from the big oak.

It was not simply this new skill which filled him with joy and excitement, but the fact that it held the key to something far more important – escape. He walked back to the house quite jauntily, not caring that his supper would not make up for missing breakfast.

'Caught yourself a little mouse for breakfast, did you?' asked the sleek woman, scraping the last globule of mush from the tin. 'There's a good pussy.'

Good pussy swallowed the revolting food. It was important now to keep up his strength. When he saw the family go out for the evening, he climbed onto the roof of the house, skirting the television aerial and leaping up onto the flat top of the chimney. He sat there for a long time, his tail neatly curled over his feet. It was not that he lacked courage; it was just that this was the first time he had contemplated jumping from anything other than a tree. And it might be that trees were a vital ingredient . . . However, he would never find out just by sitting.

He stepped off into space, automatically widening his paws, claws outstretched, tail stiffened, lifting his head. These movements slowed his free fall, then he leaned carefully into a wide arc, his brilliant eyes almost crossed with concentration. He glided across their garden, past the dahlias, rising over the hedge, then soaring up as he came face to face with an overgrown rhododendron bush. The evening air was cool and peaceful as he locked into a pure, straight, calculated climb, his whiskers twitching as the wind resistance began to increase. He winked as he passed two alarmed starlings flying home to roost. As he topped the climb, he closed in his paws, tucked his head down and streamlined his descent onto the flat roof of a neighbour's garage. Shaking with relief, he sat down and began to lick back his ruffled fur. He had done it. He did not need a tree.

After that, there was no stopping Leopold. He jumped off anything and everything. His greatest day was when he managed to climb into the church belfry and then up the narrow ladder that was steel-pinned to the side of the spire. There was precious little room at the top for him and the weather-vane. The dim metal cock spun round, creaking, obviously out of control, almost knocking Leopold off his perch. Leopold took off in a perfect swallow-dive, levelling out at about a hundred feet without any effort. The thermals of air took him up higher and he gloried in the feeling of space and freedom. Below, the neat rows of houses and gardens stretched for miles. Dark green patches of woodland were all that was left of the great forests which had once covered the hills. He flew over the top of the ugly grey gasometer, tracking for fun the snake-like train that swayed along the line. People were so small, wobbling along on matchstick legs, heads down, wrapped up in their worries and dreams. No one noticed a large ginger and white cat flying casually overhead.

He began to get more adventurous, exploring the countryside and neighbouring towns. He followed the River Thames to London, but did not stay long among the high-rise flats and skyscraper office-blocks. The air traffic bothered him and the pigeons were rude.

'I've just seen a cat fly by,' said a stunned window-cleaner in a cradle at the twenty-first floor of an office building.

'Fell out a winder,' said his pal morosely, wiping a dark mirrored pane of glass. 'Probably pushed.'

'It was flying. It was a ginger cat.'

'We gotta little tabby. Company for the missus.'

The window-cleaner screwed up his eyes against the sun. Whatever it was was almost out of sight, skimming over the top of St Paul's dome and the cross sparkling in the bright rays. Perhaps it was a ginger bird. He clamped his mouth shut and turned back to his work. He did not want to get his cards.

Of course, Leopold could not keep his secret forever. He began to get careless. The family gave a party with watered gin and cut-price whisky to celebrate the sleek man's latest promotion. As they cleared up, Leopold slid among the chairs looking for morsels of cocktail snacks. If they were anything like the general standard of catering in the house, most of the guests would have dropped them. He found a pathetic shrimp on a soggy toast finger stuffed behind a pot plant. It wasn't bad. The cheese they had used had been so stale and crumbly, it had parted company from the cubes of pineapple and there were lots of bits on the floor.

The sleek woman had also lashed out on a dip made from dried chicken soup and tinned cream. Not many people had dipped, so there was a lot left. As she was scraping it all together and wondering if she could turn it back into soup, a big dollop slopped off her finger and fell onto the carpet. Leopold raced to the rescue.

'Gerrout the way! You damned cat! Look what you've made me do,' she stormed. She swiped at him with her morocco-bound visitors' book. (Someone had written: 'Unbelievable party, darling.')

The book caught Leopold hard on the side of his head. Swift as a flash he spread his paws and leaped to the safety of the pelmet. The woman was furious and did not notice anything unusual about the ascent. She lashed out at him again and he took off, flying right across the room to a shelf on the other side.

'You wicked thing,' she shrieked, wondering if she had not watered the gin enough.

'Mummy,' said Dana, opening the French doors to let out the smoke-laden air. 'I think Leopold can fly.'

Leopold soared out into the night air. He shared a gnarled oak with an old owl and contemplated the future. They knew now. Perhaps it would not matter. After all, what could it possibly mean to them? Habit was hard to break, and at breakfast-time Leopold nodded to the sleepy owl and took off for home. He flew down into the garden and sauntered up to the back door, casually twitching his tail.

'Darling,' cooed the woman, scooping him into her arms. 'Darling Leopold, you've come back to mummikins! Nice pussy, come and have some lovely milk.'

Leopold was thoroughly alarmed, squashed against her second-best jumper with the sequin buttons. She smelled of musk and face-cream. He struggled, but she was holding him very tightly. He heard the back door shut and it was the thud of doom.

They sold him to a circus. As he was being driven away in the back of the circus owner's Cortina estate, the sleek family were hugging each other with glee, waving the fat cheque and planning to buy more cars, more televisions and a holiday in the Bahamas.

Leopold quite liked the circus for about two days. They put him in a large cage that smelt of bear, and people came and looked at him, bringing delicious things like fish and chips, beefburgers and anchovy pizzas.

Then the circus owner put him on the scales and declared a diet. Leopold must not gain a single ounce. Aerodynamics, he called it.

Leopold did not understand the circus. It was so bright and noisy, with strange animals growling in the night. They did feed him better food than he was used to, though he suspected it was left over from the lion's share.

The trouble started when Miss Dora, the trapeze artiste, refused to carry Leopold up the ladder to her platform high in the roof of the big tent. She absolutely refused even to touch him.

'I shall come out in a rash all over,' she said, every rhinestone on her brief costume quivering with indignation.

The circus hands rigged up a basket affair in which to hoist Leopold up to the platform. Leopold hated it. He felt sick as it swayed and jerked higher and higher up into the dim black regions of the roof. He stepped out onto the narrow platform and looked round politely. It was very high up indeed. Miss Dora stood as far away from him as possible.

'Shoo, shoo,' she said, her feathered headdress nodding with each word. 'Go away.'

Someone switched on a spotlight, blinding Leopold. He stepped sideways to avoid the brilliant white light, and disorientated, he fell off the platform. He fell, paralyzed with fear, like a stone, and landed with a bounce in the safety net, all four paws and his head stuck through the mesh; it was very undignified.

'Now, Leopold,' said the circus owner, speaking slowly and deliberately. 'When you get up there on the platform I want you to fly across to the other platform.' Leopold looked back at him with puzzled green eyes. 'Fly across, like Miss Dora. Only you're a clever pussy and you don't need a trapeze bar.'

Miss Dora scowled. 'I don't like sharing my act with a cat. It's ignominious.'

Again Leopold was put into the elevator and swung up to the platform. Again he fell into the net. The sweat began to come out on the owner's brow. He had gambled a fortune.

This time Leopold rolled over and got into such a mess in the netting they had to cut it to get him out. He tried not to look smug as he was returned to his cage.

'Please, pussy,' said the circus owner the next day, wringing his hands. 'Fly for me. I gotta lotta money tied up in you. You wouldn't want to see old Joss go bankrupt, would you?'

Miss Dora had covered her body thickly with an anti-bite ointment in order to protect herself from Leopold's deadly rash. The smell was awful. He couldn't stand it for two seconds. He launched himself off the platform at speed, did two fast circuits of the arena, then spotting the exit sign, made a bee-line for the opening. He dipped stylishly over the big top before heading off towards the far country. He felt the faintest twinges in his paws as he climbed higher in the sky. He had never reached this altitude before. His tail streamed out behind him, his fur filled with air, and the loose flaps of skin under his armpits belled out like a parachute.

Leopold was looking for the sea. He had had in mind for some time to learn to fly properly. He was a bit afraid of going to the mountains to find an eagle or a condor. They were so big and unpredictable. But seagulls, now they were a different kettle of fish. And there was no doubt about it, they could fly. Leopold's role would be that of ardent observer.

He was quite surprised when he eventually found the sea. It was not at all as he had expected, just miles and miles of heaving wet blue waste. But the seagulls were there in their thousands, screeching and diving and squabbling among themselves. Leopold particularly admired their precision take-offs and landings on water.

He went down onto the pebble beach to practise a few low level take-offs, but each time he nose-dived straight into the sea. It was horrid, and he soon discovered that he could not fly very well if his fur was wet.

'Scram, scram,' shrieked the seagulls as Leopold went headlong into the waves yet again. He gathered his dignity round him like a wet bathrobe and climbed into the heather to dry off.

When he found the cliffs, he knew he had the answer. Their sheer height was impressive; the grandeur of the craggy rock-face filled Leopold with quivering pride. This was going to be his home. He was going to be a cliff catperson; he saw himself leaping about the rock-face as sure-footed as Tarzan, catching his food among the gorse on the headland, sleeping in a small cave. He could watch the seagulls all day and learn their secrets. He would practise diligently from his cliff-top, experimenting, adapting their flight to his. It was going to be wonderful.

The seagulls were a bit alarmed by this peculiar flying ginger thing. They knew cats ate birds, but what sort of cat was this? They resorted to a Mafia-style protection racket, dropping Leopold the odd freshly caught mackerel in return for paws-off. This suited Leopold admirably. He did not fancy a mouthful of wet feathers.

Leopold ate well. Fresh fish, rabbits and mice; the dew to drink from fragrant morning puddles shot with silvery sunshine. He was very happy.

His flying improved. He could stay in the air for much longer and with a lot less effort. He could glide in for touchdown with fanatical precision. He experimented with stalling in the air, letting himself fall, heart in mouth, then pulling himself out of it moments before hitting the waves. He skimmed along the surface of the sea with carefree abandon. He learned to loop the loop, to power-dive like a blazing meteor; he perfected a victory roll, coming out of it to soar up into the sky until everything was so translucently blue that he could no longer tell which was sea and which were the heavens.

He was sailing along on one such routine flight, when he discovered he could no longer see land. He circled around, his green eyes searching the horizon. He could see nothing solid or familiar. He flew slowly, wondering in which direction to make tracks. He had no idea how far this sea stuff went.

He began to get tired, flying in ever wider circles. Then he realized that the sun had gone and it was getting darker. He was not alarmed by this as he could see very well in the dark. But this was not the night. It was another kind of foreboding grey gloom; the gathering of thunder-clouds laden with rain.

Leopold looked up as he heard far-off rumbling. There was going to be one heck of a storm, and he was going to be caught in it. He knew what would happen when his fur got wet. He knew what would happen if he had to land on water. Caput. End of Leopold.

He flew on bravely, his body aching. The first big drop of rain hit him squarely between the eyes. He blinked and adjusted his speed. He had to keep his head, or this thing would beat him.

He tried to climb higher to get above the storm, but it was too late. The thunder-clouds were dark and menacing; flashes of lightning lit up the rolling masses of horror. He began to wish he had stayed with the circus, or perhaps even the sleek family.

The storm gathered into a seething black mass overhead; the rain began hitting him like sledgehammers. In minutes he was soaked, his fluffy fur plastered to his skin. He lifted his head, trying to maintain height. Fiercely Leopold fought to hold his own, relying on the months of practising to come to his aid now. But he was losing speed and losing height. The dark water below was surging in great white-frothed waves, deep gullies sucking and swallowing each other. One bedraggled ginger and white cat would soon disappear beneath that hungry sea.

Leopold could hardly see now. His lids were glued by the onslaught of rain. He began to fall. As he fell, he mewed piteously . . .

'Jumping Jehovah, if it isn't raining cats and dogs! There, my fine fellow, don't struggle. Mike Kelly's got you safe enough.'

Leopold found himself caught by strong arms that took the impact of his fall. It was a miracle. He must have fallen straight into the arms of a saint.

The saint was wearing glistening yellow oilskins and a brimmed sou'wester, off which the rain was dripping. His lined and crinkled brown face had a pair of the bluest eyes Leopold had ever seen.

'And where did you come from? I suppose you done drop out of one of them aeroplanes? My word, we'd better take you down below and dry you off before you catch your death.'

Mike Kelly carried Leopold down into the tiny cabin and began to rub his coat with a rough towel. It was the smallest room Leopold had ever seen, cat-sized in fact. He looked around with interest. The room pitched and rolled in the strangest way, but it did not seem to disturb the man so it must be all right.

'Well, you're stuck here now,' Mike Kelly went on. 'Whether you like it or not. I'm sailing round the world and I shan't make landfall for weeks. You can get off if you want to, or you can come back to Ireland with me. Please yourself. I'm easy. What do you think?'

Leopold had already made up his mind. No one had ever consulted him before, or treated him as an equal.

'I'm needing a ship's cat and a bit of company,' said Mike, opening a tin of evaporated milk. 'So you dropped in just right. You'll earn your keep and I reckon we'll get on . . .'

It was the beginning of a lifetime of devotion and mutual companionship. Leopold sailed all over the world with Mike, following him round strange foreign places and wintering sometimes in Southern Ireland in Mike's cottage while his catamaran was docked for repairs or maintenance, and the next voyage was planned.

The circus owner sued the sleek family for misrepresentation and the wrangling went on in court for years. Eventually the judge dismissed the case, saying it was useless to go on when neither party could produce the evidence (i.e. the cat) in question. The costs were enormous and the sleek family, who had spent the cheque, were rather silent as they made an appointment to see their bank manager. Dana did not go. Instead she ran off with Roger and went to live with him in a caravan.

Leopold did not entirely give up flying, though it took him some time to get his nerve back after that terrible storm. He made sure he did not fly too high, or too far away, realizing that navigation was his weak point. He even perfected a new technique of a low-level approach for a deck landing.

If Mike ever noticed his cat flying round the masthead, he was too tactful to mention it. Occasionally he was heard to mutter unsaintly comments about the Blarney Stone, or wonder if it was the Irish whiskey.

One day he vowed he'd write a book about Leopold, but then, who would believe him?

Travels with Inky Packer

Inky was an extraordinarily beautiful, pure white, long-haired, pedigree Persian. She had vivid blue eyes and exactly the right short nose, full cheeks and broad muzzle. She lived at Russets, Culimore Crescent with the Packers. It was a large, comfortable house, the kind estate agents describe as 'a highly desirable residence'.

Inky could have lived a pampered existence with a cushion to sleep on, daily grooming, limitless minced chicken, and nothing more exhausting to do than stretch herself luxuriously at the occasional cat show.

But Inky, right from kittenhood, developed some odd habits. For a start she preferred to be thought human and rapidly developed a liking for many human-type occupations. She regularly went shopping every morning, paying a call at each of the various establishments in the High Street, leaving the Chinese take-away and the fish and chip shop until last.

Twice a week she went to the Public Library and browsed round the shelves. She particularly liked the crime section which had quite a different smell. She soon became addicted to the television in the evening, but turned her back and went to sleep if a repeat was being shown.

She knew her way round the neighbourhood and there was hardly a building with an open door or window that she had not visited. Exclusiveness did not deter her. She preferred eating out, and several times strolled nonchalantly into a very posh restaurant, though she was soon lulled to sleep by the warmth of the place, and curled up on a stool at the cocktail bar.

She also liked a good play, and the bright lights of the local theatre lured her to an evening performance. It took two programme sellers ten minutes to coax her out from under the seats. Inky took umbrage at this total lack of understanding and retreated to the cinema where she sat through *A Hundred and One Dalmations* for the third time, which is saying something for a cat.

But she was a happy wanderer, and the Packer family became quite used to telephone calls from a faintly bewildered librarian.

'Miss Packer? We've got your cat here at the library again. Could you come and collect her? We don't like to just turn her out into the street.'

Elaine Packer would take the car down to the library and scoop the errant book-lover into her arms.

'Inky Packer,' she would say severely. 'Stop looking so lost and helpless. You know your way home perfectly well.'

Of course Inky knew her way home. She knew her way everywhere. But she would never pass up the chance of a ride in the car. She stood on the front seat with her paws on the dashboard ledge, her vivid blue eyes alert for any jay-walkers.

The other Packers, that is, George Packer and his daughter, Elaine, were resigned to Inky's wanderings until the episode of the hospital.

Inky could not have gone off at a worse time. George Packer worked for an advertising firm which had alternately grown and been taken over, grown and been taken over again. With this last takeover, he had an uneasy feeling that his style did not fit the trendy image of the present organization, New Views Inc. George always believed in the products he advertised, and some of his accounts were very long-standing. He could not see himself promoting some tasteless product simply for a fast profit.

The word redundant had not exactly been mentioned but it hovered over his iron-grey head like a neon sign. Redundancy would not be that disastrous, but Russets cost a lot to run, there was still the mortgage to pay off, and jobs were not easy to find at his age. Fortunately Elaine was a thrifty housekeeper, and never thought of eating out or spending money on clothes.

Elaine, too, had her problems. But she did not say a word to her father for fear of hurting his feelings. She had taken over the reins of the household at seventeen when her mother died of an unexplained virus infection. Then it had seemed the right thing to do. She had no career in mind and was content to run the house and garden. But now she was almost twenty-eight, and when the children next door suddenly grew from Brownies into brides she began to feel restless.

There was very little she could do except run a household. She had not been trained for anything. But the urge to get away and do something on her own was certainly part of the reason for her restlessness.

Mr Packer invited Clive Hilton, Managing Director of New Views Inc. to supper. He had some strange idea that if he could show the young man the solid background and comfort of his home, Clive Hilton might feel less like casting him out into the street.

But it was also the day Elaine had arranged to go for an interview for a job. She had answered an advertisement for a housekeeper to a wealthy titled family with a large estate in Norfolk. It meant a long drive there and back. She wanted to look her best, so much of the evening beforehand was spent washing and setting her hair and pressing her best dress and jacket.

It was no wonder Inky decided to explore futher afield. There was simply no one to talk to, and certainly too much fussing going on for one visitor. It was best to keep out of the way on such occasions.

Elaine did most of the meal before she left. The chocolate mousse was put to set in the refrigerator, the sauce for the prawn cocktail was ready mixed, the chicken casserole and vegetables sat in the automatic oven waiting to be switched on electronically.

'Now Inky, you've got to be a good girl while I'm away,' said Elaine to the white Persian. 'No going off anywhere.'

Inky looked at Elaine with blank astonishment. What me? Never. She pounded a little circle on Elaine's dressing stool and curled up for a snooze. She had every intention of remaining there for as long as it took Elaine to drive down the road.

The interview went well, and despite her lack of references Elaine felt she had a good chance of getting the job. But she hit the evening traffic and the return drive took far longer than she expected. She flew into the house. She had very little time to get everything ready.

The chicken casserole was definitely overcooked; the chocolate mousse slipped as she took it out of the refrigerator to decorate and slid untidily up the sides of the cut-glass bowl; and the mayonnaise, made in haste, had curdled. She was just making some more when Clive Hilton arrived.

Clive Hilton was a quiet young man in his early thirties, his horn-rimmed glasses hiding the determination and burning ambition in his eyes. He had built up New Ideas Inc. himself and was set on success.

He had no room for old-fashioned operators like George Packer, and he was going to have to tell him tonight.

'I'm terribly sorry,' said Elaine, tucking wisps of hair behind her ears. 'Supper's going to be a bit late. I was delayed. Would you like to have a glass of sherry first?'

Despite the generous schooners of dry sherry, Elaine's supper was not memorable. George Packer could not think what had happened to his normally efficient daughter. The table was not even laid properly – no side plates and not so much as a daisy for a floral centrepiece.

They were trying to take Clive's mind off the dry chicken with conversation, when the telephone rang. A loud voice resounded against Elaine's ear-drums.

'One of my nurses tells me that this flea-ridden creature padding round my wards belongs to the Packers in Culimore Crescent,' she barked. 'Would you please come and remove it at once.'

'Inky hasn't got fleas,' said Elaine, not caring if Clive Hilton did hear.

'Anything that has fur and moves has got fleas,' said the matron. 'You've got fifteen minutes to come and collect your animal, or I will telephone for the vet.'

The matron's voice was indeed threatening, and Elaine found that her hand was trembling slightly as she put the telephone down.

'That was the hospital,' said Elaine. 'Inky's visiting out of hours. I'll have to go and fetch her. I hope you don't mind having your mousse without any cream on top . . .'

And it was that evening the family car went on strike and refused to start. Try as she could, Elaine could not get any life out of it. The engine turned over with an uresponsive whine. She began to panic, remembering the fifteen-minute deadline and the fate that awaited her fluffy beauty.

Elaine felt the perspiration breaking out as she struggled with the starter.

'Having trouble?' inquired Clive owlishly.

'I've got to get to Inky,' said Elaine desperately. 'They're going to send for the vet.'

'We'd better go in my car then.'

The ward sister had shut Inky into the sluice room. Inky was quite indignant about it. She had come to visit the patients, not an unresponsive collection of bedpans. Still, it was clean. She sat on the floor licking her fur into place, waiting for Elaine to collect her in the car.

'So this is Inky,' said Clive, amused.

'Inky Packer,' said Elaine, lifting the cat up with one hand. Inky hung there, eyes closed, feigning a dreadful incurable illness. 'You bad, bad thing. I'm fed up with having to come and rescue you. Why can't you stay at home and catch mice?'

Inky shuddered at the word. However, she recovered when she saw the size and make of Clive's car, and forgot her indisposition enough to purr ecstatically while exploring the innards of the vehicle.

'Can't you get your cat to keep still?' asked Clive. 'It's a little unnerving having to drive with that thing leaping about.'

'She's enjoying it,' said Elaine. 'She likes your car. She's never been in a Mercedes before.'

'I'm glad she likes it, but I'd rather she sat on your lap.'

Elaine managed to extract Inky from the glove compartment and sat her forcibly on her knee. Inky trampled enthusiastically, her claws going through the thin material of Elaine's dress. Elaine gritted her teeth . . . after all, Clive had been very kind.

'Does your cat go wandering often?' Clive asked.

'Yes, but I know why she does it,' said Elaine with feeling. 'She just wants to get out and see the world.'

'Do I detect the stirrings of a rebellion in the homestead?'

'You do,' said Elaine, glad to have someone to tell. 'I've looked after my father for over ten years. I just feel it's time I started doing something of my own. I've got to get away.'

Clive Hilton was ruthless when it came to decisions, but even he could not see a man losing both job and daughter on the same evening. So he said nothing to George, but accepted Elaine's invitation to return for supper another evening before she took up a post.

This time her preparations were well in advance, and she set the table perfectly with matching candles and flowers. She also looked very pretty. A letter that morning confirming the job had given her a new sparkle. But she had yet to tell her father.

Just as Elaine was about to serve the salmon soufflé, the telephone rang. It was the local librarian.

'Oh dear, not Inky again,' said Elaine, exasperated. 'Would you mind keeping her for another ten minutes or my soufflé will collapse?'

'Oh, she isn't here,' explained the librarian. 'I just thought I ought to let you know that I saw her boarding a 507 bus to Kestram.'

Clive was very understanding about the supper. 'This is getting to be a habit,' he said, starting the Mercedes. 'Do you know the 507 route?'

'Vaguely,' said Elaine anxiously. 'I do hope she's all right. She'll be so frightened. She's never been on a bus before.'

'If I know Inky at all, she won't be in the least put out. She's probably sitting up with the driver by now.'

'I hope she doesn't jump off anywhere.'

'What, and miss seeing the terminus? You bet she won't. That little lady can take care of herself. She'll land squarely on all four feet.'

Inky landed all right. They found her in the drivers' canteen sampling bus company milk. She'd had a lovely time. Buses were far more fun than that Mercedes. However, she was tired and quite happy to curl up on Elaine's lap for the drive home.

Seeing the contented look on Inky's face gave Clive an idea.

'I'm going to put Inky into advertising,' he announced.

Elaine stared at Clive in horror. 'Not cat food,' she said, appalled.

'Of course not. Tourism. I've a series of television ads to make for the American market to promote package tours to England. Who better than Inky, our happy wanderer to show them around? Imagine . . . Inky at Edinburgh . . . Inky at Stratford-on-Avon . . . Inky at the Changing of the Guard . . . Inky meeting Concorde. . . !'

So Inky went on the box. She took to it like a duck to water. Filming held no terrors for her. And it meant lots of lovely travelling. George Packer became her business manager and Elaine, after sending a letter of regret to Norfolk, was Inky's personal assistant and travelling companion.

Clive supervised the American advertisements himself so it meant he saw a lot of Elaine. She grew prettier and prettier. One evening when they were at Land's End he asked her to marry him. She did not say yes at first, though she knew she would eventually. She had a little wandering of her own to do first. . . .

This Man is Mine

She had been living with him now for almost a year. The time had flown and neither of them had really noticed the months passing. He was a man worth loving, a man with his head among the stars, dreaming and thinking and plucking ideas out of the bright dark night with long, slender fingers. He was an author, writing under the name of Graham Marsh, but she did not know if this was his real name.

They lived in quiet, rural happiness with never a quarrel to mar the peaceful days in that small Devonshire cottage. He asked nothing more of her than that she should always be there. And so she was, ready to greet him on his return from London, or from the nearby market town – waiting to welcome him home.

He asked that she should be quiet and undemanding when he was writing, but that she should be ready with affection during the long evenings. The perfect lover. And how she loved him on those evenings, waiting for the moment when he would push aside his papers and smile at her. Then she would come into his arms, and his soft words of love were music to her ears.

She rarely left the cottage, partly because she was still a little nervous of the outside world. He had given her a home when she was most lonely and afraid. He had offered her a haven.

She did not like travelling in his car because it made her feel sick, not did she like fishing with him in his little boat because she was afraid of the dark blue sea. So she stayed at home happy to wander round the little cottage and its sunny, flower-filled garden.

But she also liked it when they walked together into the surrounding countryside. Sometimes his long legs tired her and them, if there was a field with poppies and butterflies, she would sit and daydream and wait for him to return.

There was no doubt that Graham adored her. 'You have beautiful eyes, my love,' he would say, staring into their amber-flecked depths as if seeking some truth there. Then he would run his hands over her face and rest his neck against the softness of her neck.

And she loved him till sometimes she thought her heart would burst, and she just had to go over to him where he sat at his desk and touch his sleeve or make some small gesture of love. But when he was working, he had little time or thought for her.

'Go away, Susy,' he would say, not unkindly. 'Leave me alone, there's a good girl.'

She did not sleep with him but had her own bed in another room. Once she had come to him in the middle of a cold, wintery night when the temperature had fallen and frost was biting the air with icy needles. She had stood in the doorway of his bedroom. But he had been angry with her and had escorted her back to her own bed. She had heard his door shut firmly and had not been able to understand his harshness.

Then one day – a day in early spring – when the garden was full of nodding daffodils and the long green pods of unopened tulips, Graham came home early from seeing his publishers in London. He stood in the porch and Susy ran to him, wanting him to take her into his arms as he always did. But today he stepped back, and she saw that his arms were full. In them he held a small bundle wrapped in a blanket.

Susy faltered in her approach and looked up at him questioningly.

'I've brought a baby home for you, Susy,' he said softly. 'A little baby for you to look after.'

He turned so that she could see what was in the blanket, and the small blue eyes that regarded her were startingly clear and unafraid.

'This baby has no home,' he added, 'and you and I are going to look after the poor little mite.'

Susy saw the baby look up at him with adoring eyes, and anger began to smoulder in her heart. He was her man. He belonged to her, and no one else. She did not want to share him with anyone – not even a baby.

She backed away sullenly, not even welcoming him as she usually did, then suddenly it was all too much and she turned and ran upstairs, her heart turning over and over in a turmoil of jealousy and love for him.

'Oh, come on, Susy. Come downstairs and don't be such a silly girl,' he called out after her.

But she did not answer, nor did she come downstairs. She heard him talking to the baby then preparing its food in the kitchen, and she began to hate it. Oh, why did he have to do this to them, she cried to herself, when they had always been so happy together?

Hours later, feeling hungry and desolate, she crept downstairs. The door to his study was ajar. She stood silently in the shadows and saw that he was holding the baby on his lap and it was sleepy with milk. His papers lay on his desk, untouched.

Susy fled out into the garden, not caring where she went, running wildly through the flowers, shaking with a storm of rage. She ran to her favourite tree, a lilac, and climbed a little way, sitting and plotting against this newcomer. She heard Graham come to the door and call her name, but she took no notice. She did not return to the cottage until she saw the lights go out, then she trod softly into the kitchen.

She was very hungry by now, but was almost too angry to eat or drink anything. It would have choked her.

She wandered round quietly, looking for the baby. Where was it? She stood outside the door of his bedroom and her senses quickened. The baby was in his room! She could hear its small movements. She crept away, cowed and beaten, but loving him still despite the misery in her heart.

So the baby came to live with them, and they were three. It was female and for the time being its name was just Baby. Susy refused to look after her, and once Graham had accepted her decision, he was not angy any more but simply laughed and teased her about it.

'Why, Susy, I do believe you're jealous!' he would say. 'Fancy being jealous of a scrawny little mite with a screwed up face, when you are beautiful and I love you.'

But Susy was still and unrelenting in his arms. It was not easy to forgive him.

So Graham took care of the baby and saw to her small needs. He loved to encourage her unsteady efforts to walk and gave her a soft, woolly ball to play with. When she was tired, he carried her in his arms, while Susy sat and watched from a distance, hatred in her narrowed eyes.

Now in the evenings it was the baby he cuddled on his lap, and Susy slunk sadly away for she could not bear the sight of them together. However, if he wanted to smoke his pipe, he put Baby down, frightened that hot ash might fall on her. It was then that Susy crept back into his arms, burying her face against his neck, trying to ignore the swirling puffs of smoke from his pipe for the sake of being with him again.

'Just like old times, Susy,' he would say to her, and she would soften with love for him all over again.

One day he had to go up to London, and he asked her to look after the baby. He stood in the doorway, tall and handsome in his city suit and polished shoes.

'Now will you be a sweetheart and take care of Baby for me?' he asked. He turned her face so that she had to look straight at him. 'Can I trust you?' he added seriously. Susy turned away so that he could not see her eyes, and in answer she went over to the baby and began to wash her half-heartedly.

He sighed with relief. 'That's a good girl, I'll be home tomorrow, but there's plenty of food for you both.'

Susy waited until she heard his car going down the lane, then she stopped washing the baby and shook her rather roughly. She hit her, quite lightly at first, then harder a second time. Baby cried out with surprise and looked at her with hurt eyes.

Susy walked away, pleased. She went into the kitchen and deliberately spilt the food which he had prepared for Baby – some special mushy stuff that had no taste.

She went into the study, finding those typed sheets that were so precious to him, and she tore them and scattered the bits over the floor. The baby crawled in after her and began to chew the shreds.

Susy stepped over the baby, not caring now, bent on her path of destruction, all her unhappiness boiling over in a torrent of uncontrollable hatred.

She smashed vases, cups, a jug of water, trampled on his bed, wrecked a pile of clean shirts just back from the laundry, tore at the curtains, swept his photographs off the bureau. She was like a wild creature, her eyes gleaming, her pulse thudding, her breathing sharp and shallow.

The baby was at the foot of the stairs but Susy ran down, knocking her over in her flight. The baby started to cry but Susy did not care. She turned on her, wanting to hit her again. One of her long nails caught the baby's face, making her squeal in pain.

'Here! What's going on?'

Graham stood in the doorway, the key still in his hand.

Susy froze. His eyes went round the scene of destruction, finally taking in the baby who was still crying pitifully.

He turned to Susy. 'You wicked, wicked girl,' he said angrily, lifting his hand and striking her.

'Thank goodness I came back for my wallet. You might have killed the baby. I'll take her to Mrs Simmons down the lane. She'll look after her for me while I'm away. I'm ashamed of you, Susy.'

He picked up the baby and began to soothe her.

Susy did not move. It was the first time he had struck her. She thought the world was falling to pieces around her. She stayed quite still, thinking perhaps he would hit her again and then she would die. But he did not touch her – he simply turned and walked out.

She ran away into the woods, and when he came back from London he called and searched in the garden and the woods beyond, but he could not find where she was hiding.

At last she could bear it no longer. She would accept his terms, share him, if only just to be with him sometimes and to love him.

She was thin and cold and hungry, and she went back to the cottage to ask him to take her back. He swept her into his arms, overjoyed that she had returned.

'Oh, Susy darling, I've missed you so much,' he said.

The weeks passed and the baby grew, and Susy still hated her, though now she hid this hatred inside, growing thinner as the baby grew fatter.

One day Graham came home from the market with someone and there were happy, laughing voices in the hall.

'Well, Val, this is it,' Graham was saying. 'What do you think of it? It's certainly not a palace, but at least Susy keeps it wholesome.'

'I think it's perfect,' said the woman's voice. 'Just the kind of cottage I've always dreamed about.'

'And you don't mind about Susy and Baby? Susy might break out again, you know.'

Curious, Susy came out of the kitchen and saw a tall young woman with loose, fair hair standing in the hall, close to Graham, holding his arm. Susy withdrew slightly, suddenly afraid, wondering what this man she loved was going to do now.

'Of course they hate each other,' the young woman said with a laugh. 'It's only natural. It's like having two women in one kitchen. They never get on.'

'Am I to take that as a hint that you don't want any other female in your kitchen?' Graham asked. They were smiling at each other.

'Nonsense,' she said. 'We'll keep Susy, of course. She obviously adores you. But the kitten will have to go. I'm sure my sister would have her.'

At that moment, the young woman caught sight of Susy behind the kitchen door and went to pick her up.

'Why, you beautiful thing,' said Val gently, stroking the long black fur. 'You are a lovely creature. Now you have two adoring females to spoil you,' she said to Graham, her eyes shining with happiness.

And Susy stretched deliciously in the young woman's arms, curling and uncurling her claws among the loose fair hair purring a loud, rapturous welcome.

This was a woman after her own heart. Susy quite agreed. The kitten would have to go.

The Uninvited Guest

It was not long after we moved into our house that I saw the black cat walk into the larder. The occurrence was unusual as we did not have a cat. I thought perhaps a neighbour's pet had come to inspect the newcomers.

I could see him quite clearly from the corner of my eye . . . a large handsome black cat with long curving tail and alert pointed ears.

For a moment I paused, not wanting to scare him. Then I went over to say hello.

There was nothing. Empty air. The larder was stacked with tidy rows of bottles, jars and tins, the bread bin, vegetable rack . . . but no cat. I searched the larder thoroughly but he had completely disappeared.

Puzzled, I shut the door. We had made the larder from a large walk-in cupboard under the stairs. It was ideal; cool and ventilated and a blissful size after our cramped years in rented accommodation. Everything about the house was a long-awaited dream come true. It was old, weather-beaten red brick, brimming with character and space, with a rambling garden made for children and animals. We had the children, two daughters, Linda and Janice, and I had promised them a cat and a dog as soon as we settled in.

I began to search the house. I had clearly seen that cat, and yet there was no cat. Odd.

'What are you doing, Mummy?' asked my eight-year-old curiously, as I peered under beds.

'Er . . . just checking,' I said.

'Checking for what?' she persisted.

'Dust,' I said.

I sat back on my heels, pushing the hair off my face. I must be tired, I thought. The move had been hectic and there was still such a lot to do, getting the house straight and redecorated as well as caring for the family. Perhaps it had been a shadow, a very dark shadow.

It was easy enough to tell myself this, but I didn't believe it, not for one moment. I know a cat when I see one.

'Mummy, isn't it nearly tea-time?'

I shrugged off the incident and returned to the world of tea, baths and bedtime stories, dismissing the cat from my mind. What did it matter anyway? It had obviously found a way out of the house.

That same evening as I stood in the kitchen making a late drink, I saw the cat again. He was sitting on the floor near the larder, looking straight at me. There was no mistaking him this time . . . a big black cat with his tail curled neatly over his paws.

'Hello, puss,' I said. 'Where have you come from?'

I was talking to myself. It was ridiculous, but there was nothing there. The cat had completely vanished. I made a brief search of the kitchen but there was no way he could have got out.

'I just don't understand it,' I said to my husband, Neville, as I went back into the living room with our two mugs of hot chocolate. 'I saw a black cat in the kitchen this afternoon. It went into the larder. Then just now I saw the same cat, sitting outside the larder.'

'So? You've seen a black cat. By the larder. Perhaps he's hungry.'

I shook my head. 'No, it vanished into thin air. That's what's so strange,' I said. 'It was definitely there, and then it wasn't.'

'You're imagining things,' said Neville.

'Once perhaps, but not twice,' I said firmly.

As the weeks went by I saw the cat almost daily, but only in the kitchen, either disappearing into the larder or sitting near it. I often spoke to him softly, but soon learned that if I made any movement towards him the cat vanished instantly.

'Puss, puss,' I said coaxingly. 'Come and talk to me. I won't hurt you.'

The cat stared at me, his slanting amber eyes unblinking, thinking secret thoughts in a secret world. His coat was a furry blackness that I longed to touch, to feel its softness.

'Talking to yourself again?' said Neville, grinning.

'I was talking to the cat,' I said. 'Are you sure you didn't see it?'

'No. Nothing. Not a black cat in sight.'

Everything about the kitchen was so normal. The warmth, the delicious smell of a casserole cooking, sunshine streaming through the window, curtains moving with the fresh breeze. We were not far from the sea. It was all quite ordinary. There was no icy chill, no hush, no premonition . . . only a mysterious cat that came and went like a ghost.

I made some enquiries. There was no large black cat living in the neighbourhood; the previous occupants of our house had not owned a cat.

Linda and Janice knew nothing about the uninvited guest in our house. I did not want to frighten them, although they occasionally caught me talking to thin air. '

'Mummy,' one of them would giggle. 'You're talking to yourself again!'

I was sure that the cat could see me. It had a feline expression in its eyes as it stared across the kitchen. There was nothing unseeing about those eyes. I could not describe the look. I tried to find the words . . . the cat looked contented, almost serene.

It was some seven months later, a warm day in early summer, when my daughter Linda called from the kitchen, her voice high with excitement.

'Mummy, Mummy, there's a black cat just gone in the larder! A big black cat. It is ours? Can we keep it?'

The girls had been wanting a cat for ages and I had promised them a cat and a dog. There just hadn't been time to look for the right pets.

'Oh, really?' I said, going into the kitchen. 'I bet you can't find him in there now.'

Linda looked inside the cupboard under the stairs, clattering around, but she came out mystified, her innocent face looking puzzled.

'But he's not there,' she said. 'How funny, I saw him go in.'

'I often see this cat,' I said casually, as if I were talking about some mundane daily routine. 'But he's not an ordinary cat. He can disappear, just like that.'

The child laughed at my impersonation of Tommy Cooper.

'You mean a ghost cat?'

I nodded. 'I think so, but there's no need to be frightened of him. He means no harm. He's quite friendly in a remote sort of way.'

Linda did not seem in the least alarmed. She quite liked the idea of having a ghost cat. 'We'll call him Spooky,' she said.

Linda only saw Spooky occasionally, but I saw him often. I got quite used to the black cat sitting by the larder or walking into it. I began to wonder if the cupboard under the stairs had been used as an air-raid shelter during the war years and he was waiting to take cover; or perhaps his favourite sleeping place had been in some dark recess under the stairs. I felt sure he must have lived in the house at some time.

'Hello, Spooky,' I said, standing quite still and returning his gaze. Cat and I stared at each other. It was a strange sensation, knowing that when I moved, the cat would instantly disappear.

We had not mentioned Spooky to Janice, my six-year-old daughter. We thought she was a little too young to cope with such an unusual phenomenon, even a friendly furry one.

One evening in August, we were downstairs watching television. I was knitting and thinking about the new baby I was expecting soon. Suddenly we heard Janice calling from her bed.

'Mummy! Mummy! Mummy!'

I raced upstairs as quickly as my size would allow and rushed into her bedroom. She was sitting up in bed, her eyes wide with fright.

'Mummy, Mummy, there's a big cat on my bed,' she cried. 'Take him off, take him off. He jumped on me and frightened me.'

'Is he still there? Where?' I asked, for I could see nothing.

'Yes,' she said, calming down but still trembling a little. 'He's leaning on my legs. He's ever so heavy.'

She was obviously getting over the fright, for she put out her hand and began stroking the cat. I was amazed to see her hand making the movement of actually stroking a non-existent cat. It was to be the only time anyone actually touched or felt the black cat. And I was not surprised that it was Janice who was given this gift. For she was and still is quite mad about cats.

I almost expected to hear a purr as Janice stroked the air, but there was nothing except my daughter's cooing and coaxing voice, then the rustle of bed sheets as I tucked her back to bed. Outside the house, the summer breeze combed the long grass and whispered to the nodding leaves.

'Spooky,' I said quite firmly. 'You are not to go waking the children when they are asleep and frightening them.'

I think he must have heard me, for Spooky was never again seen upstairs. Perhaps Janice's first reaction had alarmed him. He returned to his old haunts in the kitchen and all three of us saw him often. But never my husband.

A year after we moved in, our son Bradley arrived and about the same time we got a cat of our own. She was the runt of a litter and not expected to survive, but with some hand-feeding and lots of care, she grew into a lovely little black cat with white nose and paws. We called her Snagglepuss, after the tatty old cartoon lion.

One day the girls were playing in the field opposite the house where there were some ruined farm buildings waiting for demolition, when they found the remains of a black cat. It appeared to have been squashed flat by some old machinery, although that may just have been the appearance it gave after decomposition.

The girls were very upset and wanted to give the cat a proper funeral. They dug a little hole and buried it wrapped in silver foil like a spacesuit, shed tears and said a little prayer.

'Maybe this was our Spooky,' I said, picking some wild flowers to put on the little grave. 'Perhaps he's at peace now, and won't visit us again.'

He did, but less frequently. The family were growing up and when Linda left school and began working, she brought home a stray kitten, a pretty little tabby female which we immediately adopted and called Twinkletoes, Twinks for short. Perhaps Spooky was beginning to feel crowded out in our household, for Brad was a normal, noisy eight-year-old and we also had a red setter called Crackers, short for Meadway Caractacus.

Twinks settled down with Snagglepuss and Crackers and she grew into a beautiful cat with gentle, loving ways. Spooky was part of our family too, but only females saw him, human females – or so we thought.

Brad was fifteen and getting ready for bed one night. He was on his own in the house as we were out. Suddenly he heard the most terrible racket coming from the kitchen. He hurried downstairs and on opening the door was nearly knocked flat by Twinks, who leaped out, eyes wild and staring, her black striped fur standing on end.

She flew upstairs into his bedroom and hid under the chest of drawers. She refused to come out, her eyes transfixed with fright.

Brad searched the kitchen but could find nothing amiss. Puzzled he went back to bed, Twinks still crouched in the futhermost corner under the chest of drawers.

'Mum,' he said the next morning. 'You should have seen Twinks last night. It's a wonder you didn't hear her! There was a terrible commotion in the kitchen. What a racket! I went down and Twinks shot out of the kitchen and up the stairs, breaking the sound barrier, I bet. She got under my chest of drawers and refused to come out. I wonder what on earth got into her?'

Twinks was sitting on the landing, peering down the stairs through the bannisters. She looked most unhappy. I took it that she needed to go out, having been indoors all night.

'Come on, Twinks,' I said encouragingly. 'Out into the garden.'

She did not move. I didn't have time for playing games so I went upstairs and picked her up to take outside. As I reached the hall, Twinks stiffened in my arms. I went towards the kitchen, intending to open the back door. It was too much for Twinks. With a screech, she leaped out of my arms and raced upstairs again. There was no way that cat was going into the kitchen. She was obviously terrified.

'For heaven's sake, Twinks,' I said. 'What's the matter with you?'

But I had a shrewd idea. Twinks had met Spooky.

I eventually got her out of the front door. From then on she refused to go into the kitchen. She avoided all contact with the floor, using every available piece of furniture to walk on. She insisted on being carried to bed by Brad. Her eyes always had a staring, frightened look and any slight movement or noise sent her into a panic with her fur standing on end.

During these months Spooky was never seen. Perhaps Twinks' reaction had alarmed him too. Twinks is a very pretty female cat and it could be he longed for some cat company.

Twinks has slowly recovered but still leaps off the floor as if it is hot coals. She sometimes ventures a little way into the kitchen. The encounter – or whatever it was – has changed her. She is extremely nervous.

Now Spooky seems to have gone forever and I often wonder if it was the presence of the girls in the house that brought him to us. Perhaps he once belonged to a little girl in the past.

Laura, our two-year-old grand-daughter often comes to visit us. She's a sweet little girl with long fair hair and big brown eyes. She loves pets and shows no fear, playing with Twinks for hours.

I was sitting in the living room, sewing, the sun streaming in through the window. We have half a dozen finches now and are hoping to build an aviary in the garden. Twinks is sunning herself in a warm spot.

Laura is wandering about, going into the kitchen to fetch some toys left on the floor.

'Nice pussy,' I hear her say. 'Nice pussy . . .'

I keep quite still, listening. I wonder if I am imagining things. But no her childlike voice is cooing and coaxing something.

'Puss, puss, puss . . .' she is saying.

Perhaps she is playing with her toys, or talking to Twinks through the window. Perhaps out strange visitor is back. Maybe one day she will ask me about a big black cat sitting by the larder.

The Clown

The cat knew that his name was Cecil but he could not understand why that made everyone laugh. He said the sound over and over again in his mind: 'Ses-sil, Ses-sil . . .' but he did not find anything funny about it.

Every time there were visitors ot the house, Mrs Billington would scoop him up into her arms, his four paws waving frantically and helplessly in the air like erratic windmills.

'This is Cecil,' she would say with a merry trill. 'He's such a clown.'

The visitor would tickle Cecil's tummy (which he loathed) and then laugh uproariously. He could not see what was so funny. He did not understand it at all.

They did not laugh at people called Cecil. There was an Uncle Cecil who dropped ash all over Cecil's fur; and the postman's name was Cecil, and no one had hysterics when he dropped those flat white things through the letter-box.

And clown. What did clown mean? Cecil thought he was a cat, a cat with black paws, which were mostly what he saw of himself. He was positive he was a cat. But apparently he was also a clown. Everyone said so. But it was something mysterious and beyond his comprehension.

He skidded across the hall floor and landed in a heap against the front door. Then he sat up and rearranged his ruffled fur. He resolved to spend at least the next seven, eleven or ninety-four minutes on finding out what a clown was. He owed it to himself for his own peace of mind.

Cecil looked at the kitchen clock. He knew it was the right thing to do. People were always looking at the clock. It was ninety-three minutes past half-past one. He had plenty of time. He knew how to tell the time now.

He climbed into Mrs Billington's shopping basket and closed his eyes to think. He always thought better with his eyes closed. Mrs Billington spotted him and hooted with laughter.

'Look at Cecil! He thinks he's coming shopping with me. Isn't he a scream?'

She tipped him out and he fell head first, somersaulting with a neat twist of his body. It was a normal feline four-point landing after an awkward take off.

'Cecil's standing on his head!' she shrieked.

Cecil walked away with some dignity. He was not standing on his head and never had been. He began to wonder, not for the first time, if he and the Billingtons were really compatible.

Late that night, Cecil went down to see the brown owl that lived in the copse at the end of the garden. He had heard that an owl was supposed to be a wise old bird, but Cecil doubted it, with all that pointless twit-twooing and demented staring.

The owl blinked down at the cat from the hollow in his tree. Cecil asked him if he happened to know what a clown was.

'A clown?' the owl crooned wisely. 'A clown is a clown.'

'Is that ye-ow-all?'

'Twit-twoo,' agreed the owl, spotting a field-mouse that was trying to hide under a discarded chocolate wrapper. He took off silently, his great wings casting a shadow over Cecil.

Fat lot of use, thought Cecil, wandering back to the house with a couple of jaunty side-steps. He jumped over imaginary obstacles, punching the air like a goal-scoring football player. Perhaps a clown was something anti-social. After all, none of the birds could talk to him, the dog next door was positively rude, and those foxes down by the stream had a mean look.

Cecil sat on the top of the yellow monster with four round legs in the drive and waited for morning to come. The monster was asleep, so it was safe to sit on it. The frost tipped Cecil's fur with spears of ice. He tucked his nose into the warmth of his tail and prayed not to be a social outcast.

He knew that something was happening the next day by the frantic activity. Bags, boxes and cases began to pile up in the hallway like a hastily erected flood barricade.

Cecil sat on top of the luggage, an oversized cherry on an ice-cream sundae. His rule was never sit on the floor if there was a chair, never on a chair if there was a window-sill, never on a window-sill if there was room on the bookcase, and so on up to the hat shelf, curtain pelmet and the top of the wardrobe. An unsteady pile of luggage rated about grade three.

'Exterminate . . . exterminate,' droned one of the junior Billingtons who conducted an endless war with Cecil. Cecil scrambled over the luggage in retreat, tail waving surrender, and hid inside a bag of beach gear with only his head showing.

'Eliminate . . . eliminate,' the drone went on.

Mrs Billington swooped in, putting a faded straw hat on top of Cecil's ears. She stood back, shaking with laughter. 'That cat's a real clown. Going on your holidays, are you?'

Cecil leaped out of the bag, hat askew, knocking everything over. He fled. They were going to Majorca for Christmas, they said. He was suddenly afraid. What did it mean? What was going to happen to him? For Christmas? Could they eat it?

It was peaceful when they had all gone away in the yellow monster. He sat in the garden, slowly getting cold, then hungry. It started to get dark. Perhaps he ought to go and ask the owl. He decided that at half-past twenty to eleven he would go and see the old bird.

But light footsteps came hurrying down the empty drive with a voice on top.

'Puss? Puss? I'm so sorry. I know I'm terribly late. That damned train was held up again. You must be starving – and frozen. I'm afraid I've got to feed you outside even though it's no weather for a picnic. They didn't leave me a key.'

It was a girl, a pretty dark-haired girl with rosy cheeks and smiling eyes. She pulled off her woolly gloves and started to unpack a bag. She had brought warm milk in a thermos and chicken in aspic on a bone china plate.

'I hope you don't mind party food,' she said, chatting away as she poured milk into a floral-patterned soup bowl. 'So much nicer than that tinned stuff. And this is skimmed milk. Low fat, you know. But if you don't like it, just say so, and I'll get your favourite tipple.'

Cecil was amazed. She was actually talking to him as if he was real. And party food! He forgot all about visiting the owl. He looked at the young woman closely to see if she was laughing at him. But she wasn't. She was smiling and that was quite a different sensation.

'I promise I'll be on time tomorrow,' she went on, as he ate his supper. 'It's Christmas Eve and I'll be home from work early, thank goodness. Then, of course, life is one long holiday.'

Cecil felt almost dizzy with happiness. The young woman was discussing plans with him quite seriously.

'I hate leaving you out all night. Are you sure you'll be all right? There are those awful foxes around, but I suppose you're used to it. By the way, I'm Jane. Good night, puss.' She dropped a kiss onto the top of his head and hurried away.

Cecil staggered around the garden as if he were drunk. She had not laughed at him once, not a single once, and she was coming again tomorrow and the next tomorrow. It was all too marvellous.

She kept her word. She was right on time the next day. She stomped about the garden, swinging her arms, as Cecil ate his fish canapés.

'This is silly,' she said, her breath coming like a white mist. 'We're both getting frozen. You might just as well come home with me. Would you like that? I only live two doors away.'

The number of doors presented no problem. Cecil simply followed her along the pavement to the big house on the corner. It seemed Jane lived in the downstairs, someone else lived in the middle and quite another person lived at the top. Weird, but no different to trees.

Cecil explored her flat, fascinated by the pot plants, the books, the cushions, her collection of records and tapes. It was quite different to the Billingtons'. She sat down on the floor beside him with a mug of coffee.

'Make yourself at home,' she said.

Cecil needed no further invitation. He crawled onto her lap and went to sleep.

On Christmas Day he shared roast turkey and chestnut stuffing with Jane and Philip, a tall young man from upstairs, whom Jane was also feeding. They were pulling crackers and reading terrible jokes which made them laugh. But they weren't laughing at him, even when Jane put a little paper clown's hat on Cecil's head and the elastic strap under his chin.

'You look very sweet,' said Jane with a hesitant smile. She quickly took it off him and tied the hat to the back of a chair. 'But it's much more fun to play with it.'

It was too good to be true, and too good to last. It didn't last. Cecil knew it wouldn't.

'You'll miss Cecil, won't you?' said Philip, as he helped her with the washing-up one evening. For a teacher of ancient languages he was remarkably handy with a tea-cloth.

'I will indeed, He's good company, and a nice, friendly cat. I've grown very fond of him. But the Billingtons are due back tomorrow. Their plane lands at Gatwick at five.'

Five, eleven or ninety-four . . . it all meant the same to Cecil. How could he measure his happiness when it was running away like sand through his paws? He followed her reluctantly along the pavement, trailing his tail. Every few steps Jane bent and stroked him, murmuring words of encouragement.

'We'll see each other,' she said. 'Ever such a lot.'

The Billingtons were already home, all of them. Cecil had never really counted how many of them there were; they were just the Billington *en masse*. They had brought Jane a bottle of Spanish wine and a two-foot-high grey donkey for Cecil.

They sat the donkey on the floor facing him. It had button glass eyes and a leering grin. Cecil backed off, hissing, his tail twitching. Then he fell over his tail and they all began to laugh, pushing the donkey at him. He tried to close his ears to the sound of their laughter, but there was nothing he could really do. Everything was all horribly the same again.

But something *was* different. Cecil sensed it. They were preoccupied with a new activity. It seemed that Mr Billington had met someone in Majorca who had offered him a job 'up north'. They talked endlessly about 'up north', and quite soon the house was full of more boxes, and everything was being put into these boxes. Even the despised donkey went into a box.

'Of course we're taking Cecil with us,' said Mrs Billington. 'I've bought him a lovely travelling-basket. He'll make everybody laugh up north. He's such a clown!'

She kept putting Cecil in the basket. He kept jumping out. Life became a perpetual yo-yo, in and out of the basket. Mrs Billington lost a little of her usual good humour.

'We shall have to make sure the strap is fastened on moving day,' she said, slamming the lid on Cecil.

Cecil observed the preparations with apprehension. The small boxes went into big boxes, and were then carried into a bigger box that stood on round legs and which had arrived outside the house and promptly gone to sleep. Cecil watched the procession of boxes disappearing into its inside. They had even packed his food dish and he had had to eat his breakfast out of the tin.

Cecil glanced at the clock. It was three-quarters to fifteen o'clock. He had plenty of time to think.

He was wrong. Mrs Billington produced the travelling-basket and put it on the floor. He could tell from her expression that there was no jumping out this time.

Cecil did not know what to do. For a moment, he panicked. He wanted to create some kind of diversion – anything – but his wits had deserted him. He could think of nothing. He began moving – anywhere – faster. He slid along the bare boards, his paws spread to the four winds; then he danced sideways along to the front doorstep, tumbling and somersaulting down the steps; he chased his tail, rolling over and over, shadow-boxing the air. It was all pretty normal stuff.

'Look, Cecil's standing on his head again!'

They leaned against the walls, laughing.

'My word, that cat's a clown,' said Mrs Billington, wiping the tears from her eyes. 'He's too funny for words.'

By the time they had stopped laughing. Cecil had disappeared. They searched the house and the garden, calling for him everywhere.

'Ses-sil. Ses-sil . . . Ses-sil.'

But there was no answer.

Cecil watched them go. He watched the big box monster and the yellow monster waking up and driving off. He was up the tree, watching from the hollow where the owl slept. He waited there a long time, perhaps six, eleven or ninety-four minutes before he judged it safe to climb down.

He went straight along the pavement to Jane's downstairs house and miaowed outside her door. She heard him and came to let him in.

'Hello, puss,' she said, as if she had been expecting him. 'Didn't you want to go up north?'

Cecil walked in with some hesitation, a little unsure of his reception. After all, he was uninvited. He fell over the newspaper, scattering pages all over the floor, landing on his back with the front page of the *Daily Mail* like a wigwam on his head.

He waited for Jane to burst out laughing. And she almost did. But it was a sweet, gentle sound and it did not hurt him at all.

'Philip said you were a funny cat, and you are,' she said, removing the newspaper from Cecil's head. 'What do you think you are? A clown? Everybody loves a clown, you know . . .'

Cecil closed his eyes to capture the moment. He had found out at last. At last he had found out what a clown was. He should have known that Jane would tell him. A clown was a cat that everybody loves.

White Tiger

Ebony was an ordinary black farm cat. He did not know that he was fated to cross the path of a white tiger cub, and that for a time they would live together.

The story really began ten years earlier when Dr Theodore Reed journeyed to India to escort one of the most beautiful and rare creatures in the world back to the Smithsonian Institution's National Zoological Park in Washington, DC.

Mohini, as she was called, translates as 'enchantress' and she soon became one of the zoo's greatest attractions. She bewitched people with her startling glacier blue eyes and her white fur with its glamorous greyish-brown stripes. She was a white tiger, a mutant from the better known orange Bengal tiger.

It was not surprising that such an outstanding beauty acted remote when it came to suitors. She did produce three cubs with Samson, but the only white tiger cub died of a virus.

Then she mated with Ramana and gave birth to a single female white cub. The zoo was ecstatic about the new arrival. The Indian Ambassador suggested a name for her, Rewati, meaning 'a pure mountain stream'.

It was as if Mohini knew that her tiny cub was precious and irreplaceable, very valuable and difficult to rear. She began to lick the cub excessively and pace nervously around the cage, carrying the baby in her mouth. The zoo officials were worried. It was very odd behaviour. They felt the cub was in danger. The 420–pound tigress was normally a model mother, but the tiny bundle of 10,000–dollar fluff could so easily be crushed if Mohini was disturbed.

A decision had to be made.

Dr Reed took the cub home in his car. His wife, Elizabeth, was busy in the kitchen preparing a dinner party for fourteen guests. She was up to her elbows in stirring sauces and making dressings.

'Here's your new baby,' he said, putting the cub into her arms. 'We could turn one of the bedrooms into a nursery. She has to be in an incubator till she's stronger.'

Elizabeth looked at the small white kitten in her arms, totally bewildered. Incubator? Nursery? What on earth was she being let in for?

'But what are we going to feed her on?' she asked. 'Do we know about tiger's milk?'

'I can't find any information on tiger's milk,' said Dr Reed. 'The fat and protein content of the milk of big cats varies so much. We'll just have to use a commercial formula.'

Ebony watched the new arrival, his curiosity veiled with an aloof indifference. It was not unlike his own arrival at the house. He, too, had been smuggled upstairs.

The black cat was born in a barn on a busy farm. When the Reeds were on a visit there, Maryalice, their ten-year-old daughter, pleaded to be allowed to have one of the kittens, but her parents said no. The girl was very quiet on the drive home and her father thought she was sulking. But Maryalice was up to more than that. She had one of the kittens tucked inside her coat, a scrap of black fluff with a white spot on his chest, just to take the curse off.

Elizabeth was unable to resist the kitten when Maryalice eventually confessed. It was a bright, intelligent little thing and they could not possibly take him back. Dr Reed gave in. He knew when he was beaten. They christened the kitten Ebony and he quickly became Elizabeth's cat, following her everywhere.

He loved to be vacuumed. Whenever he heard the cleaner, he came scampering over, arching his back in delicious anticipation. Ebony had the run of the house and the yard, as well as the neighbourhood. There was never any evidence that he caught mice or birds, but the chipmunks in the garden decided to make a rapid and permanent exit.

Ebony listened to the cub yowling that first night. It was an insistent sound. He heard two pairs of bare feet hurrying across to the new nursery. Ebony stood in the nursery doorway, glaring balefully as Elizabeth went to tend the tiny cub. Rewati was howling for a bottle and a dry blanket. It was the beginning of a regular three-and-a-half-hour routine of feeds.

Ebony had no objection to this middle-of-the-night routine as long as there was some milk in it for him. He padded into the kitchen, where Rewati's feed was being made up.

'I haven't forgotten you,' Elizabeth yawned. She sat down for a moment, cradling her head in her arms. She was very tired. Ebony jumped onto her lap, pretending to be a kitten again. 'It's just for a few months, Ebony. I have to look after Rewati until she's strong enough to go back to her mother, and the zoo. Then it'll be just you and me again.'

A few months . . . How long was a few months, Ebony thought without enthusiasm. He felt threatened by the new arrival. He watched every move, every feed, trying to read the signs with suspicion.

Two days after Rewati arrived at the Reeds', her blue eyes opened and she looked in bright astonishment at the world around her. On the thirteenth day, she took her first wobbling walk on cotton-wool legs. On the twenty-second day, she began to play, shaking her towel, making miniature growling noises.

Ebony watched the cub's progress with caution. He sensed that the oddly striped bundle of snowy fur was something special. So special that everyone endured the round-the-clock routine without grumbling. Elizabeth was worried by the huge responsibility. So many people enquired daily as to the infant tiger's progress. And she was the one who the cub depended upon for its life.

At first it was difficult to find a compatible feeding formula, but by varying the commercial product, they gradually found the right mixture for a baby tiger. Soon Rewati outgrew the incubator and graduated to a box. The rate of growth astonished Ebony. He sat, meticulously washing his face and grooming his whiskers, but watching all the time. It seemed that with every feed, Rewati grew an inch. She became a bouncing bundle of energy, full of mischief, lunging and rolling about like a puppy.

The big black tom-cat took no notice of these antics, but he was disturbed when the tiger cub began crawling in tight circles on the floor making small noises and dragging her hind legs. Ebony sensed that something was very wrong and he wanted someone to come quickly. He began to miaow loudly. Elizabeth hurried in.

When the zoo's veterinary specialist arrived, Ebony moved away to a distance, but they did not seem to know what was the matter with the cub. They talked in low, worried voices. They tried antibiotics, oxygen treatments, outside exercise lessons and a formula pepped up with brandy and egg. Ebony's nose twitched at the smell. He wondered if he would be fed any of that delicious yellow stuff if he fell about on the floor.

But in a week the panic was over. Rewati recovered and was running around her garden jungle again. She graduated to baby cereal and strained beef in a bowl. Rewati was a sloppy eater, leaving most of it on her nose and face. Elizabeth always had a clean-up job with a damp washrag. Ebony helped too by licking out the bowl when no one was looking.

The jungle was a paradise of shrubs for hide and seek, camellia bushes on which to sharpen her claws and a big red ball for Rewati to pounce on and attack. She roamed free in the house, much to the surprise of visitors, unused to being greeted by a hefty playful tiger cub with formidable teeth and claws.

By now Rewati was trying to be friendly with Ebony. She wanted a playmate, but the black cat was having none of it. He'd seen those sharp claws puncture the red ball. He did not want to be similarly deflated.

Rewati chose her moment. She crept up to the unsuspecting Ebony and gave him a playful nuzzle in a soft spot. Ebony leaped into the air and up onto the fence. He sat there, totally outraged, licking down his disarranged fur. He glared down at the cub, whose baby blue eyes blinked back so innocently.

'Rewati needs someone to play with,' said Dr Reed.

Ebony could not believe his eyes when a second tiger cub arrived at the Reed household. The zoo had bought an orange Bengal cub as a playmate for Rewati. This cub was called Sakhi, which in Hindi means a close and dear companion.

Ebony was disgusted. He told Elizabeth in no uncertain terms. Now he had two half-wild creatures romping round his garden. He thought briefly about leaving home, but he loved Elizabeth too much. The yard had once been his domain; then it became a jungle for one baby to play in; now it was out-and-out tiger country. It became necessary to plot a course for safety with a dozen escape routes. He wasn't black and canny for nothing.

Rewati loved company. If she was left alone, she would howl and scratch and get into mischief. But if she could see someone, even just Ebony, she felt secure and happy.

As she grew bigger she was moved into new quarters in the base-ment. Elizabeth forgot to warn the man from the electric company about the new arrangement when he came to read the meter. He took quite a while to recover from the shock.

Rewati liked Elizabeth's company in the evening. The cub would curl up on the couch beside Elizabeth while they both watched television. Even the most boring programme took on a new lustre in such élite company, thought Elizabeth, stroking the white fur. She could rarely go out now. But when she did manage to get a brave tiger-sitting friend to stay for a while, the rule was: 'If the house catches fire, grab the cub first!'

The cub was now worth 35,000 dollars.

At two months old Rewati weighed a solid fifteen pounds and was eating ground beef. She greeted everyone in the Reed household with enthusiasm and affectionate chuffing noises. Ebony kept his distance. The young white tigress was already something of a handful. Friends were less keen on visiting. The cubs were becoming a rough and rowdy pair with teeth and claws that could hurt.

Ebony sensed something was different on that last day. Elizabeth was rather quiet. The two cubs were romping as usual in the garden and Ebony suddenly knew that they were going. He thought of all the friendly overtures he had dismissed. Perhaps he had been a little too standoffish. His icy reserve melted a fraction at the thought of their imminent departure.

Crossing the yard, he stopped, eyeing a thrashing white-striped tiger tail. The temptation was too much. For a few moments he batted the tiger tail back and forth with his paw like the kitten he was at heart.

Rewati turned and looked over her shoulder, blue eyes wide with surprise. Was this a game two could play? Ebony straightened his back slowly, recovered his dignity and stalked off into the shrubs without a backward glance. He never saw Rewati again.

Two weeks later, Sakhi also returned to the zoo. The house was very quiet and empty. Elizabeth wandered from room to room, at a loss without her tiger cubs. Ebony curled himself round her ankles. Remember me, he purred.

Elizabeth scooped him up into her arms, old friends, and nuzzled his dark head. 'They've gone. Just you and me now,' she said. ' . . . until the next phone call.'

Rewati is never lonely now. She has all the company she wants: hundreds of thousands of children visit the zoo every year to admire the magnificent fully grown white tigress.

Life returned to normal for Ebony. His patience was rewarded and he regained his rightful place in the Reed household.

He no longer shares Elizabeth's lap with a frisky white tiger cub. The garden is his, and the vacuum cleaner. Peace has returned.

The Cat from Next Door

It was so undignified and that's what really got Herbie about living with the ever expanding Robinson family. Sometimes he felt he must have been delivered in a Christmas stocking, gift-wrapped, but far more durable than the other playthings.

He knew if he saw six-year-old Katy donning her nurse's outfit then he was due for a blanket bath, and that meant being swathed in towels and ignominiously anointed with water. It meant having his face and ears washed which he particularly detested, but for the sake of Katy's gentle crooning and cuddling, he put up with these atrocities.

Eight-year-old Jane had thought up a torture of a different kind. He suffered being dressed in a matinée jacket, long nightie and bootees with a satin-ribboned bonnet flattening his ears. He endured being ridden up and down the road in the basket on the front of her bicycle. This was far worse than being pushed in the pram, because at least in the pram he could take a nose dive down to the foot of the cover and leave only his tail showing, whipping the pillow.

But in the bicycle basket, he was exposed to public glare and comment. He could not even have a good scratch. At the first sign of a slackening of Jane's attention, he would leap out on to the pavement, fly through gardens and across the fields to a secret place where he would hide long enough to divest himself of the hated garments.

This went on until Jane ran out of baby clothes.

Thomas, two years her senior and lanky with it, had a habit of putting Herbie on the top of doors. Just why, Herbie did not have the slightest idea. One minute he would be curled up happily on some abandoned school blazer, then . . . whoops! He would find himself being born aloft by Thomas and deposited on the top edge of an open door, scratching and clawing to gain a balance. Once there he could remain lying along the edge with complete indifference until rescued by some adult Robinson.

Herbie was a Bi-coloured Shorthair. He could be described as a black cat with white splodges or a white cat with black splodges. It depended on the angle of viewing which colour was predominant. He had a small, alert face with intelligent eyes and neat ears. No one was quite sure of his age. He came sort of before Katy and after Jane. His birthday was celebrated on the date of the Battle of Waterloo, 18 June, when he was encouraged in vain to blow out the candles on a nice piece of cod fillet and all day it was cream, cream, cream in his saucer.

He ate well with the Robinsons. They were always saying he was the only cat in Great Britain who got meals on wheels. This was because Grandma Robinson was too old to have new teeth fitted, and anything she fancied but couldn't manage went into his bowl. Herbie was game to try anything from trifle to spaghetti bolognese. He was not fussy.

Herbie loved boxes. They were his all-consuming passion. He would get into any box, trying it out for size. He would investigate the depths of paper bags, plastic carriers, handbags, suitcases, typewriter lids . . . you name it, he would get into it.

When the crates arrived he was delighted and curious. But when he made a few tentative forays, there were immediate shrieks of 'Mind the china!' 'Off that linen!' 'Help, that one's full of glasses!' and eventually. 'Will somebody put Herbie out, *please?*'

So Herbie sat in the garden and watched. There were no blanket baths and rides on bicycles these days. Everyone was so busy. He did not quite understand what was going on.

One morning the Robinson family assembled outside with bags and parcels and he was being passed round for hugs and wet kisses. It was all very messy and he still did not understand what was happening. He hoped it didn't mean that he was going down the road. Several of his elderly friends had told him that hugs and wet kisses meant going down the road and not coming back.

So Herbie was quite relieved when it was evident that the Robinsons were not intending to put him in the car as well as all their family and the mountain of luggage. He rubbed his head against Katy's new ankle socks to show that he forgave her all the medical ministrations.

'We don't really want to leave him behind, but what else can we do?' said Mrs Robinson. 'One is always hearing about cats that walk back to their old homes and how could Herbie cope with all that ocean? We're so grateful for your kind offer.'

'Shall I have a new kitten in Australia?' asked the fickle Jane.

'Of course, darling.'

'Don't worry, Mrs Robinson, I'll look after Herbie for you,' said a new, sweet young voice. 'He'll be perfectly all right with us. I'm sure he'll soon get used to us and we'll take great care of him.'

Katy wept more water all over Herbie's ears. 'Goodbye, darling Herbie,' she whispered. 'I'll never forget you, never, never, never . . .'

It was very disturbing, and then amid a great deal of noise the Robinsons drove off, leaving Herbie and the sweet voiced young woman on the front lawn. He looked at her, wondering what was going to happen next. She was very young and quite tall. He hoped she was not going to put him on top of doors. She regarded him a little uncertainly, her fairish hair brushing her cheek like a breeze stirring a cobweb in the moonlight.

'Come along,' she said, trying to sound brisk. 'You live next door now.'

He did not move for two reasons. Firstly he did not know what next door meant, and secondly he was a mite worried about the door bit. Chrissie picked him up carefully and gave him a few little pats. 'Come along,' she said, again, more cheerfully. 'This way . . .'

The next door house was joined on to the Robinson's house and it was exactly the same, except that it was all the other way round. He discovered that Chrissie and Alan Marshall were newly-weds, that they lived in empty rooms and went out all day. It was very strange. Sometimes Herbie thought he had gone deaf.

It was an odd house. There was nothing to jump on, knock over, hide behind, sit on, scratch at, sniff at, trample on or investigate. Most of the time Herbie sat in the middle of the kitchen floor, polite and distant, grooming himself and slightly nauseated by the pervading smell of paint. He missed the Robinsons and all the noise and activity. He missed being talked to and included as part of the family.

'Herbie doesn't seem very happy,' said Chrissie for the hundredth time. 'He behaves like a visitor.'

'Perhaps we ought to show him round,' Alan suggested. 'That might make him feel at home.'

'It's very difficult when you've never had a cat before,' said Chrissie. 'I never know what to do.'

'Don't worry, darling. They are very independent creatures, aloof and stand-offish. It's probably just his way.'

Alan hoisted Herbie off the floor and carried him up the stairs. He flung open the first door with a flourish.

'Now, this is the spare room,' he announced, putting Herbie down on the lino. Herbie was amazed. It had been impossible to move in the Robinson's spare room when they had one. It had always looked like a central sorting depot for Oxfam. But this spare room was totally without interest . . . he prodded the two tennis rackets with some apprehension.

'Careful, old chap,' admonished Alan. He steered Herbie out of the spare room and into the next room. 'And this is our bedroom. We sleep here,' he added unnecessarily.

Herbie made a flying leap on to the rose-patterned duvet. It sank most satisfyingly, but before he had even done half a turn, Chrissie had whisked him off again.

'Sorry,' she said. 'Not on the bed.'

He was not allowed on the two armchairs either, or on the draining board, or in Chrissie's shopping basket, or in the linen cupboard or under the television set. So he took to staying in the middle of the kitchen floor, quiet and withdrawn, sometimes pretending to be asleep or watching a bee buzzing against a window-pane trying to get in.

The garden was immaculate and everything was in measured rows. Herbie learned to tread carefully. He found it hard to stalk tigers in an organized jungle of Tom Thumb lettuces, or scare birds who were already wary of all the flapping labels.

The best spot was the greenhouse, baking warm and out of the draught. But Alan was growing grass in trays and kept shutting Herbie out.

'Shoo . . . mind the cuttings. Off my seedlings, old boy.'

Herbie lost weight despite the fact that the Marshalls were kind to him and fed him. But Herbie's heart began to fail when he saw Chrissie reaching yet again for the tin opener. He longed for a bit of fruit cake and some cold cocoa.

He made one visit to the Robinson's old house but never again. A horrible sloppy dog with ears hanging down like soup plates had moved in. Herbie shuddered and kept to his side of the fence.

Sometimes he sat on the pavement outside and watched people go by on bicycles and in cars. One young woman with red-streaked hair always stopped and stroked him, knowing the special place under his chin just above where his purr started.

Sometimes he followed children along the road, but he was afraid to go too far. He was less trusting than he used to be. Especially after the field-mouse episode. He had only meant it as a gift for Chrissie. It was such a tiny thing and was paralyzed with terror. Yet Chrissie had shrieked as if being attacked by a rampaging bull elephant. Herbie simply did not understand her and brought no more gifts.

The situation improved somewhat when Chrissie stopped going out every day. She started to sing around the house and that was rather nice. However, although she sat around quite a lot Herbie was never invited on to her lap. He now learned that he must not sit on her sewing or try to get into her knitting bag. The tennis rackets were moved into the back of the broom cupboard and some furniture was delivered for the spare room. Alan began hammering in the evenings and Herbie watched the shelves going up with interest.

'Off you come, Herbie. They won't take your weight,' said Alan, lifting him down.

'He's just testing,' said Chrissie with new perception.

Alan kissed her tenderly.

'Funny girl,' he said, ruffling her hair.

One day a new smell arrived in the house. Herbie recognized it immediately. It was the thin, sweet smell of milk. Something stirred and breathed in the pram parked in the hallway, and made small mewing sounds.

Herbie pricked up his ears. Surely it was not another cat? He stood up on his back legs and peered in, but the mesh of the cat-net obscured whatever lay under the mound of blankets.

'Say hello to Timmy,' said Chrissie, picking Herbie up with a growing confidence. It was the first time that Herbie had felt safe and not about to be dropped. He trembled slightly with a small rush of emotion.

Now the improvements began to accelerate at a rate of knots. Chrissie left things on the floor and was far too busy to notice if Herbie sat on them. All sorts of boxes and pails and bins began to appear in the kitchen.

'What on earth shall I do with this cereal?' Chrissie wailed one breakfast time. 'Timmy won't touch it.'

'Give it to the cat,' said Alan.

Baby cereal! One of Herbie's favourites. His rough little tongue could hardly lap it up for purring. Then at teatime it was marmite soldiers dropped all over the floor in various stages of squashed disintegration.

'Oh, you. are a messy baby,' said Chrissie, hurrying to clear up, but Herbie was there before her. It seemed like years since he'd had a marmite soldier.

The baby soon began to crawl and then there wasn't a thing Chrissie could do about life at floor level. It became a glorious landscape of wooden bricks, round-eyed ducks, chewed crusts, lost shoes, sticky spoons and a fat yellow teddy bear who kept falling over. Herbie sat amid the chaos, keeping an eye on the baby, keeping his claws sheathed and never getting in the way. He was still rather like a visitor.

One afternoon Chrissie was sewing while her baby played on the floor with some empty cotton reels. Herbie was sunning himself by the window when through half an eye he saw the baby reaching up towards the flex of a reading lamp.

No one really knew whether he remembered the occasion when Katy Robinson did the same thing and brought the whole contraption crashing down on her head, but in a split second Herbie leaped off the window-sill and sent the baby flying back on his bottom on the carpet. The baby howled in surprise and one chubby fist shot out and grabbed at Herbie's long waving tail.

It hurt. It hurt very much. Herbie was almost transfixed with pain. He dug his claws into the carpet.

Then Chrissie was down on her knees, scolding the baby, hugging Herbie. Or was it hugging the baby and scolding Herbie? It did not really matter for Herbie's heart was leaping up into a joyful rumble of happiness.

For in that moment Herbie had looked into Timmy's eyes, and had seen a faint but unmistakable vision of blanket baths, and bicycle rides and door tops, and perhaps even worse. But it meant Herbie had a home. The move was complete. Next door had become home. At last.

Curtain Call

It was not that Titus was stagestruck or came of a theatrical family, but rather that he came upon the warm, steamy stage door entrance on a chilly October night when he was at his lowest ebb.

The Titus of that moment was far removed from the majestic creature that now greets patrons in the foyer of the plush Wellington Theatre as they arrive for the evening performance. He always sits a little to the side of the first step of the grand staircase leading to the Dress Circle, his brilliant lemon eyes scrutinizing each new arrival.

But on that wet autumnal night, Titus slunk his emaciated body towards the stage door, drawn like a magnet towards the light and warmth. His black fur was matted, his white vest caked with Thames mud, one ear tattered and bloodied after a fight with some Soho cats over the debris from a restaurant dustbin.

Titus had been on the London streets for twenty-seven days. It had been a terrifying experience, and one for which his suburban upbringing had not prepared him. From kittenhood he had been housed by the Carson family, fed, milked and comfortably quartered in a specially designed cat-bed lined with foam cushions. Life had been uneventful apart from pouncing on the odd bird, or an occasional night-out caterwaul.

As Titus sunned himself in their back garden, he gathered vaguely that the Carsons were going on something called a holiday. He sensed change in the bustle of packing and kept out of the way. Then the

Carsons discovered that the cat kennels had closed because of a flu epidemic.

This seemed to throw everyone in a panic, and Titus, who somehow felt responsible, kept very quiet and withdrawn. Then an old aunt appeared with an equally old wicker basket and said why couldn't they take Titus with them to the house they were renting in Cornwall?

Titus had sniffed the basket with apprehension. It smelled of long gone cats, ill cats, bored cats, tired cats. When they put him inside it, he fought and scratched and it took two adults to fasten the lid.

All the way to London in the car Titus spat and howled and they had to turn up the volume of the radio to drown his protests. Nerves began to get frayed and the children started to quarrel about silly things.

Titus scratched and chewed between howls. Suddenly the lid flew up and he scrambled out, perched for one petrified moment on the back of the driver's seat and then leaped out of the open car window. The cacophony was terrifying – buses, cars, coaches, hooters blaring from all directions . . . Titus fled along Westminster Bridge, careering between people's legs, dashing across the road, slithering down stone steps and racing along the Embankment, tail high, fur on end.

The Carsons could not find him. They spent an agonizing two hours searching and calling his name. Eventually they gave up, reported their loss to the police, and continued on their way to Cornwall, both children crying noisily in the back of the car.

Titus crawled out from his hiding place under a fruit stall near Embankment underground station and surveyed the busy street scene. It was nothing like the town he came from. At first he felt a little heady and elated with his new freedom, and he strolled the streets, taking in everything like a tourist. He was somewhat bewildered by the sheer volume of traffic, but continued sight-seeing, curious and wondering.

However, three days later the excitement of city life had worn off. He was cold and hungry, and had come across unexpected hostility from other vagrant cats. If he found a restaurant dustbin with some fish or chicken scraps in it, within seconds some huge alley-cat would turn up, hissing and spitting and claiming territorial rights.

The weather changed and it began to rain, and warm, dry places were difficult to find. The pavement was hard on his paws, and his pads grew callouses. The foam-cushioned bed began to fade from his memory.

Titus was not built for jungle warfare. His plump good looks quickly disappeared and he became scrawny and untrustful. No one spoke to him and he missed human companionship. No one stroked him with affection. His heart shrank with emptiness. Sometimes his only human contact was a boot kicking him out of a doorway.

He roamed the mud flats of the Thames shore, wondering if they might lead him to this place called Cornwall.

He had had nothing to eat all that twenty-seventh day except a rotting fish-head he had found in a gutter near Billingsgate Market, where the language addressed to him had not improved much since the sixteenth century.

He crouched against a wall where the overhanging stonework gave him some protection from the weather. His tail was curled under him, his ears flattened against his head. He watched the lights of the stage door entrance, and the orange-red glow from within. It looked warm and he could hear cheerful sounds.

People were coming out now, chatting and laughing, wrapping scarves round their heads and putting up brightly coloured umbrellas.

'Night-night. Sleep tight.'

'On my diet? See you tomorrow.'

Titus was wondering if he might be able to slip in unnoticed when the next group of people paused in the doorway before venturing out into the grey street. He slithered forward, his dark fur merging into the shadows of the night.

'Just look at that poor creature,' said one of the young women suddenly. She came out of the group, not conscious of the rain on her dark, curling hair. She did not touch Titus, but went down on one knee, approaching him respectfully like a true cat lover.

She made small encouraging noises so that he would not be alarmed, and when he made no move to escape or bite, she put out a careful hand to rub his forehead.

'There, there, puss. My goodness, you are wet. And so thin. Look, Nigel, you can see his ribs. I don't think the poor thing has had a decent meal for weeks.'

'Oh, do come along, Lindy. Stop messing about with that revolting creature. You know we're meeting the others for supper, and we're going to be late as it is.' Nigel strolled over, a tall, elegant young man turning up the collar of his trench coat.

'It doesn't seem fair,' said Lindy, straightening up. 'Here we are, going out to supper when we're not really hungry, leaving this poor cat who is starving. It's cruel.'

'What do you propose to do? Take the cat out to supper with us? Do you think it would prefer Chinese or Italian?' he asked with a calculated degree of sarcasm in his voice. He was a very promising actor.

'That's a splendid idea,' said Lindy with some spirit. 'You go ahead and join the others. I'm taking him across to Joe's for a square meal. Don't wait for me.'

'You must be joking. Lindy, for heaven's sake, you're not going to pick it up? It's filthy and it's probably got fleas. It'll bite you and then you'll get tetanus. We've no one to replace you if you get ill,' Nigel warned gloomily.

'Nonsense, he's not going to bite me. He's got the look of a perfect gentleman. And you'd be filthy too, if you were living in the streets. He's a gorgeous cat really. Look at his eyes. They're beautiful . . .'

Titus did not struggle. The young woman's arms were holding him confidently, and her voice dripped words which were honey to his soul. Her eyes were a dark hazel, flecked with amber, warm, caring and unafraid.

Joe's Café was on the point of shutting, but when Joe saw Lindy approaching, he hastily reversed his closed sign.

'Hi,' he said, casually stacking his accountancy books out of sight under the counter. He was taking a correspondence course between customers. 'What can I get you?'

'One coffee and one warm milk straight away please, Joe. Then one cottage pie with plenty of gravy and I think I'll just have a cheese omelette,' said Lindy, choosing a table away from the door and the draughts. She settled the cat on her knee, calming his nerves with gentle strokes.

'Eating alone?' asked Joe, slightly confused by the order.

'No, just me and Titus,' said Lindy, making an equally puzzling reply.

How Titus enjoyed that first meal with Lindy! The warm milk was nectar, the cottage pie ambrosia. He could hardly eat for the deep, rhythmic purrs that threatened to choke him.

Afterwards Lindy took him back to the theatre, explaining that he could not live in her high-rise flat, but that he was welcome to doss down in her dressing room. She found him an old props box and lined it with a towel. She thoughtfully left open a small top window so that he could get in and out.

Titus fell asleep immediately, hardly able to believe his luck. He felt his dignity returning. He soon warmed to this strange, rambling building where people seemed to live during the day but went away at night when it became all his. Not only did he adopt the Wellington Theatre, but he appointed himself Lindy's guardian and mentor, too.

Taking charge of the theatre was a gargantuan task. He swept it clean of mice and no rats dared to come within a whisker of the place. He checked security, superintended the cleaning women, attended rehearsals, and was in the foyer every evening to welcome the patrons.

His appearance improved out of all recognition – he was not only clean and well-fed, but he had grown in magnificence with his new status. His black fur gleamed like darkest velvet, his white shirt front was whiter than pure snow and as soft as swansdown. He held his head proudly, his shoulders haunched haughtily, his tail curved over his toes with precision and delicacy. His lemon eyes watched everybody and everything: nothing escaped him, from a spider taking up residence beind a marble pedestal to a programme wedged between two seats.

Titus ate at Joe's Café and Lindy insisted that Joe gave her a weekly bill. Joe was reluctant about this, saying that Titus mainly ate leftovers, but Lindy was adamant. What about all the extra milk, she argued? Titus guessed that Joe did not charge Lindy enough because there was often a nice piece of fish or some steak for him. So he took on the café as a side line and the mice got a salutary eviction.

However, Titus had a curious attitude towards the cats who scavenged the dustbins. He did send them flying, but not, Joe observed, until after they had found something to eat.

'It's as if Titus remembers,' Joe told Lindy, one evening over a late coffee. 'He seems to have a certain sympathy for them.'

'Of course he remembers,' said Lindy, rubbing Titus expertly under his chin bone. 'Cats have memories, and are most intelligent creatures. Why, the Egyptians even worshipped a cat-goddess called Pasht.'

It was in Lindy's dressing room that Titus overheard Lindy and Nigel having a fairly heated discussion about the play. It was a classic thriller and assured of a pretty long run with the tourists and coach parties. But Lindy was unhappy about one scene.

'The letter incident really is my best scene,' Lindy was saying as she sat at the mirror taking off her make-up. 'And I would appreciate it if you would not fidget so much, Nigel. Somehow it destroys the tension I'm trying to build up.'

Titus was only half listening. He was curled up in his prop box which by now was lined with Lindy's shawl.

'I'm not fidgeting,' said Nigel, lighting up a cigarette. 'I'm merely being natural and at ease.'

'I don't regard that messing about with the decanter this evening

73

as being natural and at ease. How can I be tense and emotional, reading the letter, when you are wandering about doing different things? It wouldn't be so bad if you always did the same things, then at least I could time my pauses.'

'I'm improvising, darling,' said Nigel, casually. 'You should be able to cope.'

Lindy turned, the amber in her eyes starting to spark. She crunched the tissue in her hand and tossed it into the wastepaper bin.

'I don't rush about madly during your confession scene,' she retorted. 'I keep still, I blend, I merge. I leave it to you. It's your scene.'

'But that's your style,' said Nigel, getting up to leave. 'You blend, merge . . . I just naturally dominate.'

'Oh!' The crash as she slammed down the jar of cleansing cream made Titus almost jump out of his box. 'How can you be so selfish?' Lindy stormed at Nigel. 'You're spoiling my best part. People will stop believing in me, and then when the c-contracts are renewed, they'll get s-somebody else . . . and I'll be out on the streets.'

Titus did not understand about contracts, but he knew all about being out on the streets. He had had twenty-seven days of it and he would not wish one half-minute of the experience on his beloved Lindy.

The following evening, once the audience was seated and he had checked the stalls, the dress circle and the upper circle. Titus sat in the wings, keeping well out of everyone's way.

It was true. During the letter scene, Nigel very craftily took the tension out of Lindy's reading. He stretched, he got up to close the curtains, he smoothed his hair in a mirror . . .

Lindy's hand was trembling as she held the crucial letter but Titus could tell that the audience had been diverted and the atmosphere in the theatre had lost its electricity.

In the interval he went back to Lindy's dressing room but he did not go in. From inside he could hear the sound of weeping. He quickly nipped over to Joe's Café to try and seek help there. Joe looked up from the text book he was studying, surprised, since Titus never usually left the theatre during a performance.

'Hello, you're early,' he said. 'What's the matter?'

Titus could not tell him, but he tried. He rubbed against Joe's ankles, miaowing desperately. Realizing he wasn't having any luck with Joe, he returned swiftly to the theatre.

The confession scene was near the end of the play. It was well-written and Nigel made the most of it. He began the speech with his usual confident skill.

At about line four, Titus casually strolled on stage. He sniffed carefully around and then decided that the upholstered arm of the settee was the best vantage point. He leapt up gracefully and got into position. Then he turned and stared at Nigel.

He stared. He kept still. He remembered what Lindy had said about blending, but it was a little difficult for a magnificent black and white short-haired cat to blend successfully.

He sat there throughout the whole speech, staring, dignified, enigmatic, ears pricked at such an angle that he looked as though he were listening politely to a vaguely amiable idiot.

Nigel fought back. His voice grew louder, his projection more deliberate. The sweat glistened on his forehead.

Then Titus yawned, a small pink-mouthed yawn of delicate boredom. The audience collapsed in laughter.

It did not ruin the play but it did ruin Nigel's scene. He stormed off after the curtain calls in a furious temper.

'I'll kill that cat,' he raged. 'Get it out of the theatre!'

But the management refused. Everyone liked Titus. The producer thought the change of emphasis actually improved the finale. He was wondering if Titus could be persuaded to do it again.

Meanwhile Titus took refuge under a table at Joe's, exhausted. Acting was definitely tiring work. And those blinding bright lights . . . the experience had been quite unnerving.

Of course it was in all the newspapers the next day, and soon the box office began to break records as people flocked to see Titus. He did not always go on. It seemed to depend on how the letter scene went, observed Joe, who came over regularly to watch the phenomenon.

Eventually Nigel's nerve broke. He could stand it no longer and he left the cast. Lindy got her contract renewed, Joe passed his exams and a few months later they got married.

Titus was guest-of-honour at the wedding reception. He decided wedding cake was overrated but champagne was delicious. Lindy looked as pretty as a picture with white roses entwined in her dark curls, and he hardly recognized Joe in a suit.

'And where are you going for your honeymoon?' someone asked.

'Cornwall,' said Lindy. 'We've been lent a very romantic fisherman's cottage. We thought we might take Titus with us.'

Titus did a standing leap which took him out of the window on to the balcony of the restaurant. He fled down the Strand, through the back streets of Covent Garden, down an alleyway that led to another alleyway that led to the back of the theatre, up through his window into Lindy's dressing room and into his prop box.

He loved Lindy. He was prepared to follow her to the ends of the earth. But there was one place where he would not go.

Cat Knievel

No one told me there was going to be an audition. Nor that I was the item being auditioned. How was I to know, as I munched my way through a man-sized breakfast, that today I was required to look sleep and athletic, and not like an over-stuffed ginger-banded bean bag?

I was aware of the air of tension in the kitchen as I polished off the leftovers in Hebe's bowl. Hebe is a black Persian queen with an appetite like a bird, which is just as well for me. I took me and my stomach to the window-sill for a tidy-up while I had the strength. My fawn paws worked overtime as I coaxed my thick russet and caramel fur into near perfect order.

'I must have been mad,' Val was saying, rushing around cleaning up the place. This meant we were having visitors. I knew the signs. 'I wish I'd never written to them. After all, I mean, what does it matter, really?'

'You knew they'd go for it,' said Robert. 'It's just the kind of thing they love. A performing cat and an idiot owner. They don't often get both at once.'

'I'm going to look a fool if Copper won't co-operate,' Val wailed. 'He'll probably sleep all afternoon and refuse to budge an inch. Oh no, we've run out of cat sweets. I'll have to rush to the shops and get some. He'll never perform without his usual bribe.'

'Bribe?'

'Reward.'

By now I had the faintest suspicion that they were talking about me partly because my name is Copper and I am addicted to cat sweeties. I need my daily fix. Sorry, folks, that's just a joke. I'm doing what comes naturally, and if a little reward comes my way naturally too, then I'm not one to refuse.

'May I point out that Evel Knievel is at present looking so unhealthily fat that I doubt if he could jump over a pincushion if you gave him a hefty push,' said Robert as he left for work.

Val scooped me up into her arms. I purred hello, patted her face gently, tugged a claw through a tempting brown curl.

'He weighs a ton,' she said, her voice doom-laden. 'He won't be able to do a thing.'

That was true. I only felt like sleeping it off under my favourite forsythia bush at the end of the garden.

A young man arrived, sleek, smooth, trendy. I could tell from his voice that he was not over the moon about cats. His name was Martin O'Connell and he was a director. Director of what? But I was only marginally curious.

'Do you like cats?' I heard Val asking him.

'I can take them or leave them,' he replied, with a distinct lack of enthusiasm.

I settled back into the warm crushed grass of my hideaway. It was nothing to do with me. The pale March sunshine dappled my coppery fur and lulled me into an unsuspecting doze.

But suddenly it had a great deal to do with me. I was unceremoniously heaved out and cajoled into my routine. It was the same old stuff – sit, beg, lie down, shake hands. Years ago, for reasons she cannot remember, Val had decided to train me in basic obedience as one would a dog. I was very easy to teach, of course, being intelligent and an extrovert. I didn't mind the treats either.

'Paw.'

I held out my left paw. Always my left. It's something to do with balance.

'Down.'

I flopped down, full length. I went through it all, trying to maintain a matching lack of enthusiasm, reacting to Val's voice and hand signals with an air of casual sophistication. I was doing it all for Val, though I do quite enjoy it. The O'Connell man was looking at me without any expression. I could do that too. I stared back at him, unflinching. I do have the strangest colour eyes; they are the colour of the underside of a new leaf, like the clear green sea off Cyprus; like a piece of polished green onyx marble in a museum. They can be disconcerting to some humans.

'Well . . . how about this jumping over toddlers you say he can do,' the director went on, continuing his laid-back attitude.

'Yes, yes,' said Val, rapidly producing our own home-grown toddler, a two-year-old variety called Jenni, and a collection of toys to add to the line-up.

'Jump,' Val commanded.

I cleared toddler and teddy with one spring. I was certainly not at my best as I was carrying a lot of extra weight. But Mr O'Connell seemed marginally impressed.

'Could we add a few more toddlers?' he suggested.

For two hours I defied gravity, heaving my great bulk over various toddlers and objects. Not satisfied with toddler-jumping, the director wanted to see stunning feats of athleticism involving various toys and children.

'Could we get him to jump over a toddler pushing a pram?' suggested Martin with signs of interest glimmering in his eyes. 'What do you think, eh?'

Val looked at me dubiously. It had been half-day closing at the shops so she was rewarding me with biscuits, most of which I politely declined. She could see that I was getting tired and bored.

'I could get some more toddlers tomorrow,' she said, frantically thinking of her friends' offspring.

Martin went into a deep directorial think. I began to slink off. There was a limit to what I would do for a biscuit.

'Okay, then. We'll call it a day. The filming will begin at ten o'clock tomorrow. Sharp.'

They let me sleep on their bed. This was a great treat and I spent the night happily tramping about, pawing, clawing, purring, first with one and then the other. Of course, I did sleep but I can purr quite loudly even when fast asleep.

'Get this cat off the bed,' grumbled Robert from under the covers.

'No, I want Copper in a certain frame of mind for tomorrow,' said Val, trying to sleep with me half sprawled over her pillow, my fur tickling her nose. 'I want Copper to be relaxed and happy.'

'Urrgh . . . tomorrow.'

Anyone would think they didn't sleep well. I don't know what they were grumbling about; they've got a lovely bed. Try sleeping in a cardboard box in the kitchen every night and see how they'd like that.

'Will you go out and buy a bribe, I mean, a chicken,' asked Val anxiously at breakfast time. 'I'd like to cook it before the film crew arrive. It's for Copper's lunch.'

Lunch? Whatever happened to breakfast? I wolfed down the meagre spoonful of Whiskas on my saucer and looked up expectantly. What was that? A sample?

'Sorry, Copper. No more breakfast for you. This is your great day. You've got to be a little peckish.'

Peckish! I was starving. I prowled around, wondering what I could find that was edible. Crumbs from under the high-chair? There were some congealed bits of boiled egg and soggy cereal. No, thank you. Whatever was going on? Overfed one day, diet the next. I looked for the Persian queen's dish but it had been whisked away. Now that wasn't playing fair.

Okay then, don't feed me, I thought. They'd be sorry. I sat aloof, grooming my whiskers and long striped tail as if I didn't care. I was looking thinner already.

Suddenly the place erupted as the film crew arrived. There were hundreds of them, at least seven. I fled, watching the commotion from a safe distance. Furniture was moved out into the garden (were the family going to live in the garden? What about rain?); tall things with white faces were installed throwing out a bright hot glare. Long black snakes slithered around the living-room floor and boxes of equipment filled every available space.

Spotlights, cables, cameras, microphones . . . I'd never heard these strange words before. And the noise! The house was full of people all talking to each other at once and stomping about. What on earth was happening? I looked at Val, but she too had caught this distraught look.

People were stepping over other people as a man fiddled with something in the hall; another wrestled with a stubborn camera in the kitchen. The house had gone mad. It was like a rabbit warren on a Bank Holiday.

I kept out of the way though my nose was twitching with curiosity. The director arrived wearing a rakish cap and carrying a clipboard of notes. He was telling everyone else what to do. My poor stomach was rumbling. I connected Val's breakfast lapse with this horde of people who had invaded our house. I slid off into the garden. They wouldn't miss me. Perhaps they wouldn't even notice my disappearance for days . . .

'Where's Copper?' asked Val.

Her voice was like a thin reed in the lull before a storm.

There was a stunned silence. No one moved. The director went white. Panic swept through the assembled crew. Even the cables twitched. They were ready to film and the star had vanished.

'Oh my God. The cat,' gasped Martin. 'Find the cat. Esther will be furious.'

The whisper went round like a word game . . . find the cat, find the cat . . . careful now, don't scare him.

'Ah, there he is,' said Val with the air of a magician. 'I've spotted his ginger fur in the bushes.'

I was brought back, limp, disinterested, but I was only pretending. I could smell chicken cooking in the kitchen. That was a good sign.

The equipment and lights had been positioned. There were a lot of extra toddlers and every imaginable kind of toy. Were we having a jumble sale? Perhaps we had become a nursery school?

'Now, Copper darling,' said Val, taking me aside. 'This is your great chance. You're going to be famous. You're going to be on 'That's Life!' Isn't that exciting?'

I nudged her chin. 'That's Life?' Never heard of it. What was it, for heaven's sake? I'd been on a window-sill, on the top of a car, on a flower bed, but I'd never been on a that's life.

For the next six hours they had me working like a horse. Sit, beg, lie down, shake hands, jump this, jump that. Every conceivable camera angle was trained on me and caught on film.

Jumping toddlers isn't that easy. They move . . . unexpectedly. An arm, a leg, and curly little head can suddenly catch me in mid-flight. Ouch. It required precision, timing and a certain expertise to cope with toddlers. I'm no amateur.

Someone crawled on the floor with this black object called a microphone and put it in front of my mouth. They wanted to catch me purring. I shook out my back leg. It's what I do when I'm embarrassed, and my goodness, was I embarrassed. It was covered in dust too. I gave it a quick lick. Then they wanted to catch me cleaning myself. Invasion of privacy, I called it. But I didn't complain. Val was rewarding me with masses of chicken morsels and I could handle quite a few.

There was a break for lunch; it was hardly worth my putting in an appearance. I got a kitten-size helping of chicken. What was going on? No proper meals but rewards coming my way like it was Christmas. Not the balanced diet I was accustomed to. Val wasn't eating much either.

Martin O'Connell was no longer so laid-back and remote. He became fired with enthusiasm for new stunts. He invented more complicated obstacles for me to jump over . . . toddler pushing pram, toddler on rocking horse, a two-storey green-tiled dolls' house, rows and rows of squirming toddlers side by side on the carpet . . . I was beginning to see toddlers coming out of the wall.

'Wonderful! Wonderful!' exclaimed Martin. 'Come on, Copper, you can do it! That's my baby! Did you catch that expression on film? I want that lion look. Again! Copper baby, you're the tops!'

By now I was like a machine, a gleaming oiled machine of muscles and sinews, my russet fur glowing in patches and stripes like fire under the hot lights. I leaped through the air, effortlessly and gracefully, my long tail streaming, a powerful beast of the jungle, a leopard in flight, muscles rippling under the taut shining coat. I was ecstatic. I could jump forever and I could jump anything. I could jump over trees, clear the roof tops, take on the moon . . .

One evening they insisted that I came indoors to watch some programme on television. Val and Robert were eagerly waiting to see what would be shown of six hours of filming. It had been weeks ago, way back in March. I'd almost forgotten all about it.

The programme began. We waited. I yawned delicately and wondered if I could ask to go out. There was far more going on in the garden.

'And now to Copper,' said Esther Rantzen, grinning widely. 'Our pet of the week. The toddler-leaping cat!'

'Jump!'

I pricked my ears. I heard Val's voice giving me my command. What did she want me to jump? But she was chatting away to Robert, not even looking at me.

'Jump!'

Hang on, now. She was doing it without moving her lips. I sat up, prepared to jump but the command simply wasn't clear. Jump what? The Sunday newspaper on the carpet . . . ?

My attention was directed to the television screen. I yawned again. I hardly recognized the splodge of ginger doing all those pathetic little stunts. You should see me now. Since then I have gone on to perfecting bigger and better jumps. Now I am magnificent.

That other stuff was child's play.

Cloud Eight

It was a forbidden place. A cold white box with the faint hum of machinery. But it held a fascination for Victcha. She often sat outside its door, waiting patiently, knowing it housed all sorts of delicacies – chicken, liver, milk, cream, cheese, trifle, butter . . . Victcha almost drooled in anticipation. Even her favourite Whiskas used to live in there if she happened to leave any – which was not often.

Victcha was not sure of the sequence of events that gave her access to this holy of holies, but perhaps someone left the door open or the catch slipped. It was about five feet high, free standing; it was easy to miss a small black and white shape crouched on a back shelf hopefully impersonating a carton of juice. Then someone shut the door without seeing the cat.

It was very dark inside and the hum was louder now. Victcha explored the shelf. It seemed to be almost empty. Only some bottles and boxes. Where had all the lovely food gone? She sniffed expectantly. But everything was covered up.

It was also cold inside, a fact which did not bother Victcha at first. Her coat kept her warm. She huddled, flipping her tail over her nose. The tips of her ears were paper thin and beginning to feel cold. It was a sensation she did not like.

She curled herself into a smaller ball, wishing the cold would go away. It was not such a nice place after all. She grew restless and scratched at the door, miaowing. No one heard.

Sleep was coming over her in waves. Instinctively she fought off the sleepiness, knowing that this was not a normal sleep.

'Victcha . . . Victcha . . .'

She heard her name, very faint and far away.

She was trembling now, an ague over which she had no control. It was becoming difficult to breathe as the cold began to paralyze her muscles. She could not fight the overwhelming sleepiness.

She was floating. It was a strange weightlessness, as if she was made of air. She did not question her new state because it was not frightening and she felt very uncurious.

There were dreams in her mind. It was like spinning back to when she was a kitten and the world was very new. Images floated in and out of her consciousness, vague but recognizable, comforting and not in any way a threat.

The cold was something she had never endured before, but it no longer mattered. She had gone beyond the point of feeling the cold; she was frozen; but the pain had gone.

The mist was a strange colour now; lavender, rose and blue, very blue . . . it was the sky, a vast endless sky, above, below and all around her.

'Her heart has stopped beating,' said the vet, Dennis Archer. 'It's not surprising. How long was she trapped in the fridge?'

'We're not sure. But she was missing for up to twenty-four hours.'

'There's not much hope, then.'

'Can't you try? Please try. There could be a chance,' urged Dorothy Wozniak. Her little black and white cat was the joy of her life. 'Please do something.'

Mr Archer tried to find the heart-beat eight times, but eventually gave up. Victcha remained icy cold. There was an odd gasp from the still form.

'I'm sorry, but she's technically dead of hypothermia.'

Dorothy was heart-broken. Her lovely little cat. They left Victcha lying on the vet's table, thinking they would never see her again.

'Look,' said Mr Archer. 'Her temperature is too low to record. But I will give her an anti-shock injection, and put her in a kennel with warm blankets and an infra-red light. If there's no change in the morning, then I'll make all the arrangements to dispose of the body.'

He always hated this part but someone had to be practical. Sometimes a grieving owner preferred to take their pet back to a familiar garden; others did not want a painful reminder.

The young art student went-home with her family. They would

never know how Victcha had got shut in the fridge. They could not forgive themselves for allowing it to happen. But the refrigerator was the last place they had thought of looking for Victcha when she went missing.

What a pity, thought Mr Archer, preparing the injection. It was a nicely marked cat with a sweet white face and big patches of black above the eyes and under the jaw. The cat would not have known much about it, or suffered. It would have got progressively colder, then simply gone to sleep. But he did as he had promised and left the cat under an infra-red lamp.

It was another busy day at the surgery; cats and dogs of all shapes and sizes came and went. Mr Archer was called out several times.

It was seven hours after Victcha had been brought into the surgery when a veterinary assistant, working late, heard a funny noise. The black and white cat had thrown off the blanket and was getting unsteadily to her feet, looking around in a dazed manner. Victcha shook her head, wondering where she was. She stretched her stiff limbs and began to stagger to the edge of the kennel.

'Good heavens,' exclaimed the assistant. 'She's alive! It's a miracle.'

Victcha began to miaow feebly. She was feeling hollow and hungry and still cold. The tips of her ears were tingling like ice.

The assistant heated some milk and Victcha lapped the warm drink gratefully. She was emerging from the strangest dreams. She could not make out what was real. They were fading now as the world became a familiar place again. The assistant wrapped her in a blanket and stroked her.

'There, pussy. You have had a strange adventure.'

'I can't believe it,' said Mr Archer, examining the cat thoroughly in the morning. 'That cat was technically dead. No heart-beat. Temperature too low to record. The odd gasp. Nothing. Somehow she's come back to life. As you say, it's a miracle.'

The Wozniak household was wrapped in gloom. They were all upset about the fate of their little cat. Victcha had meant a lot to them.

'I think I'll just ring the vet's, once more,' said Dorothy.

She listened in amazement, hardly able to believe her ears, trying to take in what the receptionist was telling her.

'It's Victcha! She's alive after all. She suddenly came back to life and started staggering around. She's all right now and we can go round and collect her any time.'

Dorothy's eyes filled with tears of joy. Her prayers to St Francis of Assisi had been answered.

Victcha came home to much rejoicing, though she did not understand what had happened. She had gone to sleep in one place and somehow woken up in another. It was all very peculiar.

She has fully recovered but is a little wary of the refrigerator now. Despite the memories of lovely food inside it, she knows it holds the cold hand of death.

Black Tom

All my life I have known the wild weather. The wild country and the wild wind are my constant companions. We exist together in bleak, raw, uncompromising closeness.

Here I wander the brown and purple moors, following solitude, finding loneliness, skirting the chattering beck which tumbles down the slope; where into the distant horizon the hills rise, wave upon wave, like the sea I have never seen. Sometimes in summer the beck is a mere trickle seeping over moss-covered pebbles, and then the air is soft and warm and the white-bibbed mountain blackbird trills a high sweet song.

But these moments are rare. It is the wild weather which dominates the moors . . . thunderstorms and forked lightning stabbing the turf, torrential rain, and wind that tears at the root of the heather and cotton sedge, and twists the gaunt trees into grotesque shapes.

Then I crouch under some friendly bush or shrub, or in the lee of a stone dyke, blinking my eyes against the furious rain, knowing that the elements and I are at war, but knowing that I can become stronger by leaning into their fierce onslaught.

When I return to the hillside village, the rain is streaming down the cobbled streets and the horses are in danger of slipping backwards. The old stone houses look as if they will topple down the steep street and fall onto the bridge that spans the rushing beck.

I have been brought to live in a house of grey stone, heavily roofed with slabs to withstand the wind. It is built on high ground, beyond the church and the crowded churchyard where the moss-covered tombstones stand shoulder to shoulder like an army of silence.

I remember the day that the family came to the house. A canvas-covered wagon lumbered up the steep incline, followed by seven carts full of their household belongings. The villagers stared from behind their curtains, for it seemed the man was of importance to their lives. A crowd of children of all sizes spilled out of the wagon, quietly behaved but excited, running all over the garden and narrow paths through the churchyard. A woman moved aside from the mountain of luggage and looked at the bleak moorland house and the rugged hills surrounding it. Her delicate features were set into a peculiar longing. This could never be a home for her. She was from the warmer, softer south.

She tried, but quite soon her spirit fled and the sorrowing children were left to play unsupervised among the hills. There were six children, five little girls and a boy.

The eldest girl strived to be a mother, and it was then I was brought into the household to amuse the little ones, who were withdrawn and quiet. It was a very cold house. But it became too much responsibility for the girl's young shoulders, and an aunt arrived who immediately lit an immense fire in the grate in her bedroom and began to turn the house back into a home.

The house was almost part of the moor, sharing its bleakness and raw weather; the doors open to its moods, a free sanctuary for the animals. There were other cats that came and went; the dogs, of course, Keeper and Flossie and Jasper; wild geese and some tame ones; Hero the hawk. We were cared for like people, not pets. They talked to us, drew sketches of us, took us with them onto the moor. It was unusual in these harsh living conditions.

'I fed Rainbow, Diamond, Snowflake and Jasper this morning,' the tall thin girl wrote gravely in a little book. It was the dogs and the moorland hawk that she loved the most. Sometimes I followed her flapping black skirts across the moor. She was like a bird herself. If the wind had taken her into its arms and borne her away, I would not have been surprised.

There was a short, plain girl called Lottie, who was too busy for much tenderness towards the animals. She drowned herself in her studies, spending hours reading and writing, then bustling about with the many household chores that fell her way. But she too escaped to the moors in all weathers whenever she could, holding her stiff black bonnet to her cheek, her short-sighted eyes raised fervently to the distant hills.

'I must escape,' I heard her saying. 'We must all escape. I shall see that we all escape . . .'

The wind carried her voice away, and she stood still, as if she could see the words escaping into the air while her body was chained to the muddy earth. She shrugged her shoulders with despair, and then set off along the track at such a pace I could hardly keep up with her.

It was the youngest girl, Anne, who loved me the most. She was violet-eyed and delicate and often ill. I would curl up at her feet as she lay on the sofa in the dining-room, her cheeks flushed with fever and a cough racking her chest.

'Oh Black Tom, Black Tom,' she said tenderly. 'What will become of us all in this wild place? If only I were a cat like you, and could bury my face in my fur to keep out the cold. Will you teach me how to do it?'

She laughed, and that started her coughing and she held the pain in her side until it stopped. She wiped the tears away with a cambric handkerchief and lay back against the pillow. The delirium took her wandering in her mind and she found herself stepping lightly into a cart that was to transport her on the long journey. It was a still dark April dawn and she had a long way to travel in her troubled dream.

I followed the silently lurching cart down the steep lane to the bottom of the valley, and then as it began to climb up the other side. But I went no further and sat in the sombre light thinking of my Anne. I dreamed I was old and thin and would not see her again, and my limbs twitched.

The father of the family was a tall, proud figure with an awesome head. He taught the children, the girls as well as the son, but he could not stand their childish prattling. After his wife died, he retreated more into his study and only shared the breakfast meal with the family.

'Tabitha,' he said sternly to the maidservant, polishing his small steel-rimmed spectacles. 'I will take my supper in my study from now on.'

The summers were a lovely time, when the becks were tumbling with clear sparkling water and the children wandered for miles over the moors. They had a special waterfall that they called their own, and often I went with them over the heather, half listening as they laughed and told each other stories. In the winter, it was often too cold and wet to walk; then they gathered in the warm kitchen while Tabitha worked, and acted out plays they had written by the flickering light of the oil-lamps.

One by one the older girls were sent away to a boarding-school;

but not the boy, who was being taught Greek and Latin by his father; and not my Anne, who was too delicate.

'We are to go to Cowan Bridge,' announced Lottie in a voice of doom, tinged with excitement. 'To a school for clergy's daughters. We have to go. An education is our only hope to better ourselves. Our only hope of escape.'

'But I can't live without the moors,' said Em fiercely. 'It'll be like a prison. I won't go. I won't. I'd rather stay here and work as a servant.'

But they went to school. One by one, the cart took them away, forlorn and desperately homesick children.

When the two eldest girls succumbed to the damp and chills and died, it was if the storm-clouds descended on the stone grey house and wrapped it in a fine black mist. May 6 and June 15 . . . two days so close and so overlapping in grief. The children wept. Anne was like a ghost herself, wondering how long it would be before she joined her sisters and her mother in the crowded graveyard.

But Lottie was angry too. She raged at the school which had hastened her sisters' deaths. Maria and Elizabeth had only just recovered from complications of measles and whooping cough when they went to Cowan Bridge, and the smell of rancid fat and unsavoury meat pies and bingy milk robbed them of any appetite even though they were hungry.

The two-mile walk from the school along unsheltered tracks to the wind-swept church was a weekly agony. The children ate their cold dinner in the porch between services, shivering with cold, longing for home. No one seemed to notice how ill they were.

'They killed them,' Lottie insisted, under her breath, as she busied her needle with repairing a torn under-garment. 'That school . . . it was monstrous . . . my poor sisters . . .'

Now the aunt gave them lessons at home and taught them household skills and her own strong Methodist beliefs. I curled hidden on Anne's lap, and her small fingers crept into my fur. I dared not purr, for then the aunt would chase me into the garden.

The father came home from a visit to Leeds with a set of wooden soldiers for his son. A gift was a rare thing in that family.

'Look what I've got,' said the boy excitedly the next morning, running into the girls' bedroom. 'A box of soldiers. You may have one each. You can choose.'

'This will be mine. He is the tallest, the most handsome, the most perfect of men and I'll call him the Duke of Wellington,' said Lottie, taking her hero immediately to her heart.

Em, gaunt and thin, took a grave-faced soldier and called him Gravey. She was always strange.

Anne took a quaint little fellow and called him Waiting Boy, though no one knew why or for whom he was waiting. But Anne smiled her gentle smile to herself as if she knew whom he was waiting to meet. Perhaps she was also waiting. I did not know.

The boy took Bonaparte.

Sometimes I could play with these soldiers, flipping them over with my paw, and that made the children laugh. They wrote and acted out lengthy plays for the soldiers, full of fighting and heroic deaths.

But life was not just plays, studies and walks across the moors. The three girls worked hard keeping the house spotless. I kept out of the way when they were scrubbing the sandstone floor. I would jump onto one of the wide window-sills and face the blue dial of the church clock. There were no curtains, because the father had a horror of fire. There was a groove in the wood where I had stretched a claw a hundred times. Lottie crouched over the mahogany table, polishing till her face was red; Anne dusted the horsehair chairs; Em wiped the bookshelves impatiently. She preferred baking and making bread.

It was a spartan household, but the moors were their personal luxury. The wind made the aunt shudder and she shut herself in her room whenever she could. But the girls ran out to the freedom of the moors, to their favourite ravines and waterfalls, their long hair blowing, eyes laughing, their voices raised in chatter. They took off their boots and stockings and waded through the streams, their voluminous black skirts getting wet. They placed stepping-stones for me, and I unhesitatingly followed them to the end of their wild and windy earth.

All nature was a lingering delight. They exclaimed over every flower and bird, every butterfly and bee, and especially the tiny mosses that clung to the rock-faces and survived despite the cruel weather. They ran like wild creatures themselves, their cloaks and skirts billowing in the four winds that joined in their games. The dogs rushed about, barking, chasing rabbits, in their simpler world of hunting.

'We will always remember this,' said Em firmly. 'We will make it remembered. It must never change.'

They were sitting at the meeting of the waters, where a space of bright lush grass was broken by small springs and flat stones. It was totally hidden. There was nothing to see but miles of hills and heather, acres of cloudless sky like a canopy of glass, warmed by an unexpected sun.

The girls sat on the stones, heads flung back to the warmth, getting their breath. I lapped water from the clear spring and I thought I had tasted nothing as pure.

'This will be my dream,' Em went on. 'Of misty moor and hill. Where every evening closes dark and chill.'

'Don't talk of death,' said Anne, combing through her curls with her fingers. 'Not now. Don't spoil this beautiful day with thoughts of the dark evening to come.'

'You're being cowardly, Anne,' said Em. 'Weak . . .'

'That's not true,' said Lottie. 'Think how brave Anne is when she is ill.'

Em rushed to hug her younger sister. 'I'm cruel, cruel,' she cried. 'Forgive me, dear Anne. Forgive me.'

Anne forgave her immediately for they were like twins, even though there was almost two years between them. They walked together, sewed together, wrote in the evenings side by side.

Lottie was the odd one out, but she had only love, no envy, for the strength they gave each other. She knew she had ambition. She did not want to stay in the stone house for ever, and yet every time she made the effort to get away, she was almost ill with homesickness. Nor could Em survive away from her beloved moors.

Laughing, they made a bracelet from strands of Anne's hair and put it round my neck like a collar. I ran through the tangled bushes and would have fled to the higher hills, but Anne caught me and pulled me into her arms.

'It was only some fun, Black Tom,' she whispered, lifting the bracelet off my neck, then stroking down the ruffled fur. 'You are still free. We were making you into a magical creature for Gondal.' She began to cough and drew a shawl round her narrow shoulders. 'I must go back . . .'

This was their only escape; their fantasies taking them on the wind into worlds of power, love and excitement. In these dream-worlds their heroines had the courage and opportunity to make their own lives; not like the three sisters, who were imprisoned by their sex.

They wrote millions of words, crouched round the dining room table in the flickering light. Their pens scratched the endless adventures of the people in their mythical countries, Angria and Gondal. I did not understand all this, but it was enough that I could curl up beneath the table where Anne would put her stockinged feet on my back for a stool.

Lottie could hardly see, even then, and peered closely, her nose almost touching the paper. Em was like a caged beast, restless even in that familiar room, wanting to be away, being called somewhere by something she did not yet recognize.

That evening there was a terrible storm and the three girls were drawn to the small glittering window. The forked lightning lit up Top Withens with jagged white flashes, silhouetting the old farmhouse roof and gaunt trees. Anne watched nervously, ready to clap her hands over her ears when the thunder broke. Em was mesmerized, hardly able to control her passion. It was as if she might throw herself out into the furious rain and run into the core of the storm with her arms open to the wildness.

Lottie stood apart, clenching and unclenching her small hands. All that power out there, and she had none. She had to do something, some work, make some place in this world. Surely her whole life was not to be given to cleaning and baking when there was so much inside her, longing to be free.

'Goodnight, my children.' The father came to the door, watch in hand. 'Don't stay up too late.'

'Goodnight, papa.'

It was nine o'clock. They heard him bar and lock the front door, then go upstairs, pausing on the landing to wind the clock.

The girls turned their faces back to the storm. Their souls were out there on the moor, succoured by the wind and rain.

'We must get away,' said Lottie. Her sisters agreed, but there was so little they could do.

The snows came hard that winter and Anne fell ill with lung congestion. She lay on the sofa, coughing and coughing, and holding the pain in her side. They brought her nourishing broths, and Tabitha brewed humble remedies. I lay at her feet, listening to her laboured breathing, unable to help, only able to offer my company.

Eventually the snows melted, leaving frozen tufts of white coarse grass among the moss. The birds had long gone to warmer climates, and only the grouse and crows flew over the moors.

As she grew stronger, Anne became more determined to find work. They could not all stay at home. She was physically the weakest and the shyest, but she was firm in her resolve. No one knew how much it cost sweet, gentle Anne. She hid her suffering. She eventually found herself a suitable post.

They were busy all week at the parsonage preparing for Anne's departure. She carried me upstairs to her room as her sisters helped her to pack. She had so few belongings: chemises, cuffs, a plain dark dress, but she also took her books, her work-basket and her Bible. I sat on the window-sill and watched. Every time she passed me, she touched my head as if to give her fingers a long remembrance of the feel of my fur . . .

She rose early the next morning and took a long last look at the moors. They were mysterious in mist and silent. She had a hurried breakfast, for she felt too sick to eat. The family embraced and Anne kissed her aunt, her father, and her sisters.

'Goodbye Charlotte,' she said, hugging her.

'Goodbye, dear Anne. Write to us. Write to us often. If only you would let one of us journey with you . . .'

'No, it's my wish that I be allowed to go alone,' said Anne. She turned to Em. 'Goodbye, Emily.'

'Goodbye, my dearest,' said Emily fiercely. 'God go with you and keep you safe.'

She picked me up and kissed me, and my black fur was lost in the blackness of her woollen shawl. 'Oh Black Tom, Black Tom,' she cried. It was a cry of despair.

She drew a veil over her face to hide the tears and stepped up into the cart that was to take her on the long journey from Haworth to Blake Hall, Mirfield, where she had an appointment as a governess to the Ingram family. It was a cold and dark April morning, and the sun did not exist even as a faint promise behind the dark mass of cloud.

I followed the creaking, lurching cart down the steep lane to the bottom of the village street. It crossed the bridge and then began the climb to the other side of the valley. But I went no further. I sat on the stones in the sombre light thinking of my dearest. I was old now, and thin, and would not see her again.

Every four years the Brontë sisters wrote an assessment of their lives, to be opened four years later on Emily's birthday or Anne's.

30 July 1841

'This is Emily's birthday,' Anne wrote from a new post at Scarborough. 'She has now completed her twenty-third year . . . I wonder what will be our condition and how or where we shall all be on this day four years hence . . . We are now all separate and not likely to meet again for many a weary week . . .

'We have got Keeper, got a sweet little cat and lost it, and also got a hawk. Got a wild goose which has flown away, and three tame ones, one of which has been killed.

'All these diversities, with many others, are things we did not expect or foresee in the July of 1837. What will the next four years bring forth? Providence only knows.'*

19 December 1848 Emily died, aged 30
28 May 1849 Anne died, aged 29
31 March 1855 Charlotte died, aged 38

* Extract from Anne Brontë's Diary Paper, from *The Shakespeare Head Brontë*, Vol. I, edited by T. J. Wise & J. A. Symington '

Independence Brown

Independence Brown was her name right from the very beginning. The name sounded like the heroine of an early American pioneer film and it suited her. They could almost imagine her trekking across the plains of Arizona in a covered wagon, repelling Indians and enduring great hardships.

The Browns called her Independence in the first place because they got her on July 4 and were sorry about the American Revolution and the Boston Tea Party. But it soon became obvious that the tiny scruff of mottled fur was a fiercely independent and ornery cuss from the word go, determined to stand forever on her own wobbly four paws.

She did everything in her own time. Lifted onto a lap, the kitten fought furiously for release, only to return minutes later, acquiescent and docile. Put on a litter tray, she scrambled out, granules flying over the floor, only to sit politely by the door asking to be let out. Food and drink were ignored: she ate when she wanted to, be it dawn or midnight.

It took the family a long time to get to know her; if they met outside, Inde merely glanced at them as if they were strangers.

'I sometimes wonder if that cat belongs to us at all,' said Mrs Ellen Brown. 'She gives us all the cold shoulder.'

Inde grew into a striking British silver tabby. The dark symmetrical markings on her grey fur were like blotting-paper images, and the lines and splodges on her small face gave her a curiously clown-like look. It was perhaps this frivolous appearance that she was determined to live down.

The only person Inde acknowledged was Corrine Brown – if acknowledge was the right word. They had something strongly in common and recognized in each other a kindred spirit. At sixteen, Corinne was going through a fight for her independence, and she often envied Inde's ruthless demolition of any Brown plans for her life.

Several times they made an appointment for a very necessary visit to the vet's. Inde refused point-blank to go. She was up and over the garden wall and into the woods, and was not seen again for thirty-six hours. Then one day she climbed into her travelling basket and sat there waiting for Mr Brown to get the car out. When she was brought home, she sat groggily licking the sore place with an air of comical sadness, as if she knew all about denied kittens and the lost joys of motherhood.

That evening she curled up on Corrine's lap all through a James Bond film. They thought that at last Inde had mellowed. But they were wrong. The next day she had recovered, and spat at anything that moved.

The neighbouring woods were her delight. She played and explored and scavenged. Every square inch was known territory. As the woods changed with the seasons, so Inde found further joys and excitements. She flew down the garden with the long rippling strides of a tiger, took the wall with the graceful leap of a front runner at the Grand National, sped across the stepping-stones of the brook with the sure-footedness of a gazelle. Corrine never failed to feel a surge of admiration watching this co-ordination of movement; it was beautiful. She would look up from her studies and watch from the window as Inde took her path to freedom. Corrine sometimes fancied she could share the joy of the cat as Inde headed for the woods. Corrine wished she knew where she herself was going, and what lay beyond school examinations and perhaps university.

Inde deliberately strengthened her independence. During her periodic disappearances, they did not look for her. Her return to bed and board was heralded by a sharp *yeowell* at the back door. She did not apologize for the wisps of dry fern and moss clinging to her fur; she had been roaming her beloved woods.

'I can't think what's got into Inde these days,' said Ellen Brown with some exasperation as she threw away an untouched dish of cat-food. 'She's always had eccentric eating habits, but she's never ignored food altogether.'

Corrine went on her knees to stroke the cat. There was something odd about Inde. She was creeping around as if half-expecting to be set upon, front paws held out in a curiously stiff manner. Inde licked the salt off Corrine's fingers with her rough sandpaper tongue. It was the first sign of affection she had ever shown.

Corrine put some morsels of chicken in the palm of her hand and held them under Inde's nose. The small tongue shot out and the chicken was gone in a flash. The cat was starving.

'Well, I never,' said Ellen from the pastry board. 'She ignored it all yesterday.'

Corrine filled a dish and put it at Inde's toes. The cat crouched down on her haunches and polished off the lot. It was the same with some milk.

'How strange,' said Corrine, worried. It was so unlike Inde, to have to be waited on. Her spirit was fiercely valiant, but something was defeating her now. 'Perhaps we ought to take her to the vet.'

'Give it a day or two and see if she gets over it,' said Ellen. 'I've a heavy week. Two committee meetings and a flag day.'

And Corrine was busy packing. She had collected the right number of grades and was to read history for three years. Her parents had hoped she would accept a place in London so that she could still live at home, but Corrine had opted for a university in the industrial north. She was apprehensive about the move. What would she find there? What would the people be like? She knew she must take her courage into her two hands and run at it, in the same way that Inde ran to her beloved woods.

Corrine took Inde upstairs with her. She felt in the need of uncritical company. She was on the defensive, with her mother still trying to organize everything for her. She started to sort out her books so that she knew which ones to leave at home, making a list of their titles.

It was an absorbing task and the two piles of books grew, hiding Inde from view. Suddenly the piles fell over and Inde shot across the room; she crashed headlong into a record case, fur flying and paws askew. Inde stepped back and crouched on the carpet, trembling, her long ringed tail swished from side to side. But it was not in anger. It was more like the sweeping of a radar beam.

Corrine walked on her knees to the stricken cat and tried to calm her.

'Easy, girl,' she soothed. 'Did the silly old books frighten you? There . . . there . . .'

She looked carefully at the cat from all angles, ran her hands down each limb. then she put a cushion on the floor and moved away to the other side of the room. A kind of chill settled on her actions. She tapped the leg of her bed with a pencil and called out: 'Inde . . . Inde . . .'

Inde got up, ears perked forward, whiskers twitching. She did not leap over the cusion or step across it. She did not side-track either. She walked straight into it.

Corrine picked up Inde gently and sat on the floor, cradling her in her arms. Silently tears fell down her cheeks. She had never felt so sad in all her life. A light had gone out, Inde's light. The light of Independence Brown. The cat was blind.

The vet thought Inde must have been in an accident during one of her disappearances. Perhaps a car wing had caught her a sharp blow to the side of the head; perhaps she had fallen from a high tree and detached the retina. They would never know. The vet suggested that the kindest thing would be to have her put down.

Inde was carefully exploring the vet's examination table, sniffing the edges, alert and curious. The afternoon sunlight streamed through the windows, catching all the silver in her coat. Her fur was alive and sparkling. No one could destroy anything so beautiful.

'Oh no, I think we'll give her a chance,' said Ellen Brown slowly. 'She's got such an independent nature.'

At first they moved every awkward object in the house out of the way – the umbrella stand, the log basket, waste bins. Then they realized that this was not really doing the cat a favour. It was better that Inde learned where everything was and tracked round them. Everyone became consciously tidier, no longer leaving shopping, briefcases, shoes on the floor.

Inde responded to noise; she recognized the sound of the tin-opener, the refrigerator door being opened, milk poured. She kept out of the way when the telephone rang or there was a knock on the door. She became far more vocal. If she was quite lost, she stood still in that foreign place, miaowing for someone to put her somewhere more familiar.

By the time Corrine came home from her first term at university, Inde had come to terms with her blindness. She still walked with a strange gait as if she was not completely relaxed, but her independence had reasserted itself and she did not want to be helped. She knew the lay-out of the house and garden intimately, only thrown occasionally by someone's carelessness. She still ruled her own life. She had no intention of being an invalid.

One day Corrine found Inde sitting by the foot of the garden wall. She looked melancholy, as far as a clown-faced cat can look melancholy. She let out a single, sad wail.

'Why, I believe you are missing your woods,' said Corrine. 'You know they are over there, don't you, the other side of the wall? Poor Inde, you can smell them and hear them but you can't cope with that wall. You need a helping hand.'

She lifted Inde up to put her over the wall, but the cat struggled and flopped out of her grasp, falling onto the waste ground the other side. Inde streaked off into the undergrowth, careering headlong through grass and fern like a demented creature. Even when she was out of sight Corrine could still hear the small sounds of her crashing progress through the woods. ·

Corrine hung about, but Inde did not come back. Eventually she gave up and went indoors. Late that evening they heard a piercing *yeowell*. It was Inde waiting to be returned over the wall. She was wet. She had obviously tried to cross the stepping-stones and fallen in the brook.

'Well, I'm much too busy to ferry her backwards and forwards over the wall,' said Ellen. 'I can't be around to do wall duty every day. What's going to happen when you go back to university?'

'I'll think of something.'

It did not seem feasible to knock a hole in the wall, so Corrine devised two planks leaning against the wall, one either side, so that Inde could get back. She wedged the foot of each plank with a stone and introduced Inde to her walk-over. Inde sniffed, then after a few hesitant, tentative steps, she understood. When she got to the top of the wall, she sniffed the air, not sure what was expected of her. She was about to leap off when Corrine restrained her.

'Oh, no, you don't. You've got to learn the way down too. Then you'll be able to get back.' Corrine guided the cat to the edge of the plank that led down to the ground. Inde stepped forward with perfect trust. She caught on immediately and sped down the plank. Without a murmur of thanks she darted off into the woods with rather more care for the undergrowth.

Corrine stood there, laughing. She had given Inde a bridge to freedom. She wondered if someone would give her a bridge into this new adult world she had so recently entered.

Inde never hesitated again. She flew down the garden, unerringly straight for the plank, up and over and into the woods. No one would have known that she was blind. It was a joy to watch the animal flying through the air.

One night there was a gale and the wind and heavy rain dislodged the planks. Inde shot out of the back door, straight down the garden but pulled up short of the wall. She sniffed around and found the fallen plank and sat on it, waiting for someone to do something about it.

A young Canadian student, Bruce, was staying overnight. After breakfast he went down the garden with Corrine to look at the damage.

'Well, if I'm going to be an architect, I might as well start my career with a cat bridge,' he grinned. He put stakes in the ground at intervals and lashed the planks to the stakes. It was firm but amateurish.

'If I had more time I'd build a brick-supported ramp,' he said, wielding a mallet on the stakes. Inde sat at a safe distance, listening to the noise with concealed curiosity. 'Though it seems a lot of work just to get one cat over one wall.'

'It's all in the name of independence,' said Corrine, mysteriously. 'You could always come again in the spring holiday,' she added.

'So I could,' he said.

The bridge was Inde's lifeline to freedom. Over the years Bruce made adaptations and improvements to its design. Inde took to each change with trust and confidence. She now knew every inch of the woods. It was still difficult to believe that she could not see. She did not let her blindness stop her doing anything she wanted to do. She even climbed trees, moving carefully along swaying branches. Sometimes Corrine watched with her heart in her mouth as Inde took a calculated leap into the air to reach another branch. Sometimes the cat missed.

She learned the size and position of each of the stepping-stones and could walk across them with scarcely a hesitation. Her mind was a complicated file of maps and routes and angles, all painstakingly learned by trial and error, committed to memory, and once there, acted upon with total confidence.

In her first year of teaching Corrine came home regularly, but gradually there were other countries with sites of historical interest to see, new friends to visit, holidays with Bruce. Inde accepted that her dearest friend should be finding new worlds and had less time for her. She turned to Ellen and grew closer to her.

Ellen was slowing down her good work for the community as younger and more enthusiastic women moved into the neighbourhood. She sat more often in the garden with her sewing or writing letters, Inde stretched out on the grass beside her, the sun warming her body.

'I'm quite glad I've given up all those committees,' said Ellen. 'I can enjoy my own garden now without having to get up and rush off somewhere.'

Absent-mindedly she put her hand down to stroke the cat's head. Inde put out her tongue and licked at Ellen's fingers. It was the first time that Inde had ever shown any sign of affection towards Ellen and she was unaccountably touched. All those years of tapping saucers and leading the cat with her voice; all those years of watching and caring for the independent creature had not gone completely unnoticed.

She stroked the cat's chin. There was the faintest vibration in Inde's throat. It was the birth of a purr. Ellen felt rewarded beyond measure.

'Both of us getting old,' she teased. 'Soft thing . . .'

Inde had an annual check-up at the vet's. He thought she was remarkably fit despite her disability and her age. 'A touch of arthritis,' he said. 'But that's to be expected at her age. Keep an eye on her if we have a very cold snap this winter.'

Corrine came home for the whole of the summer vacation. She was packing again. This time she was off to Australia on a teacher-exchange scheme. It was an exciting prospect. They were even going to exchange flats, and Corrine would be living in Sydney not far from the sea.

As Corrine's world grew, so Inde's shrank. She did not wander so far now. She had got thinner and the bright silver in her coat had dulled. She stood on the doorstep facing the garden, her face lifted towards the sun and towards the life that used to exist beyond.

'I think she wants to go to the woods,' said Corrine. 'Shall I take her? She used to love them so.' Corrine began to stroll down the garden. 'Inde . . . Come on, Inde . . .'

Inde followed stiffly. The bottom of the garden seemed a long way. Corrine bent to carry her over the wall, but the cat struggled out of her arms and insisted on crossing the bridge by herself, slowly and a little unsteadily.

'All right, have it your own way,' said Corrine.

They wandered through the woods together, the cat sniffing old haunts and new growth, remembering all the joys that had once been hers: oak moss, leaf mould, wild violets; Corrine thinking of the new paths that were opening up for her, if she had the courage to take them.

When they came to the brook, Inde hesitated. She had forgotten the exact sequence of the stepping-stones. Corrine went ahead, tapping each stone and calling. Inde followed. Once she almost slipped, but Corrine was there to catch her and set her back on the stone. Inde took a great leap from the last stone onto the opposite bank. That much she remembered.

It was a lovely afternoon for both of them, golden and warm; the silver cat's splodges and stripes merging with the dappled shadows until she was almost part of the woods themselves.

Inde was very tired by the time they got home. She drank some milk and stretched herself out before the newly lit fire and went to sleep, her paws still twitching with memories of her old exciting life.

'I suppose I may not see Inde again,' said Corrine, her hand faltering on the soft fur, feeling the gentle rise and fall of that subborn heart. How quickly the years had gone by, and Corrine had become too busy sometimes to give any time to her cat. Every day Inde had lived in her shadowy world, day after day, refusing to give in, following the promise in the wind.

'Probably not,' said Ellen, turning her face away.

Corrine continued to stroke the silver coat, remembering the cat's endless courage and determination,: her fight for everything that she had a right to have. 'You'll stay with her, won't you?' she said in a low voice.

'I'll be here,' said Ellen.

The following week Corrine left for Australia. She did not hesitate. Her plane flew unerringly straight, up and over, taking her across a bridge to freedom.

An Absolute Bargain

In a house the size of the Robinsons', it was difficult to understand why there was not room for one small kitten that weighed less than a pound. It was a weird scrap, all ears, with a tiny pointed face and a spotty patterned coat that made it look as if it had been smudged with a leaky Biro.

The Robinson house had a lot of rooms and they were filled with a lot of people, all doing their own thing. There was Mr and Mrs Robinson, three daughters – Priscilla, Augusta and Ermentrude – and two sons – James and Jonathan.

They were a family of talent. They were all so busy painting, writing, composing, dancing and sculpting that there had never really been any time for pets. And they did not see how one could fit into their household.

But Trudy, the youngest daughter, being as yet unformed in any direction, was the one person who thought there might be a corner somewhere for the small creature.

'Her name is Louella,' Trudy announced. 'She's from the Old Vicarage. They were going to drown her. They said she was retarded.'

Everyone looked at the kitten with more interest. They had never come across a retarded cat before. It was crawling between the pepper and salt on the supper-table with pathetic feebleness.

'How does one know that a kitten is retarded?' asked Augusta kindly. 'Are there tests?'

'Mrs Owen said she was the last one to be born and was slow to feed; therefore a weakling and the duff one of the bunch.'

'So why have we got it?' asked Mr Robinson, coming straight to the point.

'I thought it was a pretty hasty assessment at six weeks old. The poor little thing hasn't had a chance to show what it's made of. Believe me, I have a wide experience of unrecognized talent,' said Trudy with feeling.

'Did you pay for it?' asked Priscilla sharply. 'Mrs Owen is a professional cat-breeder.'

Jonathan choked on his chili con carne. Priscilla was not good at pronouncing her r's. He grinned at Trudy. He knew why she wanted the little misfit.

'Well, not exactly money,' said Trudy. 'But I did promise to do some gardening for her.'

'Does Mrs Owen realize that you know absolutely nothing about gardening and will spend most of the time up the nearest tree?' asked James.

'Why are you calling her Louella?' her mother asked, with a novelist's interest in names.

'Vicarage . . . parsons . . . straight and narrow . . . columns . . . the columnist, Louella Parsons. Neat, eh?'

'Classy, like all Robinson names.'

'And she's a lilac-coloured oriental tabby,' said James, who knew a little about everything. 'She ought to have a properly registered name.'

'Really?' said Trudy, impressed. 'How about Louella Parsons Robinson.'

LPR, as everyone else called her, was a weakling. She could hardly feed herself, and Trudy went straight to the chemist in the village to buy a baby's bottle and sterilising equipment.

'Expecting a happy event?' asked the chemist.

'The happy event has already taken place,' said Trudy haughtily. 'We Robinsons work fast.'

Mrs Robinson insisted that Trudy should take full responsibility for LPR; she was up to her writing neck trying to get instalments of a serial ready for an editor. Feeding the family had a great deal of random luck about it at present, without taking on a weak kitten.

'Can I have a lunch-box then?' asked Trudy, sitting on the kitchen table, the kitten asleep in her pencil-case.

'What's wrong with paper bags?'

'Paper bags are passé this term.'

Jonathan produced a Snoopy lunch-box, the kind designed for five-year-olds. Trudy took it to Augusta's studio in the garden, and bored a series of holes in the red roof of the lunch-box with some of Augusta's tools. It would do nicely.

Rumour swept round the school like wildfire that Trudy Robinson was feeding a baby behind the bicycle shed during break. She found herself surrounded by an open-mouthed audience, and fending off requests to feed/hold/play with the kitten.

'Go away,' Trudy pleaded. 'She's delicate and you'll frighten her.'

Louella sucked on the bottle, almost choking on her own small purrs of contentment. She was wrapped in Trudy's school scarf, and as far as she was concerned, the Snoopy lunch-box was home and Trudy her mum.

Trudy was not surprised when Miss Stewart, the headmistress, sent for her. Trudy was tactically ready.

'Just one week more and then I'll be weaning her onto solids,' said Trudy, who had been reading up child development. 'Then it'll be half-term. After that I should be able to leave Louella at home.'

'Very well,' said Miss Stewart, appearing to give in. 'One more week.'

She did not mention that her staff had been sending back signals about peaceful playground breaks. It was not surprising with half the school wedged behind the bicycle shed.

'Thank you, Miss Stewart,' said Trudy demurely.

The weaning of Louella was in fact quite a turning-point. Liver and bacon purée and apricot custard agreed with her. And the little baby tins were fun to play with. She grew into a remarkably handsome cat, elegantly oriental, with long legs and slanting eyes, the elusive lilac colouring giving softness to her angular shape.

The other turning-point was that, quite by chance, Trudy happened to be paying attention during a biology class; thus Louella had to tolerate an instant name change.

'Louella is now called Alphonse,' Trudy informed the breakfast gathering. 'APR instead of LPR.'

'APR,' mother nodded between mouthfuls of muesli and correcting a draft. She did not ask why. That was her trouble. She had to go to Augusta for help on the passages of purple passion in her novels.

The change of name also heralded a change of character. Whereas Louella had been weak, pathetic and possibly retarded, Alphonse was a cat of insatiable curiosity, endless vitality and a rock-like devotion to Trudy. But the curiosity, vitality, rock-like etc led him straight into trouble.

'That cat of yours has walked all over my Fort Stanley,' stormed Mr Robinson one morning. He was a naval painter. At present he was painting a Falklands scene; he was not yet onto the Caribbean.

The storm was quite unexpected, because Trudy's father was the most placid of men. 'Pawmarks all over it,' he glared.

'Couldn't you pretend they are penguin footprints?' Trudy suggested with some hesitation.

'Walking up the main street and along the harbour?' he said scathingly.

'Yesterday APR knocked coffee over chapter four and I had to type it again,' said mother, her glasses slipping off her nose.

'Ditto my current guitar composition, only it was wine,' said Jonathan.

'I found my new poem shredded,' said James.

'And you should see my third best tu-tu,' cried Priscilla, near to tears. Ruined, absolutely ruined. That cat trampled all over it. The sequins were all over the floor. It'll take me hours to sew them on again.'

'I'm terribly sorry. I'll help,' Trudy offered, hushed. She turned to Augusta. Augusta was her favourite sister, as Jonathan was her favourite brother. Augusta had said nothing yet.

'Well, I did find that my piece called Earthquake had fallen over and was a bit chipped,' said Augusta reluctantly.

'It could have been the wind,' said Trudy.

Augusta nodded. 'Probably the wind . . .'

Trudy could read the writing on the wall. All that Robinson talent was not geared to cope with an inquisitive cat. Trudy felt her nose prickling. It seemed Alphonse would have to go.

Her practical streak to the fore, Trudy negotiated swopping Alphonse for an album of The Who. Her best friend, Jane, was smitten.

'Well, I don't know,' said Trudy reluctantly. 'He is a registered lilac-coloured oriental tabby.'

'And you can have my signed photo of Tony Blackburn,' said Jane, who really wanted Alphonse.

Trudy hid her unhappiness by playing The Who very loudly all evening. It was a very good album, much better than a half-grown cat with big ears that wrecked everything, she told herself. She put on a brave face. She hung photos of Alphonse round her bedroom wall draped with black ribbon.

'He hasn't died,' said Priscilla, peering round the door. 'He's only gone to live two roads away.'

'I didn't think you would understand,' said Trudy. Priscilla was wrapped up in her dancing, and her feelings were definitely centred in her feet.

Three mornings later Trudy heard a strange noise and opened the back door. A lilac-coloured oriental tabby walked in and leaped straight into the Snoopy lunch-box.

'Alphonse, darling,' cried Trudy. 'You've come back.'

Alphonse turned round and round with difficulty, having outgrown the box, but the message was clear. He was home.

Trudy returned the record and the photograph. Jane's mother went out and bought a hamster.

Alphonse, clearly delighted to be home, had a tour of inspection of the house to make sure nothing had changed in his absence. The resulting chaos had the Robinson family signing a petition, which they presented to Trudy after she had finished her homework.

'We the undersigned,' the petition read, 'do humbly request you to remove the aforementioned APR, to the furthermost distance possible. Financial aid available.'

'What does that mean?' Trudy asked suspiciously.

'It means we'll pay the fare,' said James, who had suffered the most during Alphonse's exploration of the study, and was still retrieving sheets of poetry from the vegetable garden.

'And what's aforementioned?'

'It's legal wording,' said Mrs Robinson.

Trudy found a new home for Alphonse some three miles away. The deal was finalized with the exchange of an unwanted painting-by-numbers set and an unopened box of chocolates.

'You can have Alphonse on Saturday,' said Trudy picking out her favourite coconut éclair. 'He's got to be briefed as to the new situation.'

Being briefed consisted of being walked on the end of a piece of string the whole of the three-mile route to the new home.

'Sniff, sniff,' said Trudy at intervals along the road. Alphonse obliged. It was a long walk, but he was with Trudy so nothing else really mattered. She had to carry him the last mile.

Alphonse stayed at his new home less than a week. The stay would have been even shorter, but he was a polite cat. When he reappeared on the Robinson doorstep, paw-weary but triumphant, Trudy hid her pride in his achievement behind a dramatic display of dismay.

'Oh no, oh dear, oh heavens, glory be,' she wailed, banging her head lightly on the kitchen wall. 'Whatever shall I do? I'm so sorry, everyone. Forgive me. Just give me time . . .'

'Encore,' said Jonathan, clapping from the doorway.

'It does seem a shame,' said Augusta, stroking the cat's pointed ears. 'Alphonse seems determined to live here.'

'And we are just as determined to get rid of him,' said Priscilla. 'You'll have to advertise, Trudy.'

Trudy could not return the chocolates or the painting-set, as she had eaten the first and almost finished the last.

'It's quite revolting,' said Mr Robinson, consigning the gaudy picture to the dustbin. 'I'll draw her another one and put in lots of numbers. I hope she likes ships . . .'

Trudy composed an advertisement to go in the local free newspaper.

'Lilac-coloured oriental tabby for sale,' she wrote. 'No reasonable offer refused. An absolute bargain.'

Trudy, who rarely received any post, was delighted by the response. It was one way of getting letters. She began to wonder what else she could sell. Some of the replies were useless. One person thought Alphonse was a china cat and wanted to know if he was cracked; another misread tabby for hubby and wrote asking for a date, and please did he speak English?

It did not take Trudy long to arrange the sale. This time money exchanged hands. Trudy spent it on replacement typing-paper, manuscript sheets, sequins and a bottle of turpentine for her father. She couldn't think what to buy Augusta. It wasn't easy to buy rocks.

'You'll really like this family,' said Trudy, as they walked along the lanes that led to the next village. 'They've got lots of children. Perhaps you'll be able to play with their toys.'

Alphonse looked up, his oriental eyes inscrutable slits.

'Sniff, sniff,' said Trudy hopefully.

Alphonse stuck it for twenty-four hours. The children were unbearable and shrieked every time he went near their toys. He galloped across the fields, swift as a leopard, soaring over hedges, the dew clinging to his long spotted tail.

'He's back,' said Augusta, looking out of the window. 'He's sitting on the wall looking smug.'

'Do you think Alphonse is trying to tell us something?' said Jonathan.

Trudy stopped herself from rushing out to welcome home the traveller with a big hug.

'Perhaps he's just visiting,' suggested James.

'No such luck,' said Priscilla. 'I shall have to lock up my ballet costumes, and I don't want any more chewed ballet shoes.'

It was not easy to outwit Alphonse's investigations; it required pre-planning and the purchase of locks. Everything lockable was locked; the house began to look tidier. Fewer stories, poems, music, paintings, ballet shoes were left abandoned in rooms.

So Trudy's suspicions were aroused when one day she came home from school and found evidence of the household's customary chaos. Priscilla was sewing yards of frilly net all over the floor; father had a mural drying in the hall; Jonathan's best guitar was propped against the stairs.

'Where's Alphonse?' Trudy asked.

'Darling,' said her mother, putting an arm around her youngest daughter's slim shoulders. 'We've found Alphonse a lovely new home. They're very fond of cats and have a beautiful walled garden. I know APR will be well looked after.'

'Where is he?' Trudy was stricken.

'Oh, he's gone. They took him straight away. He was ever so good going off in their car.'

Trudy felt a cold shock wave of anguish. He'd gone. Her darling Alphonse. Some strange people had taken him away in their car.

'Where have they taken him to?' she asked in a tiny, unrecognizable voice.

'Epping, darling. It's a very nice place.'

Trudy rushed from the room. There was an A-Z somewhere in the house. Her eyes were blurred with tears as she fingered the pages. There were so many streets . . . it was the other side of London. Page after page of streets and bridges and traffic-lights, and then the Thames. Alphonse would never find his way back. She didn't even know if he could swim.

The family were very kind to her that evening. Mother cooked Trudy's favourite baked-bean pie; father, Jonathan and James made up a foursome for Scrabble; Priscilla offered the last of her best bubble-bath. Augusta had carved a tiny oriental cat with pointed ears from a piece of rosewood.

'Thank you all very much,' said Trudy, rising to go to bed at the unheard-of hour of 9 o'clock. 'You're being most kind. I just hope Alphonse will be happy in . . . in . . . Epping!'

Trudy burst into tears and ran from the room. There was silence as they looked at each other.

'Perhaps we ought to get Alphonse back,' said Jonathan.

'We can't,' said Mrs Robinson. 'I don't remember their name and I didn't get their full address. Oh dear . . .'

It took Alphonse more than a month to cross London, or perhaps he took a circular route and by-passed the great metropolis. He arrived back late one evening, thin, dirty, one ear torn where he'd been in a fight over a scrap of food, but still inscrutably Alphonse. He walked in and leaped straight into Trudy's lap, his muddy paws printing his happiness all over her English essay, which she had already copied out twice.

'Oh my darling Alphonse, you've come home,' she cried, hugging him closely which he bore with dignity. 'All that way from Epping. What a clever, clever cat.'

It was necessary to have another family conference. Alphonse was present, and insisted on sitting in his Snoopy lunch-box with his long tail hanging over the edge.

'I think that Alphonse has earned the right to live here,' began Augusta. 'Just think what he went through to get back. Such determination. Alphonse has made his point.'

Everyone agreed. Alphonse had made his point. They would have to try to live with him. It really was as simple as that.

Trudy tried not to look too pleased. Alphonse might not have talent in the normally accepted sense, but he certainly had potential.

Lucky's Story

She sat on the roof of a lorry sunning herself. She liked sitting up high, looking over the world, out of the way of the traffic, pedestrians and hotel guests.

Not that she had anything against hotel guests. They were part of her life and made a fuss of her. But there were so many of them and they were always changing.

These people were on something called a holiday. But since they ate, drank, talked and slept in much the same way as on ordinary days, Lucky could not see the difference.

Lucky dozed in the sunshine, dreaming dreams, chasing fleeing thoughts of other places that must be somewhere. She knew the world was a large place; that there were streets beyond this street, perhaps even a town beyond this town. It was all there waiting to be explored.

'One day you'll be carried away,' said the woman, lifting Lucky down from the cab roof. 'You have been warned.'

Lucky put her claws into the woman's shirt and shining black hair that hung like silk on each side of her face. Lucky called the woman Lindiladi. She liked her a lot. It was a mutual feeling.

'Come on, you soft thing,' said Lindiladi, carrying the cat indoors. 'I've enough to do without having to keep looking for you.'

Lucky was nine months old, having grown from an adorable white kitten with a black tail into a big and elegant cat with thick white fur and piercing green eyes. The top of her head was also black, and looked like a superior Frank Sinatra hair-piece. She had three pink pads on her paws and one black.

She was an affectionate cat. She knew that Lindiladi had rescued her from the RSPCA kennels, where animals disappeared if they were not claimed. But she was also very independent. Lucky had her own ideas about a lot of things, as did Lindiladi. That's why they got on so well. Lucky often jumped onto Lindiladi's knee and put her small nose right up to the woman's nose.

'You must have Eskimo blood,' said Lindiladi, amused, stroking the thick white fur.

Lucky did not understand about Eskimos but she liked to hear Lindiladi's soft laugh. The young woman was always working, so was her husband, whom Lucky called Peterman. Having a hotel meant a lot of work and no time to sit on the top of lorries, decided Lucky, as she escaped again into the fresh sea air. She stopped and sniffed; the pungent ozone was tantalizingly full of the smell of fish and seabirds and great oceans. Inland she sensed the mountains of the Lake District. She had not seen an ocean nor a mountain and she wondered why she knew these things.

It was Sunday, 21 April 1981, though Lucky did not know the date. Lindiladi put Lucky out on the doorstep. A scurry of wind whipped the woman's short hair against her face, and ruffled the cat's white fur like a flurry of snow.

'Now please be good,' said Lindiladi. 'I'm going to have a very busy day and I haven't time to waste hunting for you. Just stay around here.'

Lucky arched her back and swished her long black tail and tipped the end over into a raised question mark. Of course she would be good. She was happy to oblige. It was too windy to go exploring. She would just take a look around the warehouse and see what was going on.

Near the hotel was an antique dealer's shop and warehouse. Lucky considered this one of her favourite places to play. It had a particular smell all of its own, of houses long ago shut up and deserted, of cats and dogs and mice from the past. She sniffed at the clinging aromas of cigars and beeswax, dust and decay . . . it was all so interesting.

The owner did not seem to mind if Lucky padded around inspecting things. There was a cabinet-maker who was kind and gave her an occasional saucer of milk, but he was busy.

Lucky prowled around the antique furniture: Victorian tables and button-back tête-à-tête chairs; old pictures in heavy frames with cracked varnish; pots and bowls and old china. She liked all the different woods: rosewood, fruitwood, walnut, and ancient oak, knotted with veins of dried sap.

There was a lot of activity in the yard for a Sunday. They were packing a large container for delivery somewhere. Lucky danced across the yard chasing a woodshaving, pouncing on it as it caught against a railing. This was going to be a fun day.

It was late that night when Lindiladi finally finished work and went outside to call in Lucky.

'Lucky-Lucky-Lucky.' It was the familiar call sign. The woman peered into the darkness. No white ghost emerged sideways from the shadows, casual and off-hand as if just passing by.

'Lucky-Lucky-Lucky.'

Lindiladi was getting worried. Lucky always came when she was called. There was such a lot of traffic in Morecambe, and Lucky was only just past kittenhood. She did not have all her road-sense yet.

'I can't find Lucky,' said Lindiladi.

'Probably having a night out,' said Peterman. 'Don't worry, she'll be back in the morning.'

But she wasn't. Lindiladi was up and out early before her duties at the hotel got into swing. She searched the streets and gardens, and then went across to the warehouse. She knew Lucky played there sometimes. It was 8 a.m. A large container stood in the yard, sealed and ready for collection.

'Have you see my cat?' she asked the men. 'It's a white cat with black on its head and a black tail.'

They shook their heads. 'No, sorry . . .'

Lucky heard Lindiladi's voice, so she knew her beloved mistress was not far away. This was reassuring. The woman always found her. She would this time, too. Lucky yawned. This place was airless and making her drowsy. She had had a lovely time playing among the furniture, but now she was tired. She found some brown paper that was warm and just asking to be trampled into a bed.

A sudden jolt brought her sharply out of her sleep. Something very strange was happening.

The world was being tilted. There were harsh, unrecognizable noises. Bolts clanged. Then an engine was switched on. Lucky was confused . . . was she sitting on top of a lorry? Was this the moment to jump off into Lindiladi's arms?

But she couldn't jump. It was dark, and the darkness was full of shapes. There was no room to move. Lucky uncurled herself and miaowed loudly, but the engine revs drowned her call. A first tremor of fear ran along her spine, a prickle of alarm. This was all quite new and she was unsure how to react. She knew Lindiladi would be along for her soon. She miaowed again as she felt the movement growing within the darkness and the rattling and jolting throwing her from side to side.

Lucky crouched in her small place; two piercing green eyes searching for a solution. If only she could understand what was happening, then perhaps she could do something.

She tried to sleep again, but was unable to settle because of a growing thirst; then hunger. She prowled, squeezing herself small, sniffing and exploring. There was nothing. Pangs contracted her stomach and she miaowed helplessly, but no one heard.

Life was no longer the Morecambe sunshine and the smell of the sea in the air; it was a dark nightmare of unexpected jolts and endless vibration. Suddenly that movement stopped and, after a pause, a new sensation of swinging took its place. Lucky was thrown from her weak precarious balance, sickened as she lurched into the air; she heard the grinding and grunting of machinery: a throbbing, deafening power that grew into a crescendo of noise.

Lucky was terrified. She was convinced she was about to be devoured by some huge monster with gaping jaws. But it did not happen.

She was tortured by hunger and thirst. She sniffed dust, chewed paper, wood. Her limbs were racked with pain. Then as she lay, weak and exhausted, waiting to die, a trickle of condensation ran down the metal walls and her small tongue licked at the moisture as if it were nectar.

She followed the trickles everywhere, wiping them clean, licking and licking until her tongue was sore against the metal. But it came again, the life-saving water, replaced by some miracle that she did not question.

She was beyond all thought. Home had faded from her mind like a sweet, almost-forgotten dream. That was all so long ago, misty and unreal. Time meant nothing, stretching into a long dark tunnel of misery. She became weaker and weaker, life ebbing from her bright eyes.

But she clung to some intangible thread. She dragged herself to the trickles of moisture, her once-soft mouth now dry and cracked. A tiny flame of spirit still flickered in her heart, but it had almost gone out.

She could hardly stir herself any more. She was drifting into unconsciousness, but then somewhere it registered in her mind that all was quite still. The endless movement had stopped. She could almost hear the stillness and the silence. Perhaps this was death. Perhaps she had died.

Light streamed against her closed eyes. It blinded her. Yes, this was death.

Lucky hovered in the twilight zone between life and death. She was not aware of the strange voices, the rough but gentle hands that lifted her, the exclamations of astonishment.

'Hell. A dead cat!'

'Are you sure it's dead?'

'Yeah . . . chuck it away. Poor thing. Must have starved to death.'

'Let me look at it. I think it's still breathing very faintly.'

'Aw, leave it alone. It's a goner, Gary. We've got enough to do.'

'I'm taking it to the veterinary surgeon. It deserves a chance. It must have been in that damned container near on nine weeks.'

In the days that followed Lucky knew very little of what was happening to her, and she certainly knew nothing of the frantic searching and newspaper advertisements as Lindiladi combed the streets and pubs of Morecambe for her cat.

Lucky found herself in an amazing place. Everything smelt quite different; everything was so big. As she looked around her for the first time, it was as if an explosion had taken place and the outside of everything had disappeared, blown away. Where was she? And where was Lindiladi?

In her confusion she slipped in and out of consciousness, but gained on each encounter with this new world. She was drip-fed, injected, massaged, cared for as if she was worth a thousand dollars.

Her first sip of milk was an unforgettable moment. She almost fell out of the man's arms in her ecstasy. It tasted different, but it was milk all the same.

'Hold on,' laughed the man, Gary Fingleman. 'Not so fast. It won't go away, and there's lots more.'

When Lucky was strong enough, he no longer had to feed her by bottle. In three weeks she was able to stand and sip from a saucer. This new place had lovely food. Lucky ate well and sat in the blazing sunshine, dozing in the heat. She spent her convalescence with the man she called Fingleman. Sometimes she sat on his knee and purred, but he was still a stranger.

Lucky had always thought there must be somewhere beyond More-cambe, and perhaps this was it. People spoke differently; the cars and lorries were hugely terrifying; Fingleman had a refrigerator the size of a small room.

She liked the climate, but she missed the birds. And she missed Lindiladi. Sometimes she asked Fingleman where her beloved mistress was, but he did not understand and would just scratch behind her ear and grin, and pour her some milk from a carton.

It was August and almost unbearably hot. Lucky sat on the man's lap while he drank a cold beer. The telephone rang.

'Is that Gary Fingleman of Houston, Texas?' asked a woman. 'I know this sounds very strange, but I think you've got my cat.'

'Oh?' he drawled. 'Why should you think I've got your cat?'

'Last April I lost my cat Lucky. She just disappeared. I've just met a man who works in the antique shop opposite where we used to live, and he said an American came into the shop to buy some more antiques and said thanks for the extra package. There was a cat in his last delivery, half-dead. A big black and white cat with a black tail . . .' Lindiladi got the words out in one big rush.

'Sealand's sitting on my knee now,' said Fingleman, stroking Lucky's head. 'But how do I know she's your cat?'

'Look under her paws. She has three pinks pads, but her right paw pad is black.'

Lucky suddenly found herself upended on Fingleman's lap, her paws waving in the air. He grasped them gently but firmly. She wriggled frantically. Her paws were very ticklish.

'Three pink paws and one black. Then this must be your Lucky, and lucky she is to have survived the journey to Houston. Four thousand and five hundred miles, lady.'

Lucky did not hear Lindiladi weeping at the other end of the telephone, but she knew something was happening. Her fur crept and she ran under a table, nightmare memories of the container sweeping back.

'She was just bones when I found her, but she's putting on a little weight now.'

'But how on earth do I get her home from America?' Lindiladi asked, dazed.

'We'll see she goes home in style,' said Fingleman, knowing that he must let the cat go.

It was the media that got Lucky home. She had taken herself to America, but it was the combined forces of newspapers, television, local radio and British Caledonian who reunited Lindiladi and Lucky.

While Lucky grew stronger in the Texas sunshine, the wheels went round, forms were filled in, people wrote things, took her photograph.

She was used to the veterinary surgeon and his needles, and she thought no more than a fractional irritation when yet one more injection went into her flesh. Fingleman was holding her in a firm grasp, and looking at her with a strange, fond look. The last thing she saw before sleep overtook her was his kind, strong face.

She knew nothing of the transfer to Houston airport or the long flight. Her limbs twitched in a deep slumber; dreams tumbled through her mind: the wild, wet rain and the smell of the sea . . . the dry baking heat of the past few weeks . . . the terror of the remembrance of that other place, small, dark, endlessly jolting her towards death.

Someone was carrying her into a small room. Lucky yawned. She was dry and sleepy, barely awake, her mouth like sawdust. With a tremendous effort she opened one eye . . . Lindiladi was coming into the room with another young woman holding her arm.

'Lucky . . . Lucky . . . my darling Lucky.' Lindiladi held her for a few brief moment, tears pouring down her cheeks. Of course it was her Lucky, a very thin and skinny Lucky, but still her beautiful cat.

Lucky tried to purr, but sleep overcame her, washing her back into dreams. Her last thought was where had Lindiladi been all this time? It was all . . . yawn . . . very strange.

At the quarantine kennels in Blackpool Lucky had her first English press conference. A lot of people looking at her and expecting something.

'How do you know it's your cat?' snapped the reporters. 'How can you be sure?'

Lindiladi was asked the same thing over and over again, even though she had brought photographs taken of Lucky before she went to America.

'You can see it's her,' said Lindiladi. 'Look, the same black tail, the black head, one black paw pad.'

A man came into the back of the room, unseen.

'Lucky-Lucky-Lucky,' he called.

Lucky looked up instantly and turned her head towards the voice. It was an echo from the past. Her call-sign. It broke through the long nightmare and the unreal days that had followed in that foreign land. It brought back sunning on top of lorries, the hotel guests, the antique shop. She made as if to spring towards Peterman, a cry of freedom caught in her throat as she thought again of smelling the ozone and hearing the shrieks of the seabirds.

'You see . . .' said Lindiladi triumphantly. 'She *is* my Lucky. That's proof.'

Lucky waited out the long, boring six months' quarantine with commendable patience, reassured because Lindiladi came to see her every weekend. Lindiladi brought tinned salmon and cartons of cream, which Lucky ate because they were gifts of love and not because she was hungry.

They grew to know each other again, and one day Lucky jumped onto the woman's lap and put a small pink nose up to touch Lindiladi's nose.

'My little Eskimo,' said the woman.

Nearly a year passed before Lucky at long last returned home. She found that they now all lived in a shop. She took the new changes very quietly, sitting sometimes with a remoteness that was impenetrable.

At first Lucky would only sleep on Lindiladi's bed. The nightmares came often and her body shook. Then she would wake suddenly, sit up and look around at the sleeping figure and the dark hair on the pillow, reassuring herself that she was home; she was safe.

Sometimes Lucky gnawed thoughtfully on a piece of wood, the taste of timber still lingering in her mouth. She did not wander far. She had done her travelling.

Then, amid great activity, the shop was sold and another hotel bought. A popular feature of the new hotel is Lucky's bar.

Lucky sits on the bar counter. Persil white, poised and elegant, her press cuttings and photographs on the wall behind her. She wonders about all the fuss. Why people want to have their photograph taken with the cat who went to America on her own. Anyone knows it's just the next place on.

Scraps

He was the tiniest kitten of the litter and the last one left, an ebony black scrap of humanity, clawing at the empty air. No one wanted him. He was going to be drowned.

They had never thought of owning a cat. They were staying with her brother prior to moving to New Malden to their first house. The kitten looked so weak and appealing that they took him home. Anton, who was Dutch, had been in hospital for two years after the war and had only just started a job in the City.

'We can't really afford to have a cat,' said Anton.

'But we could feed him on scraps from the table,' said Olivia, wanting the kitten. 'He's so tiny and helpless.' Cat first, furniture later . . . her priorities were in that order.

They took Scraps to New Malden in the back of the van, on Olivia's lap. They did not have a cat basket. The kitten slept all the way.

It was a glorious August day, hot and still. They put Scraps on the lawn while they moved their belongings out of the van. The garden was an enchanted place. All they could see of Scraps was the tip of his black tail as he tentatively explored the jungle of weeds and grass.

Olivia and Anton set up home with the bare necessities. They had two beds, a piano (a legacy from Anton's mother), a statue of Nell Gwynn, an alarm clock and a set of fish knives and forks. Now they also had a cat.

Scraps was supposed to be fed from scraps from the table. He did not know but he sometimes ate better than they did. It was 1948 and rationing was still in force. Nor did he think it strange that they ate from the closed lid of the piano while they were saving for a table.

He was so tiny he could hardly climb the stairs and had to be lifted round the bend onto the landing. They took turns during the night to fill the hot-water bottle for his bed. He grew into a fastidious cat; he would not use his litter box if it was dirty; he would only eat off a clean plate.

Eventually Olivia got a job and Scraps was always waiting by the door for her return. She would get on her hands and knees for a few moments of rapturous reunion.

'Has it been a long, long day?' said Olivia, putting her face into the soft, glossy fur, knowing he would never put out his claws. 'When you've been neutered you'll be able to explore the wide world. We'll teach you how to come and go through the fanlight. Then you'll be free to do as you please.'

They began to teach him with a piece of string how to get onto the shed and jump through the fanlight. It was a wonderful game and Scraps thought it great fun. He was taught to jump down onto a low cupboard inside and then onto the floor. It took some time for Scraps to master this involved route, but they were patient and he was bright and intelligent.

He was light on his feet. He sprang through the fanlight with the nimbleness of an Olympic gymnastic gold-medallist. It was a joy to watch the performance.

Till the day Olivia forgot to open the fanlight.

Scraps knocked himself out. He lay unconscious on the floor, the world black and reeling, kitten-size stars before his eyes.

Olivia was horrified. How did one revive an unconscious cat? She cuddled him on her knees until he was less dazed, then gave him some milk.

He didn't forget. He regarded the fanlight with apprehension and it was some time before he could be encouraged to use it again. It was back to square one with the piece of string until he gained confidence. But he always made sure it was open first.

How they enjoyed that first summer in their home. They quickly became a close family, the three of them, playing hide-and-seek in the garden like children during the long light evenings.

'Where's Scraps?' they would call. 'Where's Scraps?'

A tiny black streak would tear out of the bushes, touch ankles with his nose, then bound off to hide again. The garden was one immense playground for Scraps. Anton built a trellis to hide the bottom of the garden, but they all secretly thought that the part they were hiding was the loveliest. It was a wild paradise of tangled blackberry bushes, fragrant apple trees, blackcurrant bushes and raspberry canes.

Whenever they took a walk down the local lane, Scraps came too. He did not want to be left behind. He was never far from them, yet never ventured anywhere on his own. Malden was already becoming a suburban estate, although the village itself was quaint and pretty.

Scraps developed a sweet tooth, but only for homemade cakes. He scorned shop cake. He sat on Anton's knee to share his tea; when he thought no one was looking he would swiftly hook his paw round a piece of cake from Anton's plate. Delicious. He liked queen cakes, and sponges, but shortbread was his favourite.

While he was still small he sat on Anton's shoulder for the morning ritual of shaving. Perhaps he thought the lather was a sponge mix. He liked to lick the lather from Anton's face.

'Leave off,' grinned Anton into the mirror. A small black, foam-smudged face peered back.

Scraps invented a marvellous game along the hall passage, a sort of cat ski-run. It was a Saturday and Sunday game, when Anton and Olivia were both at home and all three doors would be open.

He would take off from the front gate, gallop along the path gethering momentum, leap onto the runner and slide along the polished floor all the way into the kitchen and out of the back door. He could also do this in reverse, from the back door to the front garden. It was exhilarating. But also exhausting. After three or four runs Scraps would flop down, flaked out, panting like a dog.

Winter turned the passage into an icy blast and Scraps liked warmth. He stopped asking for the doors to be opened. There was no central heating in those days, and the game stopped.

They did not go out much as they were saving up to buy furniture. They couldn't go on eating off the piano lid forever. But one evening they decided to go to the cinema.

'The one-and-nines?' Anton suggested.

'How lovely,' said Olivia, fetching her coat.

Scraps sat alone in the empty house. They had gone out without him. How could they? He always went on their walks. How could he convey his utter disgust that they had deserted him?

He was too gentle a creature to actually cause any damage. It was not in his nature. But somehow he had to communicate the depth of his feelings. He wandered around the rooms wondering what he could do. It is not easy for a cat to get a message over to human owners.

Olivia loved flowers. They grew mostly vegetables but because it was spring and daffodils were cheap, she had treated herself to a dozen golden-headed blooms. They stood, glorious and glowing, in a vase on the piano.

Scraps jumped onto the piano and very carefully, with his head on one side, put his mouth gently round a stem and lifted it out of the vase. He moved delicately because he did not want to knock over the vase or spill water on Olivia's piano top.

He laid the extracted daffodil on the piano and went back for a second. It took him a long time to remove all twelve flowers. He laid them in a row along the top and retreated to the top of the stairs, feeling pleased with himself. He had made a statement. That would teach them for going out without him.

They came back late, laughing and talking about the film. Scraps sat at the top of the stairs, dignified and remote, not coming down to greet them as he usually would. Olivia was too happy after the unexpected outing to take much notice. She went to put the kettle on for a cup of coffee.

When she went into the dining room and saw the row of daffodils laid along the top of the piano, she knew why Scraps was looking smug.

'The young monkey,' she laughed. 'Anton, come and look at this. See what Scrap's been up to. He obviously didn't approve of our going out. Hey, Scraps, are you coming off your high horse for some warm milk?'

It was some weeks before they had the temerity to go out again. They had forgotten the daffodil incident, but Scraps hadn't. When he discovered that they had gone out without him again, he couldn't believe it. He roamed around the house, his thoughts in a turmoil. Perhaps they hadn't understood . . .

A recent purchase had been a second-hand table for the hall which Olivia had polished and polished until it shone. On it she had put a bowl of dried flowers. Scraps decided to make the same protest, but with a little variation.

When Olivia and Anton returned from visiting her parents they found a dried flower placed on each step of the stairs and Scraps sitting at the top awaiting their return, the same smug expression on his face.

'Okay, Scraps, we get the message,' said Anton, much amused. 'How about putting them back in the bowl if you are such a clever cat, eh?'

They did not try leaving Scraps again. They even took him election-eering, delivering pamphlets door to door in the village. One woman asked them in. Scraps took a strong objection to the delay and sat on her doorstep howling like a coyote. They had to make a hurried retreat.

'That's no way to win votes,' said Olivia, shooing him down the path. His glossy black tail shot up in greeting. He had only wanted to see them. Even a few minutes' separation was too much.

Some Saturdays Anton went to watch Chelsea playing. Scraps always seemed to know on which train he was returning, for the cat would move from the fire onto the window-sill to watch for his arrival. It was Olivia's cue to put the kettle on, and Scraps was always right. Moment later Anton would walk in.

'Our Lord and Master returning home from his gallivanting,' said Olivia to the cat with a secret smile as they both went to meet him.

They grew into a devoted family, a threesome. Scraps hated being away from them for any length of time. They insisted that he slept in his own sleeping-box in the kitchen, but relented enough to take him to bed for a last game of pictures on the wall.

They made shadow pictures of rabbits and dogs on the wall with their fingers. Scraps watched, fascinated, occasionally unable to resist a leap and a paw at the moving pictures.

'No more,' said Anton yawning. 'It's bedtime. Even yours, young Scraps.'

'The show's over,' said Olivia firmly, taking Scraps downstairs. 'No more television. You're a lucky puss; you have a television but we don't!'

Nor did they need an alarm clock, for Scraps woke them each morning with a gentle paw on each eyelid. He waited on a small ledge in their bedroom, watching the early morning birds flying past, wishing he could catch one but knowing instinctively that he would be reprimanded. He did not get told off for taking a nap in the airing cupboard, tucked away among the towels. He knew what he could do and could not do.

He could tell them when he was hungry and wanted to eat. They had taught him how to open the larder door by hooking his paw round the edge and pulling it open. Scraps would go in, take off the cloth that covered his plate of fish or liver and carry the cloth to Olivia, waving it like the trophy of some fierce jungle hunter.

'Thank you, Scraps,' said Olivia, taking the cloth from his jaws. 'Would you like your breakfast?'

He never took the food. After all, he wanted a clean plate. He was fussy.

One day when Anton and Olivia returned home from work, Scraps was not there to greet them. It was so unusual, they looked at each other with unspoken fears. He did not come home that night or the night after.

They searched the house and garden and the nearby lane, becoming more and more frantic with worry. He had never stayed out before.

'I can't think of anything that would make Scraps stay away from us for even one night,' said Olivia, over and over again. She could not concentrate on anything. She kept thinking of their little black cat, so small and sweet, and how he must be feeling. 'Something must have happened to him.'

It was autumn and the weather was crisp and dry. They searched as far as they could go, asking everyone they met if they had seen a small, glossy black cat . . . A young couple, desperate to find the tiny scrap who had become so much part of their lives.

'He's wearing his medallion so perhaps someone will bring him back,' said Olivia, clutching at straws.

'He wouldn't have gone with anyone. He must have been stolen,' said Anton, chilled by the thought of people's cruelty. That lovely glossy black fur had a price.

Scraps had been very wary of anyone strange since the day burglars broke into their house. They had stolen Olivia's engagement ring and Anton's suit.

Scraps had seen it all, hiding beneath Anton's wardrobe. At first even Olivia could not persuade him to come out; for a long while he never left their side, following them like a black shadow. They shut the fanlight for a time and Scraps knew why. He had seen how the burglars got in . . . He had seen the boy wriggling through and knew something was very wrong.

'He would never have gone off with a stranger,' they agreed.

'I miss him so much . . .'

'We both do,' said Anton, comforting his young wife.

The next evening they were sitting in their dining room. By now they had saved enough to buy a dining-room suite and two fireside chairs, but that night they took no pleasure in their new furniture. They were worrying about Scraps and wondering what had happened to him.

Suddenly they heard a familiar sound. The tiny scratch, the light landing of paws, the creak of wood. It was Scraps coming in through the fanlight.

'It's Scraps,' whispered Olivia, hardly daring to hope.

He did not come through to them. They waited.

'Scraps?' Anton called. But he did not come.

They went out into the kitchen. Scraps was sitting on the back door mat, plastered from head to foot in thick brown mud. It had dried on him and his tail was as stiff as a board and sticking up like a beanpole. He looked utterly dejected and weary.

'Oh my poor, poor darling,' said Olivia, going down on her knees to hug the bedraggled cat, mud and all. She felt a quiver run along his tired body. Somehow he had got himself home.

He allowed himself to be shampooed in the kitchen sink, something which he had never let Olivia do before. He knew he had to get clean, and he could not do it himself. Wrapped in a warm towel and cuddled in front of the fire, he began a low purr, which grew and grew as if he would never stop. He was home. He was really home with them again.

Scraps had obviously fallen into some stagnant pond. But there was no pond for miles around and the ditches were all dry. If only Scraps could tell them where he had been taken, but they would never know. When his fur was dry, Anton brushed him gently with an old army hairbrush, and put him to bed. He slept the sleep of the exhausted, but they took it in turns to creep down the stairs to look at him.

When winter came, they sat each evening by the coal fire. Scraps invented a new game. He would sit with his head in a paper bag. How he purred, loving the warmth. It was nice inside the paper bag and it shut out the electric light. He had got the idea at Christmas when Olivia and Anton were opening their presents and the floor was strewn with paper.

One of his Christmas presents was a piece of ribbon which Olivia would tie onto his tail. Rolling over and over, he could untie the ribbon and take it to them, asking to start the game all over again. The paper bag and the ribbon at the same time was a special party trick.

'If only we could take a photo of him,' laughed Olivia.

Olivia was the pianist of the family. Scraps knew what he liked. He liked 'When Irish Eyes are Smiling' and 'Peg of my Heart'. But if Olivia began to play the popular song 'Mares Eat Oats and Does Eat Oats and Little Lambs Eat Ivy', he would jump up onto the piano and march along the piano keys in a highly successful wrecking operation.

It had been two years of working hard and saving to get their home together, and the following year Olivia and Anton planned to take a holiday, their first.

They booked two weeks at a holiday camp at Bracklesham Bay, and left Scraps at a cats' home, kissing his sweet nose goodbye when they left.

'Now be very good Scraps and we'll soon be back,' said Olivia.

It was a wonderful holiday, all thoughts of the desert war, the pain, the years in hospital, began to fade into the past. They walked along the steeply shelving pebble beach, watching the waves pounding the shore, listening to the music of the sea. When they returned home, they immediately went to fetch Scraps. He came before anything.

The little cat went wild with excitement when he saw Olivia and Anton. Purring, climbing over them, nudging chins, kneading, burrowing deep into their arms, all with little cries of joy. But they were shocked by the change in their cat's appearance. He was desperately thin.

'He pined and wouldn't eat,' said the owner of the cats' home, shaking her head. 'We couldn't get him to eat at all.'

The happiness of their holiday fled, melting like butter in that summer's sun. They wished they had never gone. The taste of the spray was bitter now. They took Scraps home, tenderly nursing the sick cat all that night and the following day. But Scraps had been the tiniest and weakest of the litter. His heart, valiant and courageous enough to find his weary way home after being stolen, could no longer stand the strain.

He was cradled in Anton's arms when he breathed a last sigh and was gone.

He died of a broken heart, believing that they had left him. The vet said this too.

Olivia cried and cried. Scraps had been like a child. She couldn't believe he had gone, that sweet, glossy black little cat. It was heartbreaking.

For weeks they could not bear to go back to an empty house. They walked about every evening and did not eat. Nor could they have him buried in the garden where they had spent so many happy hours playing with their little black friend.

The local police buried Scraps in the garden at the back of the police station where he would be safe forever. They never had another cat. Scraps could not be replaced.

A Thoroughly Bad Lot

You only had to take a good long look at Jasper to know that she was a thoroughly bad lot. Her answering glance was always scornful, with only a flicker of interest in the depths of her almond-shaped green eyes. Her long black tail thrashed the ground in perpetual anger. She walked alone. She cared for no one. She refused to conform.

'I don't understand why you're such a bad cat,' said Jennifer. 'You have a good home and you are well fed. And yet you steal. I don't like cats who steal.'

She marched to the back door with Jasper under her arm. She hung there like a limp fur stole, only a minute flick of her tail betraying her inner fury. She did not care if she was not liked. It was quite immaterial to her.

'Stealing Candy's fish, indeed. Ungrateful thing. And it's not the first time I've caught you.' Jennifer tipped Jasper out on to the doorstep. 'Reflect and reform. You can come back when you've repented.'

Repentance. She did not know the meaning of the word. She was uncontrite, even if it was raining. She had not one fleeting whisker of regret. That Candy was going to get exactly what was coming to her.

'Is the delinquent in the stocks again?' asked Edward. 'You know it's raining, don't you? It's not like you to be unkind.'

'I've got to teach her a lesson,' Jennifer insisted, wrestling with her conscience. 'She's been stealing Candy's supper again. Of course,

Candy is a perfect lady and won't stand up for herself. Jasper gets away with it every time.'

The perfect lady sat under a chair in a corner of the kitchen, velvet-gold eyes half-veiled, waiting until it was safe to venture out.

'Come on, beautiful,' coaxed Jennifer. 'I've put that bad cat out.'

Candy broke out into a low, passionate purr. Her love was embarrassingly vocal. She could be heard on the telephone, and the mere mention of her name was enough to start the throbbing, quivering, claw-retracting fluffy black Persian on her dauntless track to the nearest soft lap. Nothing deterred Candy in her quest. She was blind to newspapers, sewing, even coffee cups in her way. She would place herself roundly on top of the lot, drooling moist words of love into the nearest ear.

Outside on the window-sill sat Jasper, balefully watching the tender reunion. Although she was nearly full grown, she was still small and sleek – sometimes she thought that one of her ancestors must have been a witch's cat . . . of course, there weren't such things now, what with radar and computers.

The rain settled on her short spiky fur like pearl onions on cocktail sticks. Her attention was caught for a moment by a shining trickling raindrop, and she licked the wet window with a small, inquisitive tongue.

Jasper looked into the kitchen at the bundle of four-inch long Persian fluff now being lovingly brushed and combed by Jennifer, and she felt almost naked by comparison. Electric sparks prickled up her spine. Her tail swung to and fro. She could not stand the nauseating sight any longer.

She jumped down and walked deliberately across a freshly raked flowerbed. Further down the garden tiny shoots of lettuce were peeping through the earth where none had been the day before. She scratched at them curiously and chewed on a tender thread of root.

The bluetits and sparrows were fighting noisily round the bird-bag that swung from the Japanese maple tree. They hung upside down, pecking at the nuts, dropping from a precarious hold, fluttering and squabbling.

Jasper watched them with narrowed eyes. Stupid, irritating things. She could not even be bothered to catch them. She had bigger prey. That long-haired layabout: the precious Candy.

Any good psychiatrist would have sorted Jasper out in a trice. Beneath that smouldering hatred lay a deep-seated inferiority complex; an unconscious distaste for her own black sleekness; a repressed wish for a coat of four-inch long Persian fluff.

Jasper did not understand this. She did not need a motive to be mean – it came naturally. She could not remember a time when she had had a pleasant thought. She had the vaguest memories of a half-wild mother, a crowded cage of stray kittens, of being handled by many strange hands.

Neither did she know that she had been chosen by mistake, nor that she was a profound disappointment to Jennifer. In kittenhood she had looked remarkably like a Persian, and Jennifer had picked her out of the selection at the animal refuge as company for Candy. But it never worked out. The sleeker she grew, the more Jasper disliked the Persian. She brooded for hours on her animosity, plotting horrendously sticky ends for her rival.

'Hello,' said Edward, scooping Jasper up against his shoulder. 'Put you out again, has she? You really will have to learn to behave.'

Jasper reared away from him, back arching, elongating her long neck like a snake. Edward scratched her smooth, almost hairless chin.

'Now you're what I call a real cat,' he said. 'Not like that other overgrown fur mat, all fuzz and fluff.'

Jasper replied with a piercing yeowl and leaped out of his arms. She could not bear all that petting and fuss. Yuck. She shook out her crumpled fur and stalked disdainfully down to the stream.

She trod daintily over the pebbles and thought wicked thoughts. She knew that by engineering something simply terrible for Candy, she would revenge herself on the humans and the pampered Persian at the same time.

She sat on a broken piece of concrete and thought. Death by drowning was a delicious possibility, but in a mere two inches of slow moving stream? Another tragic road accident – but Candy was as nimble as Jasper in dodging the traffic. Starvation? But the humans were too wily. They had seen through that one.

Jasper thought treacherously of the big golden retriever who lived down the road. Could she, without endangering herself, convince him that Candy, beneath all that fur, was a chewable proposition?

Jasper looked at her own quivering reflection in the shallow water, her eyes darting and flashing among the round pebbles like a shoal of minnows. Perhaps she could get Candy into trouble, then they might get rid of her.

She sauntered back to the house, her tail held high. She watched from the camouflage of a rhododendron bush as Candy was put out of the back door.

'There's a good Candy,' said Jennifer. 'Have a lovely run-round.'

Jasper felt sick. Have a lovely run-round . . . to a cat. It was nauseating.

Candy had a favourite sleeping place. On a rack across the ceiling of the garage were some ladders and Edward had stored the cushions of the garden swing on top of them.

It infuriated Jasper to see Candy up there on her Dunlopillow. It made her deliberately seek out the most uncomfortable box of nails to curl herself up on and go to sleep. She was no softy.

Out of slit eyes Jasper watched Candy go into the garage and climb up the shelves to her throne. She trampled it into order, settled blissfully and began her throbbing vocal appreciation.

Jasper fled down the garden. There must be some way, something that would choke off that awful racket for ever. Her claws caught in some flimsy stuff that was hanging from a shrub. It seemed to have fallen from Jennifer's washing line, and the wind had carried it away. The stuff ripped as Jasper jigged sideways trying to unmesh her claws. She bit and scratched at it, strands catching in her teeth and setting them on edge.

Wildly she leaped about, determined to rid herself of the hellish stuff. It trailed after her everywhere. She rushed into the garage where there were sharp things and it caught on some logs . . .

Some hours later, when Jasper had almost forgotten the incident, she heard Jennifer saying quite crossly: 'Candy, you naughty thing. Those were my best tights. They're absolutely ruined.

The days that followed were almost pastoral. Jasper's animosity seemed to mellow into a kind of saintly reserve. She no longer spat at Candy. She deigned to allow Candy her half share of the nourishment provided. She would sit in the same room for several minutes without provoking a squabble.

'I do believe Jasper and Candy are making friends at last,' said Jennifer with relief. 'It's a miracle.'

'Don't be too sure,' said Edward. 'This sudden change of heart doesn't ring true.'

'Jasper's being a good pussy now, aren't you?' Jennifer crooned. 'There's a darling . . .' The darling good pussy stiffened as Jennifer stroked her sleek black fur. It took immense self-control not to leap out of a window and escape to the woods.

'I think I'll go down to the shops and buy the cats some really nice fish for a treat,' said Jennifer.

'You can go into the newsagents and tell them that the new delivery boy is being highly erratic. And will you pay the gas bill? We've got a final demand. All red print and threats,' said Edward, opening his cheque book. 'You know,' he added thoughtfully, 'perhaps Jasper doesn't like her name. You must admit it sounds very masculine.'

'Nonsense,' said Jennifer. 'It means a kind of quartz, an opaque kind.'

'I know what Jasper means, but does she?'

'Or something taking a high polish. Very suitable for a highly-polished cat,' said Jennifer firmly.

'I suppose it doesn't actually make any difference, but I just wondered,' said Edward, signing the cheque with a flourish. 'I suppose it's just a sound to her.'

Jasper remained unmoved. She trod a tightrope of deception with cool aplomb. She slipped through the waving grasses in the garden, her sharp ears alert for the unexpected. She roamed the area, peering into sheds, nibbling the odd stalk.

The cuddly Candy relaxed into perpetual Elysium; her home was the enchanted fields of Arcadia; the walls vibrated with her ecstatic purring. Her complacency grew with her plumpness.

Jennifer was more surprised than alarmed when one afternoon, she found a uniformed policeman ringing the door bell. He was youngish, fresh-faced and very slightly embarrassed.

'Mrs Jones,' he asked. 'Mrs Edward Jones?'

'That's right,' she said, puzzled.

'I'm making a few inquiries and I'm wondering if you can help me,' he began.

'Yes?'

'We've received a number of complaints in this road about missing items. These complaints cover a period of several weeks. The latest was this morning when a builder working on number 23 reported the loss of a tin of emulsion paint, shade Radiant Blue.'

'I'm afraid I don't understand . . .' said Jennifer.

'There are paint tracks, shade Radiant Blue, leading into your garage.' The young policeman looked even more embarrassed. 'I wonder if you would allow me to have a look . . . er . . .'

'Of course,' said Jennifer briskly. 'Look all you like. This is absolute nonsense, you know. It was probably some children larking about.'

There were some spots of fresh blue paint on the driveway, and a larger splash by the garage window. Jennifer opened the garage doors, the policeman close behind her. They peered into the gloom. Jennifer switched on the light.

At first all seemed normal. Edward went to work in his car so the garage was empty, apart from the usual flotsam of suburban garages. Jennifer turned to the policeman, triumphantly, but then followed his gaze to the floor. A small pool of Radiant Blue was forming. They looked up at the ceiling, where the drips were coming from.

'Oh dear,' said Jennifer in a small voice, not knowing what to expect next.

The policeman climbed on to the workbench at the end of the garage and reached up among the ladders and cushions from the garden swing. Candy looked down into his youthful eyes and began to purr rapturously, soft fluff a-quiver.

'Oh dear,' said Jennifer again.

'I wonder if you would mind helping me,' he said, sounding quite apologetic.

He passed down the pot of paint, glistening with slopped Radiant Blue. Then he solemnly handed her one child's red wellington boot. Next, three copies of the Radio Times, one unopened gas bill and a dead rose bush. Dried earth showered his uniform.

Jennifer put the items on the floor. 'Is there any more?' she asked hopelessly.

'It's like a jumble sale up here,' he said cheerfully.

The pile on the floor grew . . . a knitted rabbit, a silk scarf from Liberty's, two pairs of bikini panties, one marked Tuesday and the other marked Friday, a man's vest, a brand new pair of secateurs still in their shop packaging. Jennifer went from bright pink with acute embarrassment to pale with horror.

The policeman stretched further into the robber's trove . . . a length of washing line, three odd gloves, a garden trowel, an ordnance survey map of south-west London, a tennis sock and seven pairs of sunglasses.

'I don't understand,' said Jennifer, shaking her head.

'I'm sure there must be some explanation,' the young policeman said.

The explanation sat in the middle of the garden path quickly trying to lick Radiant Blue off her paws. On the path beside her was a carton of yogurt with teeth marks denting the lid and a muddied copy of *Teach Yourself Arabic*.

'Caught red-handed,' said the policeman, almost disbelieving his eyes.

'You mean blue-pawed,' Jennifer remarked, eyeing the cat levelly. 'A serious case of kleptomania.'

Within minutes Jasper was in the kitchen sink up to her middle in warm water, struggling like a demented fiend, as Jennifer tried to wash off the paint before it dried.

'You are a very naughty pussy,' said Jennifer, unable to stop herself from laughing. 'And trying to put the blame on poor Candy. I'm ashamed of you. You're a thoroughly bad lot.'

Jennifer wrapped the cat in a towel. Jasper scowled, knowing she looked a fool with her fur all wet.

'Just you wait until I tell Edward what you've been up to,' said Jennifer, towelling her briskly till her fur shone like silk. Jasper dug her claws into Jennifer's knee. She could not understand what had gone wrong with her plan – they ought to be scolding Candy. She jumped on to the floor and shook off the towel . . . immediately in her way stood the big black Persian. She met Candy's yellow stare. There was no sympathy in the older cat's knowing eyes. Instead there was a distinctly chilly authority.

Candy sensed a momentary weakening in Jasper's fierce spirit, and stepped forward, a long hiss coming from her curled lips, her fluffy tail hoovering the floor with steady sweeps. She lifted a round velvet paw and boxed Jasper smartly on the ear.

Jasper sprang back, astonished. It hurt.

Jennifer gathered both cats up into her arms, still laughing, and buried her face in their soft fur.

'Now stop it, both of you,' she admonished. 'I won't have any more of this nonsense.'

Jasper veiled her slit eyes and arched her slender neck away from the mass of vibrating Persian almost smothering her. Then she remembered the accuracy of that unexpected wallop, and thought hard . . . perhaps there was room for negotiation after all.

Felis Domesticus Surrentum

From the age of five Elisabeth Fiorentino had been singing. The daughter of an English schoolteacher and an Italian cellist, singing came as naturally to her as breathing and she was given every encouragement. As the years went by she progressed from 'Ding, dong, Pussy's in the Well' to 'The Sound of Music', till eventually she was studying Mozart at the Guildhall School of Music and famous arias floated from the open windows of her bedroom, soaring to the treetops like birdsong.

The world of music recognized her talent as her voice grew more beautiful, and she travelled extensively on singing engagements. But Elisabeth found that the dedicated life of an opera singer was a lonely one. She desperately needed company other than that of other professional singers or her business manager. Men seemed almost afraid of her – or of the effortless sounds that came from her throat, as if she were not quite human.

The few men who did enter her life did not stay long once they discovered how many hours went into the perfecting of each note and phrase. They could not compete with her discipline, nor did they care to take second place to a voice.

So cats became Elisabeth's friends and travelling companions. The first was called simply Fluffy, then, at intervals arrived Fluffy-Two, Fluffy-Three and Fluffy-Four. They were acquired and christened because of the strict quarantine laws of great Britain. When Elisabeth first flew abroad to sing *Tosca* at the Metropolitan Opera House in

New York's Lincoln Centre, she took with her a pretty grey and white Persian kitten in a quilted travelling cat-box. It was cold in New York with dirty snow piled high on the corners of the streets. But Elisabeth loved the towering skyscrapers and walked the full length of Fifth Avenue with her small friend, learning many things about that brash and bustling city.

But on Elisabeth's eventual return to England, Fluffy had to go into cat kennels at Tunbridge Wells for six months. Lonely and depressed, Elisabeth bought Fluffy-Two, a similarly enchanting kitten. The exercise repeated itself when Elisabeth was booked to sing in Zurich, and again when she went halfway across the world to sing in the butterfly-shaped Sydney Opera House.

She was now accompanied by Fluffy-Four and recuperating from an exhausting series of recitals in Italy culminating in a gala performance at La Scala. A doctor warned her not to sing for at least two weeks and she decided to stay at the Hotel Excelsior Vittoria in Sorrento, hoping that the gloriously rugged scenery of the peninsula and the heavenly blue of the sea would restore her jagged nerves and overtired vocal chords.

The fertile plain of Sorrento was a vast terrace above the sheer cliffs that fell into the Bay of Naples, acres of orange and lemon groves, walnut, fig, cherry and pomegranate trees. The villas intruded through the flowering greenery, red-washed, faded pink or white, civilization encroaching on what nature had intended to be simply a huge garden. There were no beaches – sunbathing platforms stretched out to the sea for the tourists to invade.

Fluffy-Four, or Four, as he was more familiarly called, resented the jolting ride down the long, paved drive from the Piazza Tasso to the entrance of the hotel. It was ignominious to be perched on top of Elisabeth's matching hide luggage and wheeled in on a trolley by a porter. He protested loudly but no one took any notice.

Four could smell aromatic orange and lemon trees and he wanted to be out and exploring. Milan had been so boring. He yawned. Through the slits of his tartan-lined wicker travelling basket (Four detested tartan) he caught tantalizing glimpses of trees dripping with orange and yellow globes, of Elisabeth's pastel mink coat swinging from her slender shoulders, of her mane of honey-coloured hair tied back with a silk scarf from Yves St Laurent. He miaowed again to attract her attention to his plight.

Elisabeth turned and took Four's basket off the trolley before her luggage disappeared into the lower depths of the rambling cliff-side hotel. It had once been three imposing villas built a century earlier, relics of another era, each clinging with fortress-like buttresses on impossible sites. Two were painted red, the third was a white palace. Now all three were married into one by somewhat haphazard additions of a Swiss-style chalet and a high, glass foyer and entrance. The foyer looked like a gilded bird cage with enough magnificent potted palms to house a whole aviary of exotic birds.

'I am Elisabeth Fiorentino,' said Elisabeth. 'You have my reservation. And I trust there is no objection to my cat.'

'None at all, Signorina Fiorentino. We are delighted to welcome such a famous singer to our hotel. We have reserved the Caruso room, or you may care to see the Princess Margaret suite? Her Royal Highness stayed here in May 1949.'

'And what about Four?'

'You want to see four rooms?'

'Four is my cat.'

'You have four cats?'

'Four is the name of my cat. He is one cat,' said Elisabeth patiently, knowing she must not raise her voice.

The manager had been trained not to show bewilderment. 'Pets are not allowed in the public rooms or in the restaurant,' he said. 'There will be a charge depending on size.'

'You mean you are going to measure him? From nose to tail, or side to side?'

'Is this a small cat or a large cat?' the manager queried.

'I should say he is a large small cat,' said Elisabeth, suddenly tiring. 'He is a small cat inside a lot of thick fur.'

Each of the villas was a period piece. Marble staircases with pastel murals, grand master bedrooms, extensive balconies that took in panoramic views of the Bay of Naples, the majestic snow-tipped Vesuvius and the range of Lattari mountains.

The Caruso bedroom was a high-ceilinged confection of ornate gold and white marble, a vast gilt bed, full length brocade curtains billowing in the sea breezes, priceless pieces of furniture. Elisabeth imagined the bill if Four sharpened his claws on the legs of the antique desk and shook her head.

The Princess Margaret room was a corner sun-trap with three big windows opening on to balconies. It was large enough to hold a party in. Elisabeth and Four would be lost among the beautiful furniture, overpowered by the magnificent chandelier, awed by the palatial marble bathroom. Across a hallway that could be shut off was a private sitting room, again furnished with antiques. Elisabeth shook her head. Four yawned. He was used to this. Elisabeth was very particular about rooms.

'Perhaps one of our de luxe suites would be more suitable?' He thought . . . the Fiorentino suite would sound good.

The top floor suite in the white villa was far less overpowering – airy, more modern, with rugs on highly polished floors, a built-in-wardrobe with painted flowers on the doors, a vast double bed, a luxurious bathroom across a small hallway, and, best of all, a completely private, walled, corner balcony overflowing with urns of flowers.

Quite nice, thought Four, jumping out of his detested basket and having a delicious stretch. He could smell the sea, fish, flowers and unknown herbs, and a shiver of excitement rippled along his fur.

Elisabeth laid her cheek on his velvety coat. 'I shall get better here,' she told him. 'We will sit in the sun and wander around and be just like other ordinary tourists.'

It sounded perfect to Four, especially sitting in the sun. He began to purr and nudge her chin. He wanted to get going.

But Elisabeth had to unpack first. Four helped. He attacked her fluffy swansdown slippers, hid under a pile of cashmere sweaters, had a fight-to-the-death with a box of tissues. Finally he dragged a cobwebby shawl under a chair and trampled it into a new bed.

Elisabeth went on her knees and tugged at the shawl but his claws were firmly enmeshed in the wool. His eyes glinted with glee. He loved a tussle.

'Now you're being very naughty,' said Elisabeth sternly. It was a clash of wills that was resolved when there was a discreet knock on the door. A waiter had arrived with Four's supper served in special cat dishes, on a tray, and Elisabeth took the opportunity to disappear for her own. Four settled down to demolish flaked fish, freshly caught that morning in the Bay, artistically topped with curls of butter, unaware of the stir his beautiful mistress was making on her arrival in the elegantly-pillared dining room.

Waiters straightened their white jackets; the maître d'hotel immediately gave her the best window seat; diners stopped eating, forks in mid-air; heads swivelled to catch a glimpse. She was wearing a cream silk suit, pale and shimmering, her hair caught up in a loose knot with escaping tendrils, and dangling gold earrings.

Chester Ridgway had no inhibitions. As soon as Elisabeth had eaten and moved into the many-mirrored lounge to order coffee, he strolled over, one hand casually in the pocket of his dark blue velvet jacket. He was a handsome young man, not very tall, with curling brown hair touching his well-shaped ears; his half-closed blue eyes regarding Elisabeth with admiration.

'May I join you for coffee?' he asked, confident of his acceptability. Elisabeth shook her head.

'But you should not be alone.' he said persuasively. 'A beautiful woman should always be complemented by the rugged contrast of male company.'

Elisabeth sighed faintly. She pointed to the small cigar smoking in his fingers and then to her throat. He apologized immediately.

'Of course, Miss Fiorentino, I should have been more thoughtful. I do apologize.'

Her heart fell. He had recognized her. Now she would never get rid of him. She smiled distantly and again pointed to her throat, shaking her head in pantomime.

'Ah, I understand. You're resting that exquisite voice of yours. Then you are certainly in dire need of entertaining company,' said Chester, settling himself in the other deep armchair, and signalling to a steward. 'Two more coffees, a Drambuie and a Brandy Alexander. Ladies always like a Brandy Alexander,' he told Elisabeth, a hand sliding automatically into a pocket for his cigar case. 'My name's Chester Ridgway. I daresay you've heard of Ridgway Tiles? My father started the business just after the war. I'm a director, of course. I do a lot of travelling for the firm.'

So it seemed. There was hardly anywhere he had not been. He also knew all the local excursions from Sorrento, and seemed to think it was his mission in life to arrange her stay for her.

Elisabeth listened and sipped her frothy cream drink, wondering how she could politely take herself from this well-meaning but boring young man.

'And, of course, you mustn't miss the magnificent coastal drive to Positano and Amalfi. The views are quite splendid. Perhaps you would allow me to escort you?' he offered, his feeling of confidence growing as he marvelled at her flawless skin and tumbling tawny hair. She was a real catch.

Elisabeth shook her head and smiled politely. 'You are very kind but my husband is arriving tomorrow.' she whispered. She stood up. 'Thank you for the drink. Now I must take my cat for a walk. Good night.'

As an exit line, it was effective, whether it was the husband or the cat that did the trick, but she left Chester staring after her blankly.

The next day Elisabeth and Four set out to explore Sorrento at their leisure. They caused quite a stir. At first the Sorrentine shop-keepers were astonished and amused by the sight of the slight young woman leading a blue-grey cat on a lead. But then Elisabeth's sad brown eyes, almost hidden by her long fringe of honey hair, made each man sigh and long to bring a smile to her face. Four was universally admired by the women and petted by the children. And rightly so. He was a fine and proud Short-hair Blue-Cream Burmese, whose delicately shaded coat was like thick grey velvet. Four looked back at his admirers with large fierce eyes that reflected the elusive golden light of the Sorrentine sky.

Four strained at his lead. He was ecstatic with curiosity. Sorrento was definitely a cat place, and he could hardly contain his high spirits.

Leading from the Piazzo Tasso was the Via S. Cesareo, a narrow alley crowded with open-fronted shops. Glistening fresh fish lay on wet slabs within sniffing distance; goat cheeses swung from doorways; fruit was piled high in casual confusion still twigged with dark green leaves from the local groves.

A tortuous, twisting stone-stepped path led steeply through narrow old houses dating back to the fifteenth and sixteenth centuries, now festooned with twentieth-century washing, jeans, printed vests and drip-dry sheets.

Four's nose told him when they were nearing the Marina Grande, the original fishing harbour still cluttered with brightly painted fishing boats, yards of orange nets being repaired, and ragged children playing on the dark volcanic sand among dead fish, straggling seaweed and washed-up flotsam. Cats roamed in packs. Dozens of them. They glared at Four from under upturned rowing boats. He glared back, unafraid, a low hiss coming from his throat, thoroughly enjoying the sensation. It was a long time since he'd had a good hiss.

The little shore was bustling and noisy, cluttered with vehicles and boats, fishermen smoking and yarning and mending nets, women carrying their shopping and washing on their heads, children squabbling and chasing each other, barefooted and dirty. The closely built, red-roofed houses clung to the hillside, almost crowding out the fishermen's church on the front, cheek by jowl with dim taverns and bars, with hardly a postcard or souvenir in sight.

'The real Sorrento,' said Elisabeth, stepping carefully over the rubbish washed up on the cobbles by the night's rough seas. Four tugged hopefully in the direction of some fish-heads, but Elisabeth had glanced back and caught sight of Chester Ridgway descending down the same stone-stepped path, a suede jacket slung casually over his shoulders. It was no coincidence.

For a moment Elisabeth panicked. She darted along a lane and up some steps, only to find herself in someone's backyard among washing and crates. Another alley led to the landing of a house. Next she found herself facing a blank, sheer cliff face. Marina Grande seemed to be a labyrinth of alleyways leading nowhere. She did not want to go back the way she had come and meet Chester. The one road at the far end was a nightmare of revving mopeds, cars trying to turn, hooters blaring and no pavement. Four would be terrified out of his wits.

They were trapped, and Chester Ridgway was catching them up. He knew she could not escape. Any moment now he would stroll over, ready to pin her down with an invitation, arranging her day, planning her evening for her. At least he could see now that she really did have a cat.

A hefty fisherman's jersey suddenly blocked her way. Its owner side-stepped and started to stride away with purpose, as if he knew where he was going. His face was darkened by the sun, his grey hair roughened up by the wind, longish but well cut. Elisabeth spoke without thinking.

'Please can you help me?' She said it in English.

The man half turned and stopped. He did not look surprised, as if beautiful women were always asking him for help.

'But, of course . . .' he said, a trace of accent in his voice.

'I'm lost. There are so many blind alleys. It's very confusing and I must get out quickly. Can you show me a back way up to the town?'

'There is the road . . .'

'My cat would be terrified and there's no pavement. Besides, I would be seen.'

Chester Ridgway had seen her. He raised an arm in salute and was rapidly negotiating a route between the drawn up fishing boats, trying not to step on unmentionable debris.

The colour drained from Elisabeth's face. She turned to the stranger, trying to glean his character from his face.

'Please . . . could you pretend to be my husband . . . just for a few moments?' she asked urgently, in a low voice. 'It's very important to me . . .'

It must have been the look of desperation in her eyes, for the stranger calmly took her arm and began to guide her from the harbour front. Chester was only a few yards away.

'Did you enjoy your walk?' the stranger said casually but loud enough for Chester to hear. 'The air is very refreshing. I thought you looked a little pale last night.'

'I was awfully tired,' said Elisabeth, racking her brains for some long-married conversational phrases. 'And I had a headache. But it's gone now. Did you get the shopping you wanted?'

'No. You know I don't enjoy shopping without you to help me choose.'

Elisabeth had a sudden feeling that the man was laughing at her, but his expression was quite serious.

'Hello there,' called Chester, beaming.

'Good morning,' said Elisabeth, then turned to her newly acquired husband. 'You're a little late, you know. I thought that any moment I was going to be shouted at in Italian for trespassing on private property.'

'Forgive me for keeping you waiting . . .' He began to lead her through an archway then along a dank subterranean tunnel. It came out at some steep stone steps cut in the hillside, the back walls of houses shutting out the light. Four leaped up the steps agilely at the full length of his lead, easily keeping up with the man's long strides. By the time they reached the main road, Elisabeth was out of breath. But they had lost Chester on the way.

'Don't attempt that way on your own. Particularly at night.'

Elisabeth leaned against a wall, keenly aware that he was watching her. 'I couldn't even remember it, if I tried,' she said.

'Why do you keep your cat on a lead?' he went on.

'Because I'm afraid of losing him,' said Elisabeth. 'He is all I've got in the world.'

Four sat down and began to rearrange his fur with his pink tongue. He always felt slightly embarrassed when people began to talk about him. But he had enjoyed the chase up the hillside. He had not been quite sure what they were chasing, but it had been fun. He was not at all puffed. He hoped the man would take them somewhere else . . .

The man paused, taking in her expensive white trousers, cashmere sweater, the gold bangles jangling round her thin wrists. He seemed rough and shabby by contrast, but if Elisabeth had looked closely she would have seen that his hands were strong but not coarsened by hard manual labour. Nor was he as old as his greying hair might indicate. His accent was clipped, faintly Germanic.

'You look as if you have got everything,' he said shrewdly.

Elisabeth recognized that they were at the other end of Corso Italia, the main street. She now knew her way back to the hotel.

'Thank you for helping me.'

He nodded briefly. 'My pleasure. Anytime you have need of a husband. Bar Genny makes good coffee. Ciao.'

The man walked away without a further look. The idea of some coffee was tempting so she crossed the road to the unpretentious little café. It was crowded with locals leaning against the bar in the pleasant steamy atmosphere, talking or watching the portable television behind the bar. Thick white cups stood in a deep tray of hot water. The customers looked at her curiously, but after a first admiring glance, returned to their gossip.

The man was right. The cup of cappuccino arrived piping hot, delicious tasting with powdered chocolate sprinkled on the frothy top.

Four had seen something interesting: two lads were playing a machine which had white spots of light bouncing around and was making bleeping sounds. It was fascinating. He was mesmerized by the bobbing lights. Someone found him a stool and he jumped up on it to be nearer the game. The youths were amused by the cat's interest and put in more 100–lire coins so that they could play another match for him to watch.

Four was mesmerized, tense and excited, his eyes gleaming. Eventually he could resist the balls no longer. His paw shot out, making wild swipes at the bleeping lights. He sat back on his haunches, frantic paws windmilling like a drunken boxer. Elisabeth began to laugh at the cat's antics – it was the first time she had laughed for months.

That evening Elisabeth sat alone at her table in the dining-room, listening to the uncanny boom of the waves lashing at the rockface below, but without being able to see anything out of the darkened windows. The weather was changing. She briefly acknowledged Chester's wave, then pretended to be absorbed in admiring the vaulted ceiling painted blue with pastoral scenes of cherubs and angels. Very Florentine. Rain spattered the paved terrace outside the windows. The night was black and chilly with only the string of flickering lights across the Bay to show that at least Naples was alive.

A howling wind tore at the cliffside. No wonder the lemon and orange groves were protected from the lashing winds and winter frosts by acres of untidy bamboo mats and cages.

Elisabeth did not linger but quickly took Four for a walk along the paths that crossed the groves of the hotel's garden. Four did not like rain, and trod fastidiously over the puddles with delicate steps.

Elisabeth stood in the midst of the gale, the scarf round her precious throat being whipped away, streaming behind her. She wondered what she was doing there. Totally alone. She was famous and successful, but no one cared about her. She could disappear tomorrow and in days she would be forgotten. When she returned to the glass foyer, the kindly hall porter who opened the door did not know whether they were tears or raindrops on her cheeks.

The next morning the sky had miraculously cleared and from her breakfast table Elisabeth saw the white steamer coming from Capri. Her spirits lifted. Already a small crowd had gathered on the landing stage at the promise of a fine day and a good crossing. Elisabeth hastily swallowed her sweet roll and coffee, then hurried to fetch Four. He looked at her inquiringly as she bundled him into his travelling basket. No brush and comb this morning?

'We're going to Capri,' she whispered. 'Let's get the lift. We've just got time.'

Four did not care for the motion of the steamer, but he bore it with fortitude, sitting at Elisabeth's feet on the top deck. She found the forty-five-minute trip bracing and exciting, and her cheeks were flushed as the *Epomeo Napoli* reversed between the towering cliffs into the quay at the Marina Grande. No wonder people fell in love with Capri and returned time after time. The harbour was still small enough to be picturesque. Houses straggling up the verdant hillside in colourful profusion, the curves and soft corners of their beaten plaster walls merging with the flowers.

The steep funicular railway was a new sensation for Four, accustomed as he was to air and car travel. He was quite surprised to find how high up he was when Elisabeth took him out of his basket on the paved terrace of the hilltop town of Capri, overlooking the Marine Grande. The sea was a long way down, beyond the carpet of faded roofs and gnarled olive trees, the waves sparkling with a special luminosity.

The small, oddly-shaped Piazza Umberto I was bustling with warmly-dressed locals and cosmopolitan visitors, even though it was not the summer season. The rash of mink coats was quite startling in such a quaintly old-fashioned square, for despite the expensive dress shops and trendy boutiques in the sprouting alleyways, much of the town's eighteenth-century character was untouched. Remains of a megalithic wall were visible by the funicular railway, going mostly unnoticed and unrecognized, built into existing houses.

Elisabeth wandered into a narrow passage. She should have known it. There was Chester. He was obviously on the tourist trek to Anacapri and the famous Villa S. Michele. Elisabeth immediately chose the opposite direction, following the Via Fuerlovado to Caesar Tiberius's ruined villa on the top of Mount Tiberio. The Roman *stradetta* was only wide enough for two people to pass, covered part of the way, occasionally broadening at crossroads. The route was clearly marked with coloured ceramic tiles or the inscription 'Villa Jovis' on marble.

She climbed higher, Four leaping ahead. A twisting path took them between villas and gardens, steep enough to become steps on the bends, glorious views of the island behind and in front of them as the extensive ruins came into sight.

The last few hundred yards were all steps. She sat on a tiled base of the Imperial loggia, getting her breath, leaning her back against the cold white stone. Four lay stretched out in the sun like an emperor himself. It was still and peaceful, the sweet silence broken only by an occasional firecracker being let off by late New Year revellers. Some German students clustered beneath the greened bronze statue of a saintly Maria del Soccorso, their clear young voices not disturbing the stillness, but reassuring her that ghosts of Roman senators, togas flapping, would not stride out of the baths below, demanding that she serve wine and figs immediately.

Elisabeth understood the ageless magic of Capri. The island seemed so light, as if it were a ship moving on the oceans. Cliffs fell dramatically to the sea on both sides and, beyond the slopes, rose again dotted with tiny villas, their dark windows like cubic eyes.

The ruins of the Villa Jovis sprawled across the whole hilltop, once a dominating fortress, but now the towering stone walls were hardly recognizable as the great hall, the baths – hot, cold and tepid. A mass of stairways, terraces and promenades linked the roofless rooms, descending to the more prosaic living quarters, kitchens and sewers.

A dog had followed the workmen as they cemented the present path and 162 steps for tourists, writers and lonely singers. Its pawmarks were imprinted in the cement, more real to Elisabeth than the great Caesar Tiberius who had once strode on this same loggia, contemplating his retirement from the complicated politics of his office.

'And how is your marital situation today?' the man asked, coming into sight as he climbed the crumbling steps to the loggia.

'Safe and single at the moment,' said Elisabeth. 'But I have a feeling I may need a husband on the return ferry.'

'Then perhaps I should get in a little practise,' he said, and again she did not know if he were serious or teasing her. 'How do you explain why we are not staying at the same hotel?'

'I don't know,' she faltered. 'I had not thought it out that far.'

'We could pretend that I am allergic to your cat.'

Elisabeth shot a quick glance at him, but he was calmly taking in the magnificent view. 'Nasal or skin?'

'I beg your pardon?'

'Sneezing or lumps? The allergy . . .'

Elisabeth bent down to hide her amusement by touching Four's soft, velvety head. 'Four wouldn't give anyone lumps!'

'I think perhaps you should tell me your name. I cannot call you darling all the time, however delightful that is.'

'Elisabeth. Elisabeth Fiorentino.'

'Mixed parentage? That explains the Italian eyes and the Anglo-Saxon colouring. But not your cat on a lead. Poor cat.'

'He's not a poor cat,' she said defensively. 'I can do what I like with Four. It's a free world.'

'But not for your cat. Your cat is a prisoner.' He lifted the slack of the lead with the toe of his sandal. Four stirred and stretched, and rolling over to warm his other side, claws retracting. He liked this man's voice. He knew who it was without opening his eyes. He hoped there would be another exciting chase . . .

'I don't agree,' said Elisabeth, but guilt had crept into her voice. She knew playful, amusing Four was soon destined for six-months' captivity in a kennels where her other cats still languished. Fluffy-One's quarantine had expired and Elisabeth would fetch her as soon as she arrived back in England. But her agent had already signed up another overseas engagement – Elisabeth had no choice but to start the cat on the same merry-go-round. 'No. I don't agree,' Elisabeth repeated very firmly.

'The cat is a symbol of liberty,' said the man, still gazing into the far shimmering hills. 'The Roman goddess of liberty always has a cup in one hand, a broken sceptre in the other and a cat lying at her feet. You don't know freedom, eh, puss?'

'You're talking about statues. Carved pieces of marble. What nonsense! They mean nothing.' Elisabeth was not used to being lectured.

'You can't say that, in Italy of all places. Tomorrow you should go to see Pompeii. I will take you.'

'You sound like Chester.'

'Then you are making yourself a prisoner also.'

'But I am already. A prisoner of my career.'

He walked over to the edge of the loggia. The ruins scattered down the hillside, overgrown with weeds and flowers, almost unrecogniz-able as the luxurious Roman villa.

'We only come to this earth once,' he said, almost to himself. 'My name is Hans Johanson. I am Swiss. This much you should know about your husband. Shall we walk now?'

They walked back down the 162 steps, strolling through orchards and olive groves, flowering oleanders spilling on to the path. Hans told her about the famous people who had villas on Capri. Everyone knew about Gracie Fields and her swimming pool restaurant at Marina Piccola, but Elisabeth was surprised that Ginger Rogers also had a villa . . . bright haired, ageless, still dancing. Others who had lived their incuded the Marquis de Sade, Gorky, Chaliapin, Tchaikovsky, Alex Munthe, D. H. Lawrence, and now modern industrialists who made their fortunes from household products had moved in.

A terraced bar overlooked a steep downward path. Plain wooden tables were laid out in the open. The cooking was done in a cave, rock-walled; a woman and her daughters were chopping food on boards. Aromatic smells wafted from their cooking pots.

Elisabeth and Hans ordered a simple spaghetti Neapolitan with a bottle of local red wine. The elderly man who served them brought a dish of fish pieces for Four, and a bowl of water, without being asked. 'We have no milk,' he apologized.

Later they walked down the twisting steps, every turn presenting an even more magnificent view. They came to the Arco Naturale, a soaring archway formed in the limestone rock by slow erosion. The arch rose into the sky, but by moving to different angles, Elisabeth could look through the eye of the arch and see a vista of receding pools, each bluer than the other, unbelievably still. Four leaped on to the low wall of the viewing point, the wind ruffling his velvet coat into wavelets.

Hans was standing close behind Elisabeth. He bent unexpectedly and kissed her. It was a kiss without passion, but with a gentleness that stirred a quiver of emotion in Elisabeth's heart.

They were quite alone. They had the island to themselves. The crystal moment was handed them by the Gods.

'Just practising . . . for the return trip,' said Hans lightly, but the intensity of his expression did not match the lightness of his voice. He was searching for something he could not find. His dark eyes were unfathomable. Elisabeth found she was shaken to her very roots.

An American family joined them on the return ferry. They had two miniature-adult, crew-cut small sons and had saved for a long time for this trip to Europe.

The father was resigned to their tour operator's lightning itinerary, but still American enough to make fun of it.

'We had ten minutes of Capri,' he said. 'Or was it twelve? My wife dashed into one shop, I went into another. We threw our money on the floor and shouted "Give us something!" '

Hans and Elisabeth laughed. 'If only you had come with us,' said Hans. 'My wife and I had a most enjoyable walk up to the Roman villa on the top of the hill.'

It was almost like a stab. Elisabeth had to steady herself against the rail. He had said it so naturally, words that she had never expected to hear. Even though it was a pretence, they kindled a tiny glow within her.

Capri was slipping away from them in the distance. It had been a wonderful day, and she did not want it to end. It was cooling fast and the passengers began to crowd into the steamy cabin. She did not know which would be the most harmful, the chill wind or the incubating germs in the cabin. It had seemed pretentious to go to Capri in a mink coat, but she was shivering now. Always her voice. She must not do this, or that . . . she must cosset it, care for it. The voice was more real than she was. Elisabeth Fiorentino was simply a shell that housed the precious chords . . .

'You are cold, darling,' said Hans, draping his anorak on her shoulders and zipping it up high under her chin. She immediately felt the warmth it still held from his body.

'How about you?' She was lost inside its size.

'I am like Four. I have an in-built wind resistance. Remember, I am used to mountains and snow.'

'You must be a skiing instructor,' said Elisabeth, reminding herself of everything she had heard about skiing instructors.

'Wrong. But be careful. Your admirer approaches.'

Chester was bearing down on them, two brandies in his hand. He looked momentarily disconcerted to find Hans with Elisabeth, the wind spraying her hair across his chest in tangled locks.

'Oh. So you're the husband. You do exist then,' said Chester. 'I was beginning to wonder.'

'Most certainly,' said Hans, shifting slightly so that he shielded her from the wind. 'I exist.'

'I thought you might like a brandy,' Chester turned to Elisabeth. 'It could get rough. I'm feeling a bit queasy myself.'

'What a kind thought,' said Elisabeth, feeling safe now that Hans was with her. 'I'm sorry you don't feel well. You must stay in the fresh air.'

'Not staying at the Excelsior, are you?' Chester probed.

'No. Unfortunately I am allergic to my wife's cat.'

'Sneezes,' said Elisabeth.

'Lumps,' said Hans.

They both spoke at the same time and Chester could not understand why they started to laugh. It did not seem at all funny to him.

'What happens when you are at home?' he went on. 'You don't live in separate houses, do you? All for a cat?'

Elisabeth smiled sweetly at Hans. He could deal with that one. But he was not lost for an answer.

'No, at home, it is the cats who have a separate house. Not me. Just like some people have a granny-flat, we have a cats-flat. Is it four cats we have, darling?' Hans sounded suitably confused.

'Four,' Elisabeth confirmed.

Hearing his name, Four called out from his basket. His fierce amber eyes were watching everything. Elisabeth stroked his chin. He was a beautiful cat. He deserved more than the kind of life she was committing him to, but what else could she do?

It was dark when the ferry reached the quay below the hotel, its windows bright with lights like a many-layered birthday cake. Hans took her arm and guided her across the swinging gangway. The waves were washing over the landing stage and they ran to higher, dryer land. They walked back to the hotel along the winding Via de Maio that climbed the narrow ravine. They were strangely silent. The Piazzo Tasso was bustling with café customers sipping drinks, and Neapolitan music floated into the evening air.

'Will you be all right?' he hesitated at the drive.

'I think I can handle Chester now that he knows you really exist,' said Elisabeth, the words almost choking her. They were not what she wanted to say at all.

'I'm planning to catch the 9.55 train to Pompeii tomorrow, if you need me.' He touched her hand lightly, briefly.

Chester wanted to take her up to the crater of Vesuvius, and spent most of the evening trying to persuade her to go with him. 'Craters are just not my scene.' she kept refusing.

He followed her from the dining-room into the lounge. They made a handsome couple, reflected in the gilt mirrors on the walls. The romping, round-cheeked cherubs were still absorbed in their everlasting game of draping garlands of rosebuds from mirror to mirror. How solid everything was . . . cast iron free-standing radiators decorated with scrolls, almost museum pieces; even the blanking nut was faced with petals of a flower. The handles of the tall glass doors opening on to the terrace were the two halves of an oyster shell. Everywhere were signs of long lost workmanship. . . .

'You can't come to Sorrento and not see Vesuvius,' Chester insisted. He waved over the steward to give his order.

'I can see Vesuvius from my balcony,' said Elisabeth. 'Besides, I am going to Pompeii with my husband tomorrow.'

'I don't understand this marriage of yours,' said Chester.

'Hans is allergic to Four. It's quite simple.'

'It's a ridiculous arrangement,' he said laconically. 'Get rid of your cats. Or get rid of your husband – I daresay you would soon find a replacement who even liked cats.'

'I find that remark offensive,' said Elisabeth rising. 'Goodnight, Mr Ridgway.'

Elisabeth locked the door of her room and took Four up into her arms. It was so silly to be upset by Chester, when when she did not even have a husband. She had even started to think that Hans . . . 'Oh Four, I wish you were a big fierce Alsation dog to guard me,' she said vehemently. Four felt a tremor of alarm. He didn't like the idea of dogs at all.

He was even more alarmed when Elisabeth hurried to the Circumvesuviana station the next morning. He was jolted about in his basket and had to protest loudly before she slowed down.

'Oh, I thought I might miss you,' she said as a tall figure, reassuringly familiar, came from the booking office.

'I came early,' said Hans. 'I have bought two tickets. It's quite a short journey really. Ah, I forgot my duty . . . good morning, darling. Did you sleep well?'

He took her hand quite naturally. It felt warm, firm and comforting. Elisabeth had a heady feeling, as if she were suddenly sixteen again, and singing was no more than a girlish daydream.

Pompeii was a humbling experience. The splendid Roman city still lived on in all its pomp of long ago – when senators strode among the columns of the great Forum, the Roman ladies took the baths, servants tended the lordly villas, townsfolk sold wine and baked bread, the priests prayed, the gladiators fought their bloodied battles in the vast amphitheatre.

Elisabeth found it affected her deeply, especially the small things – the worn stepping-stones across the cobbled streets, the deep ruts made by the chariot wheels, the ancient graffiti scrawled in red dye on the walls, small household articles found intact in the ashes . . . bottles, pots, combs, tear phials . . .

A guide took them round the better preserved villas which were protected from the general public.

'Oh, it is locked,' he exclaimed theatrically outside an ornamental portico. 'I have forgotten the key. The key is with my brother who is visiting a sick aunt in Padua . . .' His face was as wrinkled as an old walnut.

Hans put his hand casually in his wallet and pulled out some torn lire notes. The guide's expression lightened.

'Ah . . .' he sighed with elaborate relief. 'Of course, I have, after all, another key in this pocket. Come . . .'

Four followed curiously. He loved exploring but he knew something was desperately wrong here in this strange hollow place of broken walls and crumbling marble columns. The volcanic ash still lingered in cracks and crevices, with all its sense of imminent death and disaster. He kept close to Elisabeth, getting right under her feet, to feel safer.

Hans caught her from stumbling. She picked Four up and he dug his claws sharply into her skin. 'You are in a funny mood,' she chided.

Suddenly a Roman deluge began. Vesuvius was lost in cloud. They ran for shelter to the cloisters of the gymnasium, which at least had a roof. The Grand Palestra had housed the crowds watching athletic feats held round the now empty marble-walled pool. Rain poured through gaps in the roof. Elisabeth wandered away from Hans, trying to bring her thoughts under control. Her heart was aching. This quiet man was stirring emotions in her that had lain hidden for years. It seemed she knew every line of his face, every curve of his shoulders, every inflection of his accent.

Through the grill of a wooden side-door, a small figure lay on its back in the grey dust, its skull broken open. It looked very small. A femur lay on the ground alongside. Other bones were piled in the dust. As Elisabeth's eyes grew accustomed to the gloom of the storeroom, she saw with horror that the yellow plastic trays were stacked with bones. Excavations were still being carried out. She shivered and hurried back to Hans.

'Your boyfriend is following us,' said Hans.

'I thought he'd gone to Vesuvius.'

Chester appeared at the far end of the cloisters, waving a large, coloured golf umbrella. The rain dripped off his brown curls, making him look like a Greek god in modern dress.

'Are you sure you still want me to act the husband?' Hans asked dubiously. 'He really is a most attentive young man, and he does have a very capacious umbrella.'

'I'd rather get wet,' said Elisabeth, tucking Four inside her jacket and pulling up the zip so that only his furry face was showing. He flattened his ears in disapproval of this whole rain business. He did not mind being carried about like an Eskimo baby, but he had a feeling he was still going to get very wet. He eyed the bright umbrella weaving its way towards them. It seemed a sensible solution. As Chester neared, Four did an elaborate gyration and slithered out from the bottom of Elisabeth's jacket. With one bound he cleared the nearest puddle, scrambled up Chester's suede coat and clung on to his shoulders.

'Ouch! Get off! Drat the creature!' Chester felt Four's claws dig into his neck. He tried to shake the cat off its perch, but Four was not going and hung on to Chester, his back arched, his wet fur spiked like a porcupine.

'Four, come down at once,' said Elisabeth sharply, but inwardly she was laughing at Chester's predicament. The umbrella rolled wildly, sailed out of Chester's hands and landed wrong-way up in a rushing stream of water. Hans waded after it as it drifted away like a gaudy boat.

Chester was nearly doubled over, trying to dislodge Four, almost blinded by the rain, staggering from one slippery ridge to the next. Four felt decidedly unsafe and with his usual quick thinking leaped back into the shelter of the cloisters, picking up his paws and shaking them delicately.

'You are in disgrace,' said Elisabeth, catching him up into her arms. 'I'm ashamed of you.' Four was not at all taken in by the tone of her voice. It had all been great fun, and he felt better for it. Now Hans had the umbrella and that meant it would soon be sheltering Elisabeth. He poked a wet nose into Elisabeth's ear, asking forgiveness.

'You'd better have the umbrella,' said Chester, wet and practically choking. 'Because of your precious voice . . .'

'Thank you, how kind. Perhaps we had all better get back to Sorrento,' she said hurriedly. 'This rain looks permanent.' Hans was looking at her strangely. 'What does he mean about your voice. . . ?' his eyes were saying. The journey back to Sorrento was strained. A chill settled on the group and they were silent. Elisabeth looked out of the train window at the grey suburban flats and houses and wondered where the colour of Italy had gone.

On her last evening in Sorrento Elisabeth sang in the cathedral. Three professors from Naples were to give a recital in the warm toned, pink and brown marble church, and when they heard that Elisabeth

Fiorentino was staying at the Excelsior, they asked her to sing just one aria.

She sang the Easter Hymn, her voice soaring to the vaulted ceiling like a bird's, while the chandeliers shone and twinkled like stars in the heavens. Hans sat unseen in a pew at the back, Four curled up beside him. Hans did not know how he would be able to live without her. Each flawless note took her further and further away from him, underlining the difference in their lives.

Afterwards, as they walked slowly back to the hotel, she told him about her singing, about her career, her loneliness and her many cats. Tomorrow she would be flying back to England.

'Now is the time for our divorce then,' said Hans. 'Tomorrow you return to being the big star, Four will begin his six-months' quarantine, and I suppose next week you will go shopping to Harrods for number five.'

'Oh Hans,' said Elisabeth, shocked and hurt. 'What a cruel thing to say.'

'But it is true. You are using your cats as you would not dare to use a human. Or do you also cast off human relationships as quickly when they have finished their usefulness?'

'Why are you talking to me like this?' Elisabeth cried. 'Why are you being so unkind?'

'Because you have finished with me too. I am cast off like Four. I am fallen in love with you, Elisabeth, but I know it is no use. Our lives take different paths. You know nothing about me . . . I am a farmer. I have a small farm in the mountains. I work in the open air. We make good cheese. My house is of logs and when the snow comes there is no way down to the village. Sometimes I do not see another person for weeks. It is not your world at all . . .'

She was crying silently. Of course, it was true. How could she have thought, even for a moment, that Hans could fit into her life as a singer? But that kiss on Capri had been a miracle, when she had despaired of ever feeling love stirring within her.

'I'm not really like that,' she whispered. 'I don't want to leave you. Hans . . . please help me.'

Her eyes swam with tears as she fumbled with the collar round Four's neck. She picked the cat up and hugged him ferociously, kissing his soft grey forehead, stroking his ears with trembling fingers. It was a long moment when time seemed to stop.

Then she put him down on the paved path between the orange and lemon trees whose sharp fragrance drifted in the wind. 'There you are, Four. You're free. No nasty cage for my beautiful puss.'

Four shook himself. It felt strange without his collar. He had never been without that narrow leather strap before. The air lifted his fur and ruffled his neck. He turned himself round Elisabeth's ankles lovingly, and licked her hand with his rough moist tongue.

Then with one bound he was away. He knew where he was going. He streaked out of the hotel drive and down the Via S. Cesareo. His nose led the way. A right turning took him past the fourteenth century cloisters of Saint Francisco, down the cobbled steps to the Marina Grande. All the grand, tantalizing smells of the harbour wafted up to meet him.

A quiver of excitement rose in his throat. This was to be his life now! He was free . . .

These days Four lives with a pack of half-wild cats that roam the harbour, well established as their leader. Often he can be seen sunning himself on the keel of an upturned boat, a beautiful Short-Haired Blue-Cream, a little out of place among the mixed breeds but obviously well-fed and content with life as a Neapolitan gipsy. And there are quite a few younger cats playing around him with a definite look of Blue about them.

Elisabeth and Hans come back to Sorrento regularly. It is their special place for holidays and the odd weekend break from her singing engagements. It took Elisabeth over a year to decide to marry Hans, but she found it was not so difficult after all to combine her career with being a farmer's wife. She can commute from Zurich easily. She loves Hans' log-built farmhouse in the mountains and the clear, sweet summer air is marvellous for her voice. But the time she likes best is when the snows come and there is no way down to the village. The fir-clad slopes stand white and silent, and she and Hans are together.

Chester returned to the Rome headquarters of the Italian police to whom he was on temporary loan. His next assignment was less glamorous – a wealthy Brazilian industrialist and his wife who were visiting Rome. The Italian Government, concerned by the number of kidnappings and ransoms that plagued their country, took what steps they could do to protect potential victims.

Four always seems to know when Elisabeth and Hans are returning to Sorrento for a visit. His special sixth sense wakes him from his sun-baked slumbers, and, leaving his large family to tumble on the sands, he bounds through the back alleys up to the Piazzo Tasso. Then as their car turns into the drive of the Excelsior Vittoria, he emerges nonchalantly from the flowering bushes as if he has been there all the time.

Then, of course, Elisabeth rushes from the car, gathering him into her arms and covering him with joyous kisses and tears.

Four always stays at the hotel with them. He enjoys the occasional taste of luxury, but he knows that it is like all holidays. It is not real life. And for every cat, life is liberty.

Nirvana

The man stood staring out of the window. She had been gone some months now but still her fragrance lingered in the house. It was so empty and quiet. He was used to the two cats chasing each other up and down the stairs, the scampering feet on the wooden floor, the mock fights and hissing, then the chorus of catcalls when his wife took their supper out of the refrigerator.

He missed them curled together on his lap, replete and sleepy, each trying to push the other off, striving for extra space even in sleep. The two Burmese had been delightful innocent witnesses to his disintegrating life.

They had been a present to her, so she took them along with her other possessions. Taking the cats had been a knife turning in the wound. He was lonely. He found it difficult to work. He was a fine print photographer and worked at home. He was used to cats around, helping him at his desk, sometimes providing inspiration with their fine eyes and ethereal beauty. He could not bear life without having a cat.

Many miles away in Bedfordshire, a tiny female lilac Burmese kitten stirred in milky sleep. She had been bred from Bathsheba, a queen of rare beauty. There were four kittens in the litter, two small bundles of pink and grey fluff, two of the palest milky chocolate. They stretched their tiny pin-pointed claws into the warmth of their mother.

The breeder wanted a home for the lilac female with someone

particularly loving and understanding who would give her the kind of extra care she would need.

'I've got to find someone very special for you, little one,' she told the kitten, examining the tiny creature again.

She was expecting a visitor that day, a man who had telephoned earlier asking particularly for a lilac Burmese female. He sounded weary but was prepared to drive a long way to see her kittens. She tried to explain the circumstances but he seemed undeterred. It was almost as if he was not listening to her.

'We used to have two Burmese but my wife's taken them with her,' he explained somewhat incoherently. 'I can't blame her, of course, they were a present to her, but I miss them . . . I've . . . I like . . .'

'You like having a cat around,' she finished for him. 'Especially a Burmese. I understand. They are so affectionate and make good pets. But this lilac female kitten, as I was saying, I don't know whether I should let her go . . .'

'I'd like to come and see her anyway. Please.'

She heard the despair and loneliness in his voice. It seemed this was another marriage break-up that had included not only the loss of a marriage partner, perhaps children, but also beloved pets. People rarely thought about the impact of losing pets.

The man must have started the long drive soon after talking to her on the telephone. He was a small, stocky man, dressed in jeans, sweater and sneakers, the past few months clearly etched on his face.

'Hello. You're here already,' she said in the doorway. 'What a long way to come. I hope you won't feel it's a wasted journey. Of course, I've other kittens – but only the one lilac female. Will you come this way, please?'

She took the man into the garden room, where the newest litter were lying in a heap on the sofa.

The man sat down on the floor in a slow movement of tired limbs folding up under him, wishing he had his camera with him. The heap of kittens rolled over and the lilac female detached herself. She pushed her way out of her squirming brothers and sister, an unsteady puff-ball of lavender fur, tiny tottering legs trampling over the vast expanse of the sofa towards the man.

They held their breath. They had done nothing to encourage the kitten, or attract her attention. The kitten went straight to the man. It seemed like an abyss between them, an unequal descent to reach the man's lap. There was nothing tentative about her movements or her determination. She was set on her objective . . . the man sitting on the floor.

To a kitten of that size it was a journey of immense proportions. But she made it, kneading the warmth of his sweater, a throaty purr growing in the fragile bird-like throat, blinking mistily into his eyes. The man was enchanted.

'But she's beautiful,' he said, unbelieving. 'How can you say she's deformed? She's quite perfect.'

The kitten had done her choosing and, satisfied with her choice, she curled up on his knee, exhausted by the effort. She went to sleep, trusting, ready to devote her life to his companionship.

'She certainly seems to like you. Rapport at first sight. It's amazing. I always think cats choose their owners, not the other way round.'

The man looked content, stroking the kitten. Before her eyes the breeder could see him relaxing. Animals could be therapeutic. The kitten was already weaving a spell round the man that would last for years.

'I'd like to have this kitten,' he said. Then he murmured into the soft fur. 'Princess Esmé . . . you will have a crystal bowl to drink water from, and one day, when you are used to a collar and lead, you will sail on the Thames with me . . .'

'I do insist on you thinking it over for a night,' she said. 'Just to make sure that her defect isn't going to worry you in the future. I can't take any chances with this kitten. She has to go to a very special person. Please look at her foot.'

She turned the sleepy bundle onto its back and found the front left foot, pushing aside the pale lavender fur. The kitten had two shell-pink pads and two claws instead of the normal pad and four toes.

It was a strange sight on the kitten, a rare deformity. Perhaps it would put the man off; perhaps he would find it distasteful and take one of the other kittens.

'I knew there was something,' he said mysteriously.

'I beg your pardon?'

'We have a bond,' he said.

He held out his left hand, pushing up the sleeve from his wrist. He turned his palm to the light, showing the line of a surgical scar.

'I was born with two thumbs.'

She let him take the kitten. There was simply no question about it. They were soul-mates. Some divine instinct had led them to each other.

Perhaps the kitten would change the man's future, open new doors, point new paths, make things happen that in some way would restore peace and tranquility to his life. She knew the kitten would bring him happiness. It was written so.

The Vanishing Act

She was born in a theatrical hamper in the chorus dressing-room at the back of the Royal Variety Theatre on a cold December morning. She could not help having the theatre in her blood from the moment the dancers found her among the costumes and reared her on a diet of milky coffee, cottage cheese and ham rolls.

No one knew how the little ball of silver fluff got there. The mother disappeared as silently as she had arrived. It seemed as if the kitten was the result of some tempestuous love affair that was quickly over, and once the kitten was born – the wrong side of the blanket – the mother returned swiftly to her old life.

The chorus girls knew little about pedigree cats. This one was a rare and beautiful long-haired silver tabby with large lustrous hazel eyes and clearly defined tabby markings on her dense and silky coat. The girls called her Silvikins.

The dancers came and went with the seasons, but there was always someone, perhaps a little homesick, who liked and would look after Silvikins. Babs was such a person. She was a tall, long-legged brunette, but perpetually in the back row because of her height. She was never quite going to make it, even though her dancing was slick and her stage smile as dazzling as any other.

'I wonder what it is about me?' she asked Silvikins, gently disengaging the cat's claws from the mesh of her black fishnet tights. She couldn't afford another new pair this week. 'I sometimes think I'm invisible. The director never notices me.' The choreographer can't remember my name. I'm going to be in the back row until my hair goes grey and my teeth fall out.'

Silvikins sprang off the young woman's lap. She knew it was curtain-up soon, and then it was wiser to keep out of the way of all those high heels and hurrying legs. She prowled into the wings, keeping well back in the shadows. She looked up into the tangle of ropes and wires and acres of canvas in the flies. There were so many favourite places for Silvikins to view the show among the jungle of lighting equipment.

She was incurably stage-struck – every night she watched the jugglers, comedians, magicians and dancing girls. Her bright hazel eyes closely observed the scenery changes, quick to get out of the way if she was liable to be toppled from her perch.

She loved all the bright colours and the movements. Her paws twitched to catch the flashing silver balls as the juggler threw them into the air. She blinked at the magician's tricks, wondering where the bouquet of flowers had suddenly come from, how objects appeared and disappeared, and even more miraculously the vanishing of people from a big black cabinet.

The cleverest of the magicians was a young man called Monsieur Herriot. His real name was Henry, and somewhat like Silvikins, he came from a good family who had now disowned him for not going into the family stockbroking business. His magic art was particularly exciting to watch because he used a lot of white doves and tiny yellow canaries, and a white pom-pom poodle with a bow tied on its head. One night when Monsieur Herriot produced a moon-faced goldfish swimming round in a bowl from out of nowhere, Silvikin's mind was made up. All her latent ambition came rushing to the fore. She was going on the stage. She wanted to be part of the magic act.

But how? Henry had hardly spoken to her, beyond the odd pat on his way to the dressing-room. He had a black velvet jacket with lots of pockets and Silvikins wondered if she could fit into one of those pockets. She doubted if she could get down his sleeve. No, it would have to be the black cabinet. It drew her like a mysterious magnet. She would like him to make her appear and disappear, to hear the gasps from the audience and then those waves of applause. Silvikins knew she would be able to do it with far more showmanship than the dim poodle. And she wouldn't need a bow on her head.

The first bit of luck, if it could be called luck, was when Joyce, Henry's shapely assistant, slipped on the pavement outside the theatre, breaking the stalk-like heel of her shoe and her ankle, in that order.

'I'm going to sue,' Joyce howled in pain and dismay.

She wondered if Henry would let her hobble on stage with her ankle in plaster. But understanding as he was, Henry did point our that National Health plaster, however imaginatively decorated with gold spray, was not glamorous. And a magician's assistant had to be glamorous.

The second piece of luck was when he knocked, somewhat hesitantly, on the door that led to the chorus dressing-room. He hardly expected to find any of the girls in early. But Babs was there, feeding Silvikins a tin of pink salmon that cost almost as much as a new pair of tights.

'Hello,' he said. 'So you feed the cat.'

'Yes,' she said. 'We take turns, but it's nearly always my turn.'

'Tough.'

'I don't mind,' she said. 'I like animals.'

'Do you like doves, canaries, goldfish and poodles?' he asked.

'Yes . . .' she replied, bemused and still not recognizing him.

'I'm the magician, Monsieur Herriot,' he said, introducing himself. He did not look much like a magician off-stage in his casual jeans and sweat-shirt, and rather quiet, shy manner. 'Henry to my friends.'

'I'm Babs. Back row, third on the left. Red feathers in the last number.'

'Very nice,' he said at a loss.

'Don't try to make out you've noticed me,' she said, scraping out the last of the tin for Silvikins. 'No one ever does. I'm one of the perpetual invisibles.'

'Perhaps you're the very person I'm looking for, then,' he said instantly. He was very good at rapid decisions. It was all part of being a magician. You had to be quick, and he had noticed that she had a lovely smile and legs to match.

'I need an assistant tonight,' he said. 'Joyce has broken her ankle. Have you seen my act? Do you think you could do it?'

'Of course I can do it,' said Babs immediately, seeing herself at last coming out of nowhere into somewhere. 'Do we have time for a quick run-through of the sequence?'

Silvikins took a gulp of her salmon and followed them onstage. She knew that one of the first rules of the theatre was to be in the right place at the right time . . . you never knew who might notice you.

She watched Henry do a brief run-through of his act. She knew from his actions just when he was about to produce the white dove from a top hat, the row of wine bottles from a single container, the canary in a light bulb, the goldfish in a bowl . . . and then of course, that snooty poodle disappearing and reappearing in the black cabinet, not a hair unruffled.

Henry really did have magical powers, Silvikins was convinced. It was amazing. And now Babs was going to help him. Silvikins watched the show that evening with a small throaty purr of contentment as Babs handed him props with an elegant flourish and turned this way and that to milk the applause from the audience. She was born to it.

'You were absolutely stunning,' said Henry, after the show.

'It was fun,' said Babs. 'But I'd like to rehearse again tomorrow. I know I was a little slow at times and I want to get it quick and slick.'

'Yes, of course. But . . . I say, er . . . would you like to come out for a coffee and a hamburger?'

Babs lowered her stage lashes. She'd had dozens of invitations from men for after the show, but never one from a nervous young magician with a dove up his sleeve. It was rather touching.

'Thank you,' she said demurely. 'I'll get changed.'

Silvikins prowled the empty theatre, seeing off the mice that dared to sneak into the labyrinth of corridors in the basement. She liked it when she had the stage to herself. It was all so vast and exciting. She dreamed dreams, not quite sure what it was all about, but uplifted by all the waves of enjoyment and appreciation that came over from a happy, laughing audience.

Babs had an inventive mind and came up with a few ideas which Henry worked into his act. Silvikins liked seeing the professional way they worked together, and at one rehearsal she jumped onto the black cabinet and sniffed around. She really did wonder what vanishing was all about.

'Silvikins is curious,' said Babs. 'She wants to know how to vanish.'

'A pleasure to oblige,' Henry grinned. Silvikins sat in the small space, a little alarmed, wondering what was going to happen. If she was going to disappear, would she be able to come back? But she was not that frightened, because she could hear Babs' reassuring voice. Suddenly the blackness changed and she was sitting in the open cabinet looking out at the empty auditorium. Why, it was quite easy after all . . .

'Do you think it's possible to teach a cat anything?' Henry asked. 'I mean, well, it would be different.'

'No,' said Babs, shaking her head and lifting the silver tabby into her arms. 'Cats are much too independent. They do just what they want to do. Silvikins only cooperated today because she was curious and she wanted to know what was going on. But it might never happen again. They are not like dogs.'

'I suppose not,' said Henry, giving Silvikins a small tickle under her silvery chin. 'But she is a beautiful cat. She'd give my act real class.'

He saw the hurt expression flash across Babs' face. For all her glamour and harsh years in the theatre, Babs was as sensitive as any woman would be.

'Oh, I'm sorry,' said Henry with a groan. 'I didn't mean it like that. You are a marvellous assistant and your ideas are terrific. I just thought that being a pedigree cat, she would . . . well, she's streets ahead of a canary. I could teach you some of my tricks if you like . . .' he offered.

'Yes please,' said Babs, before Henry could change his mind. 'How do you do the one with the linked silver rings? That's always puzzled me.'

'That's easy. You just need to be fast.'

Silvikins began to wash her ears. She was very fastidious and the inside of the black cabinet had been a little dusty. She sneezed in a refined way and they both laughed and said 'Bless you,' which she thought very odd indeed.

She sat and meditated, front paws placed neatly side by side, while Henry gave Babs a lesson. She was very quick to catch on and resolved to practise and practise.

'Do you think I'll be good enough in time for the Command Performance,' she asked, hardly daring to voice the hallowed event.

'We'll see,' Henry promised. It was going to be a big occasion in his career. A Command Performance in front of Royalty; a big charity night to raise money; television cameras transmitting the show into millions of homes. He was praying a lot of prayers. Babs was quite lovely and intelligent, which added an extra zing to his act; she was not just a pair of long legs and a few sequins. But to let her do a trick . . . it was a bit risky.

Henry thought about it and hated having to disappoint her. The Command Performance was too big and too special. Babs took the news like all the other disappointments in her life, with a smile and a little tilt to her head.

'Another time, eh? She said.

'Yes, another time.'

Everyone was nervous before the big night. The theatre had been searched for bombs and Silvikins had done her best with the mice. The Royal Box was decorated with garlands of flowers and draped with satin, and special brocade armchairs were put into place.

Silvikins sensed that something was different. The air was tense with electricity. It made her fur stand on end, and she licked it down with infinite patience.

The girls were all on edge with excitement, borrowing each other's make-up; in tears if something snapped; re-painting their faces till every blush was perfect.

Babs had an extra change of costume for Henry's act. He had lashed out on a gorgeous gold lamé outfit for her, and she was very touched.

The responsibility was making her extra nervous, and in her haste to give herself plenty of time to get ready, she forgot to bring in any supper for Silvikins.

'I'm really sorry,' she told the cat. 'Can you wait till after the show? Then I'll pop out for some fish and chips.'

She looked up to see Henry waving at her from the doorway in an agitated manner. She hurried over, pulling a thin wrapper round her flimsy costume. That was another thing Henry liked about Babs: she still retained a sense of modesty.

'It's the poodle,' he said. 'He's being sick. God knows what rubbish he found to eat.'

'Perhaps he'll get better.'

'I can't have him being sick on stage.'

'Scrap the trick.'

'But it's my best,' Henry despaired. 'You know it's my best trick. No one expects to see a fully grown dog suddenly appear.' His capacity for instant decisions seemed to have disappeared with his trick.

'Wait until the interval,' said Babs, hurrying back to the mirror to fix her headdress. 'At least you're on in the second act.

Silvikins sat on the long dressing-table, being careful not to disturb the pots of powder and paint. She closed her eyes, blissfully content just to be where she was, among people she knew, to be part of all that was happening.

'There's the cat,' said Henry.

'No,' said Babs firmly. 'That time was just a fluke. She would never do it again and it wouldn't be fair to expect it from her. She's a cat not a dog.'

'I suppose you're right,' Henry agreed with a sigh.

Babs was too busy to see Henry again. The dancers had a lot of numbers and changes of costumes. By the time she was putting on the gold lamé outfit, Babs supposed that the poodle had recovered. They stood in the wings, their nerves in their throats, waiting to go on.

'Is the vanishing act still in?' she whispered.

Henry nodded. He was too uptight to speak. Suddenly their music began and Henry strolled on, tall and debonair in evening clothes, top hat and flowing operacloak. Their act had begun.

It went very well. His new tricks were daring. The audience gasped at his ingenuity as doves and canaries appeared rapidly from anywhere.

Then it came to the vanishing act. Babs wheeled the mystical black cabinet forward to the centre of the stage. The drums began to roll. Henry began the routine of showing how empty it was, opening all the sides and whirling his magic wand around in the black voids.

Silvikins sat in the small cramped space, hungry and a little puzzled. It was too tight a fit to turn round and her tail was twisted uncomfortably under her. The way Henry had sneaked into the dressing-room was puzzling too. She could hear a lot of noise, music and clapping. That was familiar enough, but it seemed louder and closer than she was used to. Still, she trusted Henry and Babs. Then something happened . . .

Silvikins was transfixed with terror. The blackness was suddenly flooded with light as powerful spotlights beamed in blinding and dazzling her sight. A primeval fear of werewolves, monsters and great beasts surged into her mind in a tumultuous rush. She saw great white eyes gleaming, lurking high in the dome of the theatre, growling, poised to pounce on her. Her jaws opened wide.

With a shriek Silvikins leaped out of the cabinet. She landed on a trolley, sending a chrome container flying, and dozens of bottles spilled from its inside all over the stage. She fled, knocking over Henry's top hat and bouquets of bright flowers sprang out in all directions. she skidded into a curtained box and a flurry of doves rose into the air, flying straight into the light.

The panic-stricken cat, still blinded and dazzled by the light, blundered about the stage, scattering tricks and equipment like some four-legged bulldozer.

Babs and Henry watched in horror as his set was demolished. Without a second's hesitation Babs ran to the five silver hoops which were still at hand. She tossed them into the air with a flourish, pressing the secret spring which would loop them together into a chain.

The cat heard the noise. The clinking sounded vaguely like the bracelets that Babs often wore on her wrists and Silvikins homed in on it, springing through the centre hoop with all the grace of a flying panther. It was a spectacle of utter beauty, Her silvery fur sparkling like moondust in the light.

The audience rose on a wave of thunderous applause. Gloved hands clapped enthusiastically from the Royal Box. Henry blinked, unable to believe his ears as he stood among the chaos on the stage. The camera crews were giving each other the thumbs-up. It made marvellous television.

In the wings, Babs and Henry hugged each other in a fever of excitement. They had to run on stage again because the applause would not die down. Their hands touched, and it was not just in the excitement of the moment. They had suddenly discovered something else.

Silvikins had escaped from the two-eyed monster. She sat halfway up the flies in the gloom of the fly floor among the counterweights, licking down her disarranged fur. She hoped Babs would remember about the fish and chips after the show.

They all knew it was a one-off trick, but Monsieur Herriot made his reputation on it. He never looked back, and when he got his own televison series, Henry and Babs decided to make their partnership into a relationship.

Silvikins, however, refused point-blank to join them in their little mews house. The theatre was her home.

Besides, she had her eye on the new juggling act. She realized that she might have problems tossing the silver balls, but she reckoned she might manage to spin a plate.

The Window-Dresser

She was almost at the end of her tether when a helper from the Cats' Protection League found her, cold and hungry, huddled on derelict ground, and took her to the local branch. Her fur was matted and full of fleas; her eyes were stuck together, and her ears torn and bloodied where the irritation from mites had nearly sent her mad with scratching.

'Well, you're a sorry sight,' someone said, trying to put a comb through her coat. 'I wonder where you've come from.'

The cat could not say. The weeks of starvation had robbed her memory of details, but she remembered a special diet of minced chicken, vitamin pills and loving, although almost clinical care.

They fed her from an enamel dish, and although she could not see properly through her stuck-up eyes, her smell was as keen as ever and she did not turn up her pert little nose at a single morsel. She finished the lot including a large saucer of milk.

'Poor thing, starving as usual,' said the vet. 'And yet this one looks as though it could have been shown. It's probably got a pedigree.' She sat obediently still while he cleaned out the eyes with swabs of cotton wool. 'She's got beautiful eye colour,' he went on. 'A long-haired cream under all that flea-ridden matt. Sorry, puss, but this is going to be a scissor-job.'

It was some days later that a business-like young woman in sharp knee-breeches and a leather jacket came striding into the CPL, swinging her crash-helmet against her long black boots. 'I want a working cat,' she said. 'My shop's got mice.'

Kate Windsor was not a cat person. She had not been brought up with pets, and the nearest she had ever got to owning one was winning a goldfish at a fair, which had expired on the way home. She knew nothing at all about cats except that they caught mice. And her second-hand shop, in which she had invested £250 borrowed from her bank manager, was overrun with mice. She could not afford to have her stock nibbled or eaten, and when she found a 1930s beaded evening dress ruined by little teethmarks, Kate decided it was time for a cat.

'Any cat will do,' said Kate. 'I don't care which one. It's an emergency. I'm under attack.'

At that moment she caught sight of the long-haired cream – or what was left of the pale fur. It had been quite a drastic scissor-job and the cat looked more like a skinned rabbit.

'Is that a proper cat?' Kate asked. 'She looks a bit like Snoopy. What happened to her?'

'The poor creature was in a dreadful state when we found her, but the coat will grow again. She's actually a very beautiful cat, as you can see by the eyes.'

Two wide eyes looked up at Kate with a touching dignity, without a trace of pleading. They were haunting eyes, a pale amber with a hint of green depths, like clear meadow-stream water with freckled sunlight plying on it. The woman and the cat looked at each other and it was something at first sight; something that neither could define. Kate only wanted a cat to catch mice. The cat stretched out a paw against the wire of the cage in unspoken appeal.

'I suppose that one would do,' said Kate dubiously.

'Are you sure its fur will grow? It looks awful. My friends will laugh.'

'She's very intelligent and sensible.'

'That would help,' said Kate, convincing herself. 'I need an intelligent, sensible working cat. Have you got a box I can put on the back of my moped? Come along home, Snoopy, you've got yourself a job. You'd better wear my scarf or you'll catch cold.'

Snoopy had never been on the back of anything before. It was not unpleasant; in fact the ride was exhilarating. She had complete confidence in the young woman, and the fresh air blowing through her whiskers was like angel's breath.

Home was a tiny flat above Kate's shop. It was up to its ceiling with unsold stock, boxes and crates of memorabilia from the 1920s to the 1950s.

'It's not actually a second-hand shop,' Kate explained as she unlocked the door and carried Snoopy inside. 'But the period's not old enough to be antique. It's in between. That's why I call it the Between Shop.'

Snoopy jumped out of the cardboard box, the scarf still wrapped around her. It looked interesting and she sniffed politely, not terribly sure what was expected of her in this new place. The young woman was not used to cats, anyone could tell that, but Snoopy trusted her to do the right thing.

'How about a cup of tea? Kate said as she put the kettle on. Snoopy was game for anything. Her supper of fruit cake and salt and vinegar crisps was an entirely new experience, and one to which she felt she could become quite accustomed. She went to sleep in a large paper bag, dreaming of glorious rides, of catching her claws in the young woman's long windblown hair, of that warm laugh that echoed sweetly in her clean and nearly healed ears.

The next morning Kate shared her bran flakes and milk with the cat. Snoopy was a neat eater, not a drop spilled onto the floor. She wondered if Kate had heard about minced chicken.

'Now sit still and be good,' said Kate, lifting Snoopy awkwardly onto her lap. 'I'm supposed to brush you every day. As if I haven't got enough to do.'

Snoopy felt a little growl grow in her throat as the brush gently went through her new fur, massaging the skin. She shut her eyes in bliss as Kate grew more confident with the grooming.

'I wish someone would brush my hair for me,' said Kate, shaking back her heavy plait. 'You're just spoiled. I hope you'll show your gratitude by getting rid of those mice. That's your department, Snoopy. I'm relying on you.'

Snoopy went downstairs with Kate into the shop, ready to start work. Kate began to unpack a parcel of hand-stitched, parlour-maids' aprons which she had bought at a house clearance. The workmanship was exquisite. It gave Kate a feeling of satisfaction to have saved them from the recycling mill.

'Right, Snoopy,' she said cheerfully, giving the cat an encouraging shove. 'Now it's up to you. Go catch a mouse.'

Which was easier said than done. Snoopy had lived a mouseless existence before: without mice, without fleas, without dust, boxes or crates, and totally without anything second-hand. It had been a scrupulously hygienic life, and the only mouse in sight had been the little pink rubber shape they had given her to play with in her pen.

Still, Snoopy was eager to help. She padded around, sniffing, made a mild attack on an Alpine walking-stick, practised a few growls at a feathered cloche hat and, after exploring the shop from wall to wall, fell asleep exhausted in the drum of an ancient spin-drier which Kate was selling for a friend.

Strangely enough, Kate sold the machine that morning. The lady who bought it wanted to know if the cat went with it. Kate pocketed the notes with a quick smile.

'Sorry,' she said. 'But that's my assistant. Mouser in chief. Although she hasn't caught anything yet.'

'Sometimes just the smell of a cat around is enough to get rid of mice,' said the woman. 'Anyway, she's got beautiful eyes.'

Snoopy gazed at them, clear-eyed and trusting, the little tufts of fur in her ears sprouting like feathers, her white whiskers twitching like fairy aerials. Kate bent to touch the short cream fur on the top of Snoopy's head. It was the first time she had ever stroked a cat. The softness was unbelievable, swansdown. Snoopy arched her neck so that the fingers continued down her back. The purr began again, low and throaty, threatening to break out.

'I'll go and buy us a quick lunch,' said Kate, straightening up in a matter of fact way. 'Would a cheese omelet suit you?'

Snoopy curled up in a cracked flower-patterned china wash-bowl and kept an eye on the shop while Kate was out.

That afternoon a schoolgirl rushed in to buy the bowl. It would be perfect for her plant garden, she said.

It was quite late that evening before they could share a supper of fish fingers and chips, then sit together and count the takings. It had been a very good day.

'Didn't notice you catching many mice,' said Kate, peering over her book-keeping. 'That's what you're here for, you know.'

Snoopy looked faintly apologetic. She hated letting Kate down. She would try harder tomorrow. She must catch something.

The next morning she roamed the shop, playing and pouncing, getting into training. She chased motes in the air, boxed a few rounds with silk tassels, leaped to catch at price-tags. Then she was wholly successful. She dragged a dead pair of evening gloves to Kate's feet and sat there growling with pride.

'Oh, Snoopy, you horror. They cost me a pound!'

But Snoopy's sharp eye-teeth had not damaged them. She had a very gentle mouth. Minutes later she returned with a suffocated bundle of lace curtains, closely followed by a throttled Chinese fan. She couldn't understand why Kate was not pleased.

'I think I'd better go to that auction before you assault all my stock,' said Kate, tucking her long hair inside her helmet. 'And you can come with me. You're not safe to leave anywhere.'

Snoopy leaped into her cardboard box and stood obediently while Kate wrapped the scarf round her. The scarf had become obligatory. Snoopy wouldn't go anywhere without it. And she had no fear of travelling. She would have followed Kate to the moon.

The auction was being held in an old country barn, and people brought goods to sell from miles around. Kate was a regular buyer of the periods she specialized in, but there were lots of household goods which were of no interest. There was one item she really wanted. It was a miscellaneous collection of pre-Second World War children's games – lotto, dominoes, snakes and ladders, happy families, ludo, tiddly-winks – all old but so well made, despite being worn with use. They were all jumbled together in a large oval-shaped wicker basket with lid, the sides patterned with close and open weaves. Kate bid for the collection and it was knocked down to her. 'Does the basket go with them?' She asked the auctioneer afterwards.

'All yours, miss,' he nodded.

'Good,' said Kate in a stage whisper to Snoopy. 'You can have the basket instead of the cardboard box before it falls to pieces. Good idea, eh? Brainwave, in fact.'

Kate spent the evening making the basket wind-proof and cosy for Snoopy to travel in, and a foam cushion for her to curl up on. Snoopy inspected the transformation and decided it was not bad, not bad at all. A test trample passed A1.

Kate remembered the vet's instructions and got out the ointment for Snoopy's eyes, the drops for her ears and the spray for her skin. 'I am beginning to wonder,' she said, unscrewing the silver tube, 'just who is working for who. I haven't stopped doing things for you since you arrived.'

Snoopy licked up the last crumb of crisp. A few crisps were her reward for keeping still while Kate did her treatment. Her eyes and ears were almost better, and her coat was growing again with the help of the daily brushing. It was a delicate cream colour, pure white in places, touched with the palest fawn in others. It was growing long and soft, floating round her like a halo of light.

She spent all day in her playground: the shop. There were so many delightful things to amuse her . . . velvet pincushions, fringes and beads, china dolls and ancient teddies, wooden ornaments, macramé and wool, knitting-needles, and glass marbles that scattered beneath her paws.

As she played, dancing and prancing, light as a thistledown, people gathered at the shop window, drawn by her unconscious innocence and artless grace. They came to watch, lingered and often stayed to buy. Kate's business flourished. It seemed that whatever Snoopy touched, Kate sold. Soon she was able to pay back her overdraft at the bank.

It was at an antique fair that Kate met Peter Madoc. He was one of the sons of Madoc & Sons, a well-known firm of London antique dealers. He noticed Kate the moment she got off her moped in the driveway of the old mansion; she shook free her long hair from the confines of a helmet and then took a cat out of the basket on the back of her bike.

She held the cat high and close to her face, and he was struck by the look of understanding and love that the cat and the woman exchanged. There was a magical rapport between them that he knew he would not easily forget.

She took a bag from her pocket, and the cat was eating from the palm of her hand.

'Hello,' he said, strolling over. 'I've never seen a cat eating crisps before.'

'She's addicted to them,' said Kate, turning away. He was a very attractive man with a thatch of prematurely grey hair above a young face. He wore rimless glasses that were held together by a double bar of gold across the bridge. 'They're a treat, a reward, but I can't think what she's done to deserve them. She is supposed to catch mice in my shop but so far she hasn't caught one.'

'Have you still got mice?' he asked, following her.

'I don't really know. I think they've gone. Perhaps Snoopy's scared them off.'

'She's a lovely cat.'

'Do you know anything about cats?'

'A little,' said Peter Madoc. 'I've an aunt who breeds cats. Cats like yours, actually. Long-haired creams. She shows them at shows and gets lots of prizes. Has your cat got a pedigree?'

'I haven't a clue,' said Kate. 'I got her from the CPL. She's a stray. She was in a terrible mess and they had to cut off her fur. That's why she's called Snoopy.'

Peter Madoc tilted Snoopy's chin, looking for the shape of her head and staring into her fearless eyes. Snoopy recognized the hands of an expert. She had been handled like this before. She wondered what was going to happen next.

Peter Madoc was also wondering. He was in a quandary. He knew what he should say next if he was to be honest, but he was also remembering the moment when the woman held the cat against her face. And then there was Kate herself. He found himself more disturbed by her than he cared to admit.

'A few months ago my aunt lost one of her queens, a beautiful female cat called Honeymist Sherrypuff. She was being taken to a cattery to a stud cat, when somehow she escaped. I hate to tell you this.' He was still hesitating. 'But I know my aunt's long-haired creams. I think this is her lost cat. I think this is Honeymist Sherrypuff.'

Snoopy maintained a perfectly blank expression, while Kate's arms tightened round her. 'What nonsense,' said Kate. 'Of course this isn't your aunt's cat. You must be mistaken. There must be thousands of cats that could look like this Honeymist cat. This is my cat and no one is going to take her away from me.' She marched off, head held high, Snoopy peering over her shoulder with a look of complete satisfaction.

'Stop spitting at me,' Peter Madoc called out. He came after her with long strides. 'I wasn't going to take your cat away from you. I can see with my own eyes what you mean to each other, and my aunt has half a dozen other cats. But I'll make a bargain with you.'

'A bargain? I don't understand,' said Kate.

'My silence for that hat-box.'

'Hat-box? What hat-box?'

'The hat-box you're trundling around on the back of your moped. I just hope Snoopy hasn't chewed the edges.'

'Snoopy never damages anything,' said Kate haughtily. 'She's very well-behaved.' Suddenly she was all business woman. 'Is it valuable?'

'My dear young lady, that box is an eighteenth-century travelling hat-box. They were mostly used on the Continent by middle-class folk: country doctors, farmers. Because they were not durable, they are very hard to find.'

'What a nerve,' Kate stormed. 'In the first place, they're my hat-box and my cat. You can't have either. I could complain to someone about this. You're being very unethical.'

'No, I'm not. I believe that to be my aunt's cat, a valuable breeding queen. But the situation is negotiable. Will you start by having lunch with me?'

'I don't blame your aunt's cat for escaping,' said Kate fiercely.

They stopped arguing and began to laugh and Snoopy did not understand why. The negotiations seemed to take quite a long time. Peter organized many visits to the shop, drives to the coast, candle-lit suppers, riverside walks and picnics in the hills. They came to a very amicable arrangement. Peter would sell the hat-box for her, and buy Snoopy a new ultra-modern, super-hygienic, wind-proof, scenic-sided carrier out of his percentage. And not a word to his aunt.

'He must love me,' she confided happily to Snoopy one day. 'Now if only you would catch a mouse, life would be perfect.'

Down the street was a big silver tabby tom who was keen on Snoopy. He thought she was the cat's whiskers. He was also an excellent mouser, but thick with it. It was child's play for Snoopy to take his latest catch off him. She patted the revolting thing up the back lane to the shop, through the rear entrance and pushed it in a casual, off-hand manner towards Kate's feet. She then sat back to clean the labour off her paws.

'You've caught a mouse!' Kate shrieked, before picking it up with tongs and putting it in the dustbin. 'You clever puss,' she said, giving Snoopy a crisp. 'Your very first mouse.'

And my last, thought Snoopy. Thank goodness that was over; she need never think about mice again.

She jumped up onto a fretwork table in the centre of the shop window and began washing the salt off her whiskers. She did not know she was reflected in the shell-edged mirror on the side shelf, nor that people were gathering to watch. Snoopy had found her true vocation. No one had told her that window-dressing would be such fun.

Chimneys

It was a blustery November day when we drove down to Surrey –
the wild wet leaves hurled themselves against the windscreen and
fouled up the wipers. Jenny and I were going to Chimneys, outside
the village of Lambhurst, to look after Aunt Polly's house while she
was away in Florida for a month.

It was an arrangement which was convenient to us all. Our North
London flat was being pulled apart while workmen put in a new
central heating system, and I was only too happy to leave my landlord
to sort out all the problems and clear up the mess.

Aunt Polly, like many house owners had a fear of burglars, and
was loath to leave her house empty for so long. Jenny was recovering
from a bad bout of measles and the doctor agreed that a few weeks
running free in Surrey would probably do her more good than a hasty
return to school.

'Besides, one of those weeks in half term,' Jenny told Dr Stuart,
sitting up in bed, her long fringe spiking her lashes. 'So I really shan't
be missing that much.'

'Don't worry,' I said firmly. 'I shall be taking your school books
with us to Chimneys so that you can start catching up, young lady.'

Jenny pulled a sweet, pert face. She was tall for her age, with
Stephen's candid brown eyes and my silky dark hair, still pallid from
her illness but already restless and fidgety with sudden surges of new
energy.

'Aunt Polly's new house is lovely,' said Jenny, turning to Dr Stuart with enthusiasm. 'You must come and see it. We went there once last summer for tea and had raspberries picked from the garden.'

'Perhaps your mother won't want to be bothered with visitors,' said Andrew Stuart, packing his stethoscope away in his slim, executive version of a doctor's black bag. 'She could do with a rest as well. You are both too pale and skinny for my liking.'

'Oh, Mummy, did you hear that?' said Jenny cheekily. 'Dr Stuart thinks that all women should be pink and fat.'

Dr Stuart was new to the group practice and certainly Jenny had become very friendly with him during her illness. Perhaps it was not surprising, because there was no man in our life. Ours was a one-parent family.

I went cold, even now, six years later, whenever I thought of my handsome Stephen's death in a mid-air aeroplane collision over Tokyo. What could have gone through his mind in that moment, that split second of knowledge before the disaster? I could only hope that there had been no moment, that he had been engrossed in the paperback thriller I had bought him at the airport bookstall; or perhaps he had been dozing on the long flight and the whole event had been no more than a slipping into a deeper, lasting sleep.

Dr Stuart had come into our lives along with Jenny's spots and he had been a reliable guide through the worst days of her fever. He was in his early thirties, often bone weary, but with disarming laughter crinkles round his deep set eyes which could chase away the weariness. He looked as if he could do with a month at Chimneys.

'Of course we should be pleased to see you,' I said. 'Anytime.'

'Thank you,' he said. 'That's very kind.'

Chimneys stood behind a high stone wall outside the village near woods, draped in trees like a house in a fairy tale. As we drove along the lane that skirted the wall we could see the top half of the long, rambling, mellow red-brick building with its odd, disjointed roof slopes and small, square, lattice-paned windows that glinted in the watery late afternoon sunlight.

'Oh, Mummy,' said Jenny, clutching my arm with sudden excitement. 'It's going to be lovely here, I know it is.'

Aunt Polly had found the house on one of her erratic car-wandering Sundays, and fortunately she could afford to buy it. In her youth Aunt Polly had wandered a lot further afield than Surrey, sometimes dressed as a man, sometimes only with an Arab guide, and her travel books had brought her a steady income ever since.

'Mind you, they're old hat these days,' she was fond of saying. 'It's package tours everywhere. There's nowhere left to explore. It's such a shame.'

We drove past a small, narrow door set in the stone wall, its wood warped and weatherbeaten, the brick supports and overhead archway listing dangerously. I smiled to myself. I liked to think of all the slippings-in and out that might have occurred through that convenient little exit.

'Here we are,' I said, driving into the courtyard.

The beginnings of Chimneys went back to Elizabethan times when a wealthy and perhaps titled family decided to have a small hunting lodge in which to eat and rest after a tiring day's hunting over the North Downs, or in which to spend a month in the country away from London's pollution or plague.

Instead of the usual timbered Tudor style, they built a cosy tile-hung, double fronted lodge with four angular bay windows and a great central chimney.

The rooms were of unusually pleasant proportions; the ceilings ranged from low, black beams to delicate, high scrolled plasterwork; every room had a wealth of oak joinery and panelling; a wide oak staircase was lightened by an eight-foot, coloured glass window with a golden winged horse and the inscription *confido conquiesco;* then the staircase narrowed, twisting and turning its way up into a warren of little rooms in the roof.

The gem of the lodge was an original hand-painted stained glass window set into an internal wall. It did not belong to any room so one could only guess where it might have been in the original structure. Now it was part of the hall and the centre panel opened out on to the modern kitchen with washing machine and working tops, a far different view from the rolling Surrey hills it must once have overlooked.

The window was nearly four feet square, the upper three panels half the size of the lower three. Each had an exquisitely hand-painted scene – an Elizabethan huntsman, in velvet coat and plumed hat, seated on a heavy chested, pawing horse; a demurely-dressed woman offered a jug of refreshment to a seated rider; another woman waited alone with a small spaniel at her feet – the painting was delicate and fine, the colours still as fresh as if they had been painted yesterday.

Each scene was set into small rectangular amber panes, each glowing with captured sunlight; then round the outside of each of the six panes was a row of clear bottle-top shaped glass, the blunt broken-off stalk of each round piece of glass now worn smooth and harmless by time.

I could pass my hand over the entire structure with out fear of a scratch or a nick.

'Oh, Mummy, it all looks like necklaces,' Jenny had said, the first time she had seen the window. 'So pretty, like big glass necklaces for horses or cows.'

She ran straight to the window as we let ourselves into the oak-beamed hall.

'It's still here,' she cried, laying her cheek momentarily against the cold glass. 'Oh, Mummy, I love it . . .'

'Of course it's still here,' I said, carrying in our cases and a basket of shopping. Aunt Polly would probably have left a full refrigerator but then she might have turned it off in the flurry of her departure to the States.

At some point in time the original kitchen and outhouses had been pulled down to make way for an elegant high ceilinged Regency extension to the south of the lodge. The thirty-foot-long drawing-room had a high, wood-panelled ceiling, square lattice-paned windows with cosy window-seats and a massive fireplace to take huge Surrey logs. The long bedroom above had another such fireplace to take off the chill. Other additions were three chimneys and a timbered bell-tower with a sweet sounding brass bell to summon wanderers to their meals or remind them that dusk was imminent and it was no longer safe to roam the Surrey lanes.

Much later a Victorian family took over the house, seeking the unsullied country air for their growing family of children. On the other side of the hunting lodge they built another extension in mock Gothic, adding the necessary enormous kitchen, a large, square, tiled dining hall with the five angels of war represented on one set of stained glass windows and the five angels of peace on another. The doors had gothic arches and carved over the stone fireplace was the motto *Virtue et fide vinco* – 'By virtue and faith I win'. With all those angels, such an awesome inscription and a bell to summon them to church, I felt the Victorian family must have been models of propriety. And they added two more chimneys.

When Aunt Polly found the house it had been owned by two sisters for years. They had lived in a couple of rooms and the rest were shut up and neglected. A builder wanted to pull it down, already having parcelled off most of the extensive grounds for a modern housing estate.

However, he had reckoned without Aunt Polly. She had lovingly restored the place, modernizing the kitchen and bathrooms, put in central heating, and removed various monstrous 'improvements' so that each part of the house was as near to the original as possible.

'Don't tell me it's too big for me,' Aunt Polly said defiantly whenever she caught that look in someone's eye. 'They won't get me to move. So they needn't even try. I like space. I couldn't live in a pokey place.'

Our North London flat was certainly a pokey place by comparison and another reason why Aunt Polly's invitation had been so welcome.

'I want you too look after all my plants while I'm away,' she said over the telephone. 'I could get someone from the village to come in, but they might forget. And I've one or two rather delicate specimens.'

I guessed that might be an understatement. It was. The conservatory was a semi-jungle. I could see I was going to spend half my time indoor gardening.

Jenny immediately threw off all lingering effects of measles and took to the woods. From the kitchen window I could keep track of her bright red anorak as she ran and skipped, exploring the walled garden and the wild land beyond.

'Aunt Polly's got the sweetest little cat,' said Jenny, bursting into the kitchen, her cheeks rosy from running.

'I didn't know Aunt Polly had a cat,' I said. 'She didn't mention it to me. Only her plants . . .'

'I expect she forgot because she's getting old,' said Jenny, well aware of my poor memory. 'But we will look after her, won't we, Mummy?'

'Of course we will. I'll buy some cat food when we go into the village.'

'Can I go and play with Mopsie until tea is ready?'

'Mopsie? Is that what you are going to call her? What a funny name!'

But Jenny was quite firm about it. 'Oh no, she likes the name. When I told her, she looked pleased. She looks just like she's made of tinsel, Mummy. All Christmassy.'

I had to laugh. 'A tinsel cat?'

'She's so pretty, almost white but sort of tipped with red, like tinsel. And she had lovely turquoise eyes.'

Jenny did not play outside for long as the November evening darkened suddenly, and she came scurrying indoors for hot crumpets toasted in front of the fire, smothered with butter that dripped between her fingers. She sat in front of the log fire, licking her fingers, mesmerized by the flickering shadows cast by the flames. She looked better already. I felt some of the tension ease out of my neck and shoulders – I was always so frightened when she was ill. I could not bear to lose her as well.

It seemed a bit ridiculous standing outside calling 'Mopsie' so I compromised with the universally-understood 'Puss . . . puss,' wondering if the cat missed the warmth of Aunt Polly's fireside and the old lady's flow of chatter. The cat did not come. Perhaps she had a hideaway in the unused stables or the garages.

But obviously the cat knew some secret way in and out of the house because most nights she slept on Jenny's bed.

'She's lovely and warm,' said Jenny. 'I can feel her weight. Then if I wake up, I can hear her purring.'

The wind seemed to drive Mopsie wild. I could hear Jenny laughing as she chased after the cat all over the house.

'Mopsie? Where are you now?' Jenny scampered up the narrow staircase to the attic bedrooms. 'Are you polishing the floor with your tail, Mopsie? Whoops! Off we go again . . .'

Jenny came flying into the kitchen and went straight to the tap for a drink of water. 'Oh, Mopsie's been so funny this morning! I think she was chasing the wind! Sliding and leaping all over the place. Eventually she jumped on to a window seat and I had to let her out. She danced away across the lawn, playing with the leaves, her fur all sparkling.'

'I know,' I nodded. 'The wind does something to some cats. Perhaps it affects their acute hearing.'

Mopsie never came into the kitchen for anything to eat. The catfood in the dish went stale and I had to throw it away. Nor did she touch any of the milk I put down.

'She hunts,' explained Jenny. 'She catches all her own food. And she drinks water. I've seen her lapping at a little puddle.'

So I gave up worrying about feeding her. Cats can always look after themselves and this one seemed to have adopted a more nomadic life while her mistress was away.

'Mummy, she's sitting on the stairs looking just like one of those big china cats. Come on, Mopsie, let's go and explore . . .'

I heard the back door close as the pair of them went out. Mopsie kept out of my way. Perhaps she did not trust strange adults. Perhaps she only liked children and mildly eccentric old ladies.

I spoke to Dr Stuart on the telephone and he agreed that Jenny did not need her prescription renewed. Her appetite had returned and she was once again the energetic little girl she had been before the measles. In fact I wished she would spend more time with her books, but she seemed so happy chasing about the garden and woods that I let her be.

'Don't worry,' said Dr Stuart. 'She's an intelligent child. She'll soon catch up.'

'I wish I shared your confidence,' I said. 'It's these end-of-term exams. It's not right that children so young should be put under such pressure.'

'Then don't put on the pressure,' he said. 'Jenny will find her own level.'

But every evening I made sure that Jenny did spend some time reading her school books and writing some of the exercises which her teacher had set. While she worked quietly in front of the fire, I sewed or knitted, making new clothes for Jenny's return to school. We always sat in the Elizabethan room for it was smaller to heat, and we both loved the pretty, ornate ceiling. When my eyes were tired from sewing it was so restful to gaze at the delicate roses and sprays of wild blackberries with which those craftsmen had decorated the ceiling so long ago.

Jenny let out a long, exaggerated sigh as she chewed the end of her pencil.

'I'm not surprised you're finding it difficult,' I said a little primly. 'You spend all day playing when you should be working.'

Jenny snuggled back against my knees. I pushed my finger through her silky hair. How lucky I was to have this precious child.

'But we've had such a lovely day,' she yawned. 'Mopsie and I found a frog. It really made me jump, but Mopsie wasn't frightened at all. She's not frightened of anything.'

I smiled and gave her a little push. 'You obviously don't intend to do any more work, young monkey. You'd better go and have your bath.'

I opened the heavy velvet curtains and sat in a deep leather armchair by the window, watching the ferocious wind whipping the last of the garden leaves in the semi-darkness. The withered leaves flattened themselves against the little panes of glass, only to be whisked away by the next gust. I switched off the table lamp, enjoying the leaping shadows from the fireplace.

Something brushed my leg and I looked down. A beautiful pale cream almost white cat was padding silently across the carpet. The fur on her head, back and tail was delicately tipped with red, the colour of a cameo. As she moved the fur rippled and sparkled in the firelight, catching the glow, yet the light shone through the fine furry coat making her beauty almost ethereal. The cat turned and looked at me. She had the strangest eyes, almost emerald or blue-green, a kind of luminous turquoise. She had an air of quiet dignity, an expression of sweet repose. I could understand why Jenny loved her.

'Why, hello Mopsie,' I said, for it could only be her. 'So we meet at last. Will you come and say hello to me?'

I held out my hand and moved forward to stroke the cat or perhaps just to see if she would let me touch her. At the very instant I moved there was a fearful crash and the window in front of which I had been sitting shattered into a thousand pieces. Long slivers of glass pierced the chair, the arrow-like shafts slicing through the leather.

A huge branch swayed against the window, brittle grey branches poking through the lattice. The wind had torn a limb from the dead elm at the far wall and hurled it against the window.

I knelt on the floor, shaking, as the glass settled with tinkling fairy-like sounds. I broke out into a clammy sweat. I could have been cut to ribbons. If I had not moved towards the cat, the glass would have torn through my flesh as swiftly as it had ripped the leather of the chair.

Mopsie had vanished, frightened probably by the noise of the falling glass.

When I collected my senses, I put on some kitchen gloves, fetched a dustpan and brush and began clearing up the glass. It took a long time. I searched the carpet thoroughly for fragments which might injure the cat's paws. Aunt Polly had mentioned the dead elm; some tree-loppers were due to come and take it down. It had stood like a stark grey skeleton for over a year. I dragged the chair back into an alcove; it would have to be re-covered.

Jenny came down in her dressing-gown, her face pink from her bath. 'Whatever happened?' she asked, her eyes round. 'I heard the most awful crash.'

'A branch of the dead elm crashed against the window. Don't come in here without any slippers on. I have cleared it up but it's so easy to miss a little piece of glass. It gets everywhere, so be careful, won't you? By the way, I saw Mopsie.'

'Gosh, what a mess.' Jenny seemed more interested in the broken window. 'Oh, did you?'

'She's a very pretty cat.'

'I told you she was. Can I have some milk and biscuits? I've had my bath and I've washed and dried my hair.'

'All right, but have it in bed. I think it would be better if we did not use this room until I've had a chance to clear up again in daylight.'

I drew the curtains across the broken window and dampened down the fire.

Before I went to bed I searched the house for Mopsie, but she had gone out her own secret way, and as I closed the front door I thought I saw a shadow streak through the distant trees.

Andrew Stuart came down the following weekend and we all went on a long, muddy trudge along the ridge of the hills. He seemed quite different in old corduroys, a thick jersey under his anorak and a tweed cap pulled down against the stinging rain. He was delighted by Jenny's recovery. She had more energy than either of us and covered twice the ground, dashing off at tangents to explore. We walked more steadily, discovering things that we liked talking about.

'I thought you would be bringing a wife and a car full of kids,' I said, as we turned for home. 'I've made a mountain of rock cakes.'

We laughed at my silly joke and he said; 'I've never had time to meet anyone. A GP's social round is somewhat limited, unless you happen to fall for a nurse. And I didn't.'

He was standing in the hallway taking off his muddy boots when he noticed the tall stained glass window, the coloured glass lighting up the opposite wall with a kaleidoscope of pastel pinks and greens.

'*Confido conquiesco*, he said, reading the inscription under the winged horse. 'My Latin is a bit rusty but I think that means "I believe in being still . . . in taking rest, in repose, in quiet. I believe firmly . . . " ' he went on, almost to himself.

His words found a response in myself. I had seemed so much more contented these past few days, more relaxed, as if the long, heavy burden of grief I had put upon myself was beginning to ease. Perhaps my own miraculous escape from injury and disfigurement had something to do with it.

'Take care of yourself,' said Andrew, touching my hand. The touch was half professional, and half something quite different.

Aunt Polly returned from America with a Florida tan and armfuls of gift-wrapped surprises for us. Everything over there was 'wonderful' and she was full of plans for returning next autumn.

'And sometime I'll take you with me, young lady,' she said, pulling Jenny to her. 'If you are a good girl with your school work and pass all your exams.

'She won't do that here,' I said drily. 'Her concentration has only been a few degrees above nil. She has spent all her time playing with your cat.'

Aunt Polly was taking off her hat and fluffing out her tinted hair. She paused before she answered. 'Oh?'

'I'm afraid we didn't know her real name, so we've been calling her Mopsie,' I went on.

'One name's as good as another,' said Aunt Polly enigmatically.

When it was time for us to go and the car was packed up with our luggage and a bunch of late chrysanthemums from the garden Jenny detached herself from us and wandered away. For a moment she stood by the little door in the wall as if she were listening.

'I'm just going to say goodby to Mopsie,' she said. There was a little quiver in her voice and I ached for her. She was too young to begin sad partings.

She ran off and we saw her disappear into the trees.

'My dear, before you go, I must tell you something.' Aunt Polly's tone was troubled. 'I don't have a cat.'

I didn't understand. 'Oh yes, you have,' I said.

'The only cat in this house is the one in the hall,' she said strangely. I followed her back into the house. We were in the Elizabethan hunting lodge, the oldest part, where the unusual stained glass window now opened out on to the modern kitchen area. I had passed it a hundred times a day, always with a glance of admiration for its glowing brilliance.

'Look carefully at the hunting scene,' said Aunt Polly. It was the largest of the painted scenes, showing the hunt in full flight, a leaping deer followed by sturdy horses and lean hounds caught in mid-bark.

Aunt Polly drew my gaze to the lower left-hand corner of the scene where a small crack had been repaired with leading. Watching the huntsmen from a safe and secret hiding-place was a creamy, almost white cat painted with the finest streaks of red tipping its fur; a cat with eyes the colour of bright turquoise. She glowed in the painting, like a cameo.

I said nothing. What could I say? I remembered the way Jenny had embraced the glass on our arrival. I touched the cold painting lightly with the tips of my fingers. I was trying to say thank you to Mopsie.

Some weeks later Andrew brought Jenny a kitten. She had been abandoned in a dustbin by some youths. She was a daft little thing – a tabby with pretty silver streaks. Jenny called her Moppety.

When the wind blew Moppety went wild. She would dash all over the flat, her small paws skating on the polished floors sending mats a-flying, curtains flapping. I could hear Jenny laughing as she scram-bled after her kitten.

Moppety would eventually scratch at a window to be let out on to the balcony. Then, with one carefree glance back, she would dance away, chasing the scurrying dust, knocking over flower pots, her feathery tail held high like a sparkling plume.

The Terrible Three

They became known as the Terrible Three following the afternoon they dug up Mr Arkwright's prize cos lettuces and left the helpless threads of leaf strewn across the garden like the trail of a scavenger hunt.

'It's those terrible three,' Mr Arkwright stormed, as he went down on his knees to lift the chewed stems of the seedlings. But even his green fingers couldn't give them back life and he consigned them to the compost heap, wondering if he would have anything ready for the horticultural show in July.

'I know it's you,' he shouted, as he caught sight of three long tails whisking to and fro in the hedge. 'And I'll catch you at it one day. You've been warned! Dratted cats.'

The lettuces were only one incident in a long line of delinquencies. They terrorized the local goldfish; they knocked over milk bottles; any washed car immediately invited a muddy game of pawball. They jumped on unsuspecting dogs; chased the postman; and regularly pilfered anything worth taking from the bird tables along the road. They particularly like fruit cake and canapés.

'Oh no, you must be mistaken,' said Lavinia Robbins as the neighbours queued up to complain. 'Not my three little angels . . . look, there they are in front of the fire. You couldn't have three more darling little cats.'

The Terrible Three looked smugly at each other. They were indeed angelic: clean, dainty, affectionate and not a whisker out of place.

They washed their faces with soft paws that couldn't hurt a fly, and purred gently songs of happiness in front of the glowing flames.

'There you are,' said Lavinia, going on – and she could go on – quite a bit. 'It must have been some other cats. Your best lace curtains? Oh no, it wasn't my pussies.'

Lavinia had acquired three cats practically by accident. When she retired from a nursing post in Penang and returned to live in England, she was quite lonely and thought a cat might be company. She read an advertisement in a shop window for a litter wanting good homes, and she thought she could indeed provide a good home.

She had an adequate pension, and with her carefully hoarded savings had bought herself a small timber-framed house and tiny garden. Everything in it was spick-and-span, and the idea of a spick-and-span cat for company was pleasing.

There were only two kittens left when Lavinia went round to see the litter. And she couldn't make up her mind which one to have. When two pairs of sapphire blue eyes gazed up in wonderment at her, Lavinia realized that the choice was not which kitten to have, but which one to reject. It was a cruel choice.

As she watched the tiny tumblers skating over the floor, attacking each other in mock combat, minute teeth gripping soft furry necks, she realized that it was impossible to separate them. So both kittens went home with her in a shopping basket.

The third cat chose her. Lavinia did not even really like Siamese. She thought them too skinny and sharp-faced for a proper cat. But one drizzly morning she opened the back door to fetch the milk, and a thin, wet Siamese cat stalked into the kitchen, calmly sat down in the middle of the floor and howled in protest.

'Shoo . . . shoo . . .' Lavinia said ineffectively for three days, but the Siamese was not budging. As fast as she carried him out into the garden, so he streaked back in at the first opportunity.

The three cats got together and formed a tableau, the two tabby kittens sitting either side of the stately Siamese, like bookends. Lavinia's heart contracted and she gave in. She was not to know that they had actually formed an unholy alliance.

'Well, since you all get along so well together, you may as well stay,' she said to the Siamese, who forgave her for the three wells. He leered and wound his long whip-like tail round her ankles. She rubbed his bony head and marvelled at the turquoise glint in his beautiful eyes. 'But you have got to behave,' she added, as if reading the future.

The tabby kittens were called Tiggy and Daisy. Tiggy was a well-marked silver and black tabby, with dark rings down his long tail; his sister had a lot more white on her body, with the tabby markings endearingly smudged on 'her little face, giving her a look of elfin charm. The Siamese was a seal-point, with rich brown fur shading into pale cream down his elegant body, and big pointed ears. For a long time Lavinia could not think what to call him. Then, remembering her days in Penang, she called him Chang. He quite liked it . . . if you can tell when a Siamese likes anything.

Chang was, of course, the leader of the Terrible Three. He assumed the position by virtue of size, age and intelligence. He led the kittens into terrible scrapes as soon as they were old enough to stagger outside. Even the sweet-faced Daisy was game for any mischief. She became the gang's moll, ready to follow her peers anywhere.

They had one unwritten law. They never did anything dreadful at home or damaged any of Lavinia's possessions. That was why she simply couldn't believe all the accusations levelled at her pets. Her neighbours must have a grudge. But what?

It took Lavinia a long time to work that one out, but she came to the conclusion that it must be something to do with the horticultural show. There were several elderly people in the road, and retired people like to grow things to prove that life still goes on. They took the show very seriously.

Lavinia had brought with her from Penang the knack of growing orchids. They flourished on her window-sills like an exotic tropical garden, their gorgeously fragile flowers blooming one by one throughout the winter, much to the envy of her neighbours. There was no doubt in their minds that Miss Robbins would scoop many of the prizes with her orchids. They did not know that she had no intention of showing them. She grew them only for her pleasure.

This, decided Lavinia, must be the link. She had no way of knowing that the Terrible Three deserved every harsh word thrown at them.

'My very good pussies,' she said absently, Putting down three equal saucers of milk. 'That Mr Arkwright doesn't know what he's talking about. What a lot of fuss about a few lettuces. There's plenty of time to sow some more if he's that keen on them.'

The three cats lapped their milk in unison. They had not thought the lettuces up to much – definitely not worth a prize. Now that custard-coloured canary over the road was worth a prize – it would make a tasty snack any day of the week.

The catalogue of crimes continued, and although it was an excellent way of becoming acquainted with one's neighbours, Lavinia had the feeling that it was not going to improve her social life. She became accustomed to opening the door and finding an irate person with ruined tights, or broken flowerpots or chewed geraniums.

'But I assure you, it's not my pussies,' she insisted, shaking her head sadly. 'They've been at home all afternoon, as good as gold.'

The fourth time Mr Arkwright came round, he was almost incensed with rage. In his hands he held the snapped necks and crushed heads of his giant shaggy dahlias. He had been nurturing them carefully, waiting for their perfection to peak exactly the week of the show. Now the whole flowerbed looked as if a herd of elephants had been playing leapfrog over them.

'Where are they?' He exploded. He had once been a major in the Marines, and he had a voice to match. The tabbies heard the angry tone and cowered nervously nearer to Chang. The Siamese merely sniffed and looked out of the window. It was so uncouth to shout.

'I'll kill them,' he bristled, shaking the ruined blooms under Lavinia's nose. 'Those damned cats of yours . . . Look what they've done. Months of work . . . absolutely ruined.'

'I'm terribly sorry, of course,' said Lavinia. 'But it wasn't my cats, really it wasn't. It was probably a fox.'

'Ever seen a striped fox? Two striped foxes playing hide-and-seek with a Siamese? How about that?'

'Well, I'm sure they'd never . . .' Lavinia began.

'They did. And one day I'll prove it to you,' said Mr Arkwright, marching down the path. 'Wait and see. I'll prove it.'

She watched his retreating back, thinking he must have been a fine man in his prime. She had nursed many such fine men, but there had never been anyone special.

Joss Arkwright stomped back to his garden, determined that he would nail those cats to their own whiskers. He would catch them out. He would prove to Miss Robbins that she had been giving houseroom to a feline branch of the Mafia.

His chance came sooner than he expected. It was one of those luminous English afternoons when cotton wool clouds floated in the azure of the sky and birds flew around with dazed expressions. Bright-winged butterflies hovered with quivering excitement over pools of nectar, their brief life-span seeming like an eternity.

Gardening provided Joss with his best thinking times, as he balanced on his heels on the grass, his fingers deep in the warm brown earth. Joss thought a great deal about his days in the Marines, the cruelty of war, the dirt and squalor endured by innocent victims.

Yet in the same world were flowers . . . petals of amazing diversity and fragility; fearless robins, like the perky male watching from the handle of the spade; a tiny spotted ladybird crawling up the outside of his sleeve. Joss was watching the ladybird negotiating the chunky cable rib with fascination when he heard a clatter and a din.

Looking across the garden to his neighbour's downstairs window, he saw mayhem breaking loose on Lavinia's windowsill. Her precious orchids were flying in all directions; flower-pots crashed to the floor; earth flew up like dust caught in a whirlwind. Joss jumped to his feet, breaking into a grin.

'Those cats. It's those damned cats. Now perhaps she'll believe me!'

Daisy peered distantly at him from among the blooms, her blue eyes wide with fright. She clawed at the window-pane. Then she leaped from sight, her tail straight and rigid, sending another plant flying as she vanished.

Joss went to Lavinia's backdoor, relishing this moment of triumph and vindication. It was swinging open.

'Miss Robbins,' he called out. 'Miss Robbins?' But there was no answer. He went further into the house.

'Oh my God,' he said.

An hour later Lavinia was sitting in Joss Arkwright's sitting-room, drinking Marine-strength tea from a thick mug, a Marine-style bandage and dressing on the cut on her head. The police had been and gone, but she was still shaking. She had told them her story and a young sergeant had written it down.

But now she was telling it again, and Joss let her. He knew that talking would help with the shock.

'I was just returning from the village when two young boys followed me up the path. They asked it I had anything for their jumble sale, and I couldn't remember whether I had anything or not, but I said I would go and look.'

She stopped to take a deep breath, and Joss waited.

'When I returned with a few little bits and pieces, these boys were in my kitchen, looking in my shopping basket. One of them had his hands on my purse. Well I told them to stop that at once and go away, but they didn't. They just laughed at me and took out my pension money, which I had just collected from the post office.'

At this point Lavinia had to put down the mug, her hands were shaking so much. She was remembering the boy's eyes, shifty and insolent, their loud and callous laughter. They were so young, and yet they had frightened her. Lavinia had nursed during the war, then lived for years in a foreign country, far, far from home, and never once been afraid; now two boys from an English village had brought fear into her home.

'How about stewed cat, missus,' one of the boys had jeered swinging Chang up into the air by a leg.

'That, of course, was their mistake,' Lavinia went on. 'I rushed to save my darling Chang, and the other boy pushed me over and hit me with his clenched fist. Chang went wild. The lad was holding him by one paw, but that still left Chang with three – and he's a very strong cat.'

Joss nodded. He wouldn't argue with that.

Lavinia's voice warmed with pride. 'Chang dug his claws into the boy's legs. He was wearing those tight jeans and they weren't much protection. He yelled out, and that frightened Tiggy and Daisy. They jumped onto the window-sill and my poor plants went flying. I don't know what happened then . . .'

Joss refilled the mug of tea and handed it to her. Obediently Lavinia sipped the hot brew, trying to remember the last time a man had done anything for her. It wasn't something that was easy to recall.

'I found you lying in a pool of blood on the floor,' He said. 'You'd obviously fainted. The boys had gone, but I caught sight of them running down the road. I've a good idea who they are.'

'How lucky I am that you came along,' said Lavinia. 'I might have lain there for days, or bled to death. It really was most fortunate.'

'It was your cats,' said Joss grudgingly. 'Caught my attention, so to speak.'

'My poor darlings were so frightened,' Lavinia sighed.

The Terrible Three hesitated in the doorway of Joss's sitting-room, like uninvited guests waiting to be asked in. They sat, one tabby either side of the Siamese, giving credible impersonations of meek and innocent pussies.

'Oh look,' said Lavinia, her eyes lighting up. 'There they are. They must have been wondering where I was. They've been looking for me.'

Joss looked down at his three enemies. They stared back at him unflinching; three Davids meeting their Goliath. He had to admit they had courage.

He scooped up the two tabbies, one in each big hand, and deposited them on Lavinia's lap.

'Here, take them. They'll keep you company while I go next door and clear up that mess for you. Orchids don't like being treated rough. I'll see what I can do. Replant them for you.'

'How very kind,' said Lavinia. There was something in his expression that stirred her; it ignited a small current of affection that she quickly hid. This was not the time. They were in no hurry.

As Joss went to go out of the room, he came fact to face with Chang. The narrow glinting turquoise eyes were sizing him up, orientally inscrutable.

Man and cat stared at each other. Chang stepped aside. It was a movement executed with elegance and a certain amount of dignity. Joss understood. He was being offered a negotiable truce.

The Highland Hunter

Towser lived in the still house. It is normally very warm, but in deference to her great age, she also has her own electric fire on twenty-four hours a day.

She emerges from her bed located under a big onion-shaped copper still and stretches herself, shaking out her magnificent tortoiseshell fur. She is a long-haired cat with orange and black fur, tabby markings on a sweet, gently face, and a white bib. Her long white whiskers twitch in anticipation of breakfast.

She is totally unaware of her champion status and that her photograph appears in full colour on the cover of the *Guinness Book of Records* for 1984.

Her life is spent prowling the dark wooden halls of Glenturret and the forested hills that surround the ancient distillery. Breathing in the whisky-laden fumes is as natural to Towser as inhaling the crisp Highland mountain air that blows down the slopes.

The huddle of two-hundred-year-old whitewashed stone buildings has been her home since kittenhood. She was born behind a wash charger, a big warm container that was the perfect hiding place for the four kittens. The stillman had been hunting for Colette, the mother cat, when he found the kittens.

As soon as she was big enough, Towser began exploring the rambling distillery, up and down stairs and steps, along the many passage-ways. Once she found a room full of grain that was nice and warm, but then she could not find her way back to her mother. She was completely lost. The same stillman found her.

'Are you lost, wee kitten?' he said, scooping her up in his big hand.

Transforming the barley into a smooth Scotch malt is a long slow process; it ages for fifteen years in the huge oak casks. The rich smells from the distillery promise a feast of top-quality barley for families of woodmice descending in droves from the heathery hills.

It was not long before the kitten caught a mouse bigger than herself. This mouse changed the direction of Towser's life.

'We need a really good mouser to help Colette,' said the stillman. 'We ought to keep you.'

So Towser followed in the pawprints of her ancestors, who had patrolled Glenturret since 1774 when the distilling of whisky began on the banks of the tumbling River Turret, near the Scottish market town of Crieff.

She would not dream of missing her daily dram of whisky. It was every drop as good as a saucer of milk. She loved the taste, curling her tongue round the last sip of vein-tingling golden liquid. It was always a fifteen-year-old malt, but no one thought it wasted on a cat. Towser earned her dram.

Towser thought it was a day like any other day. She sniffed the fumes of the 130–degree-proof malt and it went straight to her head. She prowled her domain in the sheds storing barley, purring and growling, softly through her sharp teeth. There would be breakfast waiting for her in the canteen, but first she had work to do.

It was all too easy, almost like swatting flies. She sat as still as a statue until her long white whiskers signalled a sighting. She pounced. Victory! A mouse dangled lifelessly from her jaws. She went on a triumphal parade with her trophy, growling at anyone who might dare to take her catch away.

Charlie got out a sheet of paper and a pencil.

'One,' he said, marking it on that day's log.

For a number of weeks they had been keeping track of Towser's mousing. It began as a joke, but as the tally rose, the distillery workers realized that they had a potential champion under their roof. Towser was catching an average of three a day; but she also caught pheasants and baby rabbits when she escaped from the distillery and raced to the dark roots and wet mosses of the woods, her shaggy coat flying in the bitter Perthshire wind.

There was a workforce of six at this time so there was always someone who had an eye on Towser's activities. She pounced. Again!

'Another mouse. Aye, chalk it up, lad.'

Towser crouched in the shadows of the pipes carrying water, steam and whisky. She knew there was a nest somewhere near but it was well hidden. She decided to try a little subterfuge. She climbed up onto the pipes to take a nonchalant walk. It was a tricky balancing act, not made easy by the alcoholic fumes fuzzing her keen eyesight. But she was a sure-footed alcoholic, practically weaned on whisky.

She dived off the pipe, fast as an arrow, silent as a ghost; her paws cupped the mouse delicately in a death thrust.

'Another one. How many's that now?'

'Three. And all before breakfast.'

It was not long before word went round the distillery that Towser was onto a winning streak. The tally rose steadily . . . four, five, six.

'This is amazing,' said Peter Fairlie, the managing director as he made his morning round of the distillery. 'We've got a real champion here. It must be the fumes that keep her fit for the job!'

For Towser was now no young cat in her prime. She was already twenty years old and had been catching the Glenturret mice all her life.

She became aware that she was being watched. Visitors were nothing unusual for more than 70,000 people a year toured the distillery, enjoying the occasional glimpse of her orange and black fur. Towser was happy to be the centre of attraction, stroked by her admirers. Sometimes she sat in the picnic area, watching the arrival of the cars and coaches, unashamedly cadging treats from the picnickers.

This was different. She was being shadowed. The stalker was being stalked and it was an uncanny feeling. She peered over her shoulder. A pair of jeans were not far behind. She blinked in case it was the whisky. But no, she was being followed by a pair of jeans.

She was intrigued, mystified. She took them on a fair old dance, behind casks, under pipes and through gullies, clambering over mountainous sacks of barley, through fanlights, over roofs, and into every dark corner. Her yellow eyes brightened with a gleam of mischief. It was something to do with hunting, she felt sure.

She pounced on an idle dormouse. Wham! She hid her catch neatly under a pile of sacks. That was one they weren't going to know about.

The day's happy hunting continued. The blue jeans, obviously exhausted, were replaced by a pair of white sneakers. She took them on another wild-mouse chase. It was such fun. She was almost giddy with excitement. She was chasing around the distillery, fur rumpled, her long plume of a tail carried high like a flowing banner.

'That cat's tiddly,' said Mr Fairlie, as if it was the most normal thing in the world.

Towser came back, a little wobbly on her feet, growling a low throaty sound, another victim in her jaws. She laid it at his feet as a gift.

'Thank you, Towser,' he said.

'Fourteen,' shouted Hugh triumphantly. 'Fourteen mice in one day! It's a record.'

Towser grinned smugly. Little did they know.

She took the next day off. All morning she lay draped dangerously over a pipe, letting the frail sun warm her fur. Later she ran across the fields that rose from the cluster of buildings, through the trees and up rolling heather-clad hills into the Highland mountains, a bird's eye view above the still loch and swiftly running River Earn.

Her ancestors had lived wild in the hills, she knew that. The knowledge pounded through her veins. She ran like the great cat she was, shaggy coat flying, big paws hardly touching the ground, every muscle moving in perfect coordination.

Down below in the distillery, the workforce had their calculators out. They reckoned that Towser caught an average of three mice a day. It did not sound much as a bare fact. But some bright spark was multiplying that by her age and came up with the astounding total kill to date of over 22,500 mice.

'Twenty-two thousand mice? You must be daft.'

'Work it out for yourself. She's twenty years old. Multiply the number of days she's lived by three, and that's the answer. I reckon she's the world's top mouser.'

The world's top mouser yawned and blinked against the mountain wind and thought about a nice saucer of her favourite condensed milk. She did not know that they were contacting the editors of the *Guinness Book of Records;* that a new cottage industry was about to spring up, with tee-shirts and mugs, life-size posters and postcards of the champion, newspaper interviews, TV appearances and a fan club.

She wandered down to the distillery. She wanted her wee dram, and the warmth of her electric fire on her back. She was beginning to feel her age.

Towser was billed as the greatest mouser on record in the *Guinness Book of Records*, and the 1984 *Guinness Book of Pet Records* acknowledged a total kill of 23,000 mice. Journalists came to get the inside story. Often she kept them waiting; then brought them a mouse as a peace offering.

In April 1985 Towser indirectly received a letter from the Queen.

They had something in common. They shared the same birthday, 21 April.

The Queen's Private Secretary wrote from Windsor Castle saying that the Queen hoped that Towser, like herself, would celebrate the day with all possible happiness.

Photographers came to take birthday pictures of the grand old lady – Towser, not the Queen. Towser loved every minute of it. She was used to this admiration. And for a twenty-two-year-old (154 cat years), she was keeping her good looks. Her coat was still beautiful and fluffy, her prowess at hunting unimpaired.

But something was amiss. Earlier that day she had fallen off a steam pipe which she had walked safely every day of her life. She had almost fallen into a wash-back container. Hanging on by her claws, she managed to pull herself up. It was not the alcoholic fumes, for she was nowhere near the stills, and she had not had her daily dram. She was not in the least pie-eyed.

Towser righted herself and shook out her fur, pretending that she had intended to jump anyway. No one had noticed. She was aware of something wrong with one eye. Puzzled and blinking, she began washing carefully with a curved paw, hoping to wash away the irritating blur. Eventually she gave up. Nothing seemed to make any difference. Perhaps she would sleep, and when she woke up the mist would have gone.

Birthday cards arrived from as far away as America, Canada, Australia and New Zealand. That evening there was going to be a party in her honour. She wouldn't miss a party. She would keep awake for that.

It was a grand party, but Towser got a little carried away with high spirits. She jumped out onto a window-ledge and along a gutter, then climbed the sloping roof to the top of the distillery. It was an exciting, mad birthday gesture. She was twenty-two years old! She wanted to admire the sky and glory in the magnificent Highland panorama.

It was very exhilarating, the wind streaming through her long fur, until Towser decided it was time to come down. It seemed far steeper going down than it had coming up. Somehow the roof had changed. Towser found she could not get down. Apprehensively she looked around for another route and sniffed the air. She could smell thunder in the distance, and already grey clouds were gathering overhead. There was going to be a storm.

She panicked and began yowling, loudly and insistently. People came out into the yard, talking and pointing upwards to where Towser was perched on the roof, silhouetted against the sky.

She heard the scrape of a ladder and a familiar voice saying: 'Okay, Towser. It's all right. I'll get you down in a minute.'

It was her old friend, the stillman. He clambered over the roof, put Towser inside his warm tweed jacket and took her safely back to earth.

Some days later she was patrolling her territory when suddenly she saw a mouse. She was after it like lightening, across the still house, out into the yard. A van from the *Strathearn Herald* swerved wildly and slammed on emergency brakes. The driver got out, shaking, while Towser continued in hot pursuit of her prey.

'I nearly ran over your ch-champion c-cat,' stammered Peter MacSporran, the driver. 'Why doesn't she look where's she going?'

'Because she's almost blind in her left eye,' said Peter Fairlie coming out of his office. 'When she runs from right to left she can't see what's coming. But she doesn't seem to know it, and keeps on mouse hunting with as much vigour as ever.'

'And I nearly ran her over!' Peter MacSporran had had a terrible fright.

'Come and have a wee dram to settle your nerves,' said Mr Fairlie.

Towser pounced on the cheeky mouse and held it down with one big furry paw. That was mouse number twenty-five thousand, two hundred and seventy-seven. They weren't the only ones who could count.

Towser died peacefully in her sleep, of old age, on 20 March 1987. She is buried on the hill above the Distillery, her favourite hunting ground. Her final score was 28,899 mice.

Flat Cat

She trod rapidly but warily over the cellophane tops of the preserve jars, right to the furthermost reaches of the long, dark wall-cupboard, curled herself up into the smallest possible ball and tucked her nose into her long, quivering fur.

She was hiding from the world.

Cindy did not understand what was happening. Suddenly she had been catapulted out of her secure five years of existence with Lisa into a vast alien world that simply terrified her with all its grotesque peculiarities. It was as if something had exploded in her mind and pitchforked her into another universe.

In the fog of her bewilderment she retreated into the darkest space she could find and hid her face in her fur. She was totally alone. It was very frightening.

And why? What had she done wrong? Was she being punished for some heinous sin? If so, she did not know what she had done. Had she sat on a book, knocked over some perfume, scratched the baby?

A kaleidoscope of distorted images swam round her brain: what were those tall rustling giants that swayed in the air? The thick, uneven walls of green bits that buzzed and hummed with flying things? That funny, spiky floor that bent when trodden on? And even more startling, the enormous empty blue ceiling that stretched forever, making Cindy feel that the sides of her world had fallen outwards?

Then the place to which she had been brought: there was room after room, one leading from another. She had never seen so many rooms. She had crept through their strangeness, trembling, always expecting something new and terrible to happen round each corner. She hid under a table in the quietest room wondering if it was all a bad dream, and she would wake up soon within the safety of the four walls of Lisa's tiny studio flat.

'Let's leave her there under the table,' said the strange woman who had brought her to this place. 'Everything is so different to that London flat. She must be very frightened.'

The experience had begun in a very ordinary way. The woman had arrived at the flat, and Lisa had asked her in and made a cup of tea. Cinnamon Rhama had greeted the visitor with her usual party trick, a series of pretty rolls, a kind of floppy somersault on the carpet that usually elicited murmurs of admiration and did so again in this instance.

'Oh, she's really beautiful,' said the visitor. 'What a lovely cat. Gorgeous fur . . . is her colouring sealpoint? She's like milky coffee, and those lovely dark brown paws!'

'She's a tortie colourpoint,' said Lisa, turning Cindy's gentle flat-nosed face to one side. 'There's a little bit of tortoiseshell in her face, and see the spot of pure white on the top of her head?'

'What beautiful eyes . . . so blue. No, they're more a pale aqua-marine. And those funny tufts in her ears!'

'That's the sign of a true Persian,' said Lisa, sitting companionably on the floor beside her cat. 'She's an almost perfect colourpoint. Her registered name is Cinnamon Rhama, but we call her Cindy.'

Cinnamon knew nothing about being a perfect colourpoint. Her world revolved around Lisa and the baby and the restricted view from the studio skylight. She did not know that any other world existed. Even the birth of her two litters of kittens had been by Caesarean section, and her matings had merely been a necessary ruffling of her dignity and an affront to her ravishing beauty.

But maternity had suited her gentle nature, and she had loved her kittens, and the high-protein diet of stewed steak, minced chicken and brewer's yeast tablets. But the kittens were taken away and she had almost forgotten them.

The woman visitor did not pick her up or maul her in any way. She also sat on the floor and held out a hand for Cinnamon to sniff.

'I don't think I can bear to let her go,' said Lisa, her voice impassive. 'I love her so much.'

'I won't try to keep her,' said the other woman. 'She'll always be your cat. You can have her back whenever you say. I promise you that.'

'I really do have to go back to America,' said Lisa, more to herself. 'I really do have to go, me and the baby. We have to get away.'

'And it's only Cindy that's keeping you here?'

'Yes. I can't leave her . . . unless . . .'

'I'll take great care of her.'

'I know you will. You're the right person. I can feel it.'

When her wicker travelling-basket came out of the cupboard, Cindy knew exactly what to do. She jumped into it and curled round into a small fluffy ball. She did it so innocently, as if it were just a routine visit to the vet's.

The two women closed the lid on her and tied it with extra string.

'I don't want her leaping out in Victoria Station,' said the woman, with a nervous laugh. 'I think I'll carry it in my arms. I don't trust the handle.'

She lifted the basket, wanting to leave now, to cut short the painful scene, to make the parting easier for Lisa. There had been no last stroke of the long pale fur, no last kiss on that sweet face. They had simply closed the lid. It was cruel, but the kindest way in the end.

'You'll need a bag of litter,' said Lisa, suddenly practical as they were leaving. 'Cindy's a flat cat. She's never been in a garden.'

This journey's amazingly long, thought Cindy, curled up in her familiar basket. She could hear the woman's voice talking to her soothingly, and fingers stroked her through the slat in the wicker. Eventually Cindy went to sleep, lulled by the motion of the train. She did not know the woman was taking her to a new life.

The new life began with a series of sharp, horrendous shocks. She tore panic-stricken round the garden on the end of a lead, her heart pounding wildly as trees, grass, hedges, flowers, sky, birds, insects flashed across her eyes as distorted visions, sounds and smells. What was it? What were these things?

She shot back into the house, the woman close behind, knowing only the safety of concrete and bricks.

She roamed the rooms restlessly, looking for Lisa's flat, which must be somewhere inside this building. She sniffed for Lisa's divan, Lisa's tiny kitchenette, the baby's cot, the baby's pushchair . . . They had all gone.

Instead there were new things: furniture she did not recognize, flat white fingers that made a noise as she ran across them, a rocking machine with a round face that imprisoned water, a box with moving pictures. Part of the floor was broken into small pieces and put one above the other. This led to more rooms, and beds that had space beneath them.

She leaped up onto a window-sill and came flat against a glass pane. Outside was the same great vastness that frightened her. She ran trembling into a cupboard and burrowed her way to the back among the shoes and handbags, hiding herself from the terrible sight of the sky.

'She's hiding at the back of the wardrobe,' said the woman gently. 'Leave her. She obviously feels safer there.'

At first Cinnamon Rhama would not eat or drink. They put down tempting dishes and warm milk. But her appetite had vanished. The other cat, old, short-haired and sleek, her blackness tinged with ageing brown, finished it all up. The two cats eyed each other and hissed, but they did not fight. The black cat was old and beyond fighting. But her green eyes narrowed with hostility and her stubbly fur stiffened, despite the many strokes and reassurances from the family.

'This is Cindy. She has come to live with us for a while. You must try and be friends,' said the woman hopefully.

The black cat recognized youth and beauty, and sat with her long rope-like tail flicking with suppressed anger. This was her house, her garden, her family . . . The stranger was an enemy. She hated the woman for bringing her. But she was also old and loved food, and when she found herself being fussed over and given special tit-bits while the newcomer was in hiding, her resistance mellowed to the odd hiss.

It was during the night that Cindy found a way into the kitchen wall-cupboard where the woman stored home-made marmalade. Despite the cat's haste to find a new hiding-place, she was light-footed and only stepped into one jar. In the morning she heard their voices and the familiar sounds of tea being made.

'But where is she? She must have gone out. Did anyone let her out? Who opened the door? No? Then she must be here.'

They went round the house, upstairs and downstairs, calling. 'Cindy, Cinnamon. Cindy, Cinnamon.' The cat froze.

'I can't have lost her!' The woman was dismayed, her voice rising. 'Lisa will never forgive me . . .'

'Everybody look. She must be somewhere.'

'Supposing she's got out.' The woman was close to tears. 'Perhaps she's trying to walk back to her old home.'

Someone was opening cupboard doors, getting nearer. Cindy crouched back into the darkness, watching the shafts of light growing closer.

'Well, I never! Come and look at this!'

Faces peered at her from a distance, but they could not reach her. She was still comparatively safe.

'How on earth did she get there?'

'She jumped onto the working-top, then onto the dishwasher, and up onto the plant shelf. One of the cupboard doors must have been left open.'

'How are we going to get her out? If we chase her, she'll just run down to the other end. She could evade us for days.'

'Lisa told me that she's addicted to Munchies.'

It wasn't fair. The laid a trail of Munchies, each tiny biscuit a few inches further on. Cindy was hungry and she did love them. So this place had them, too. It was the first good sign.

She was tempted beyond her fear. She ate her way out of the cupboard, and the moment she was within reach, she was lifted down by firm hands.

'Make sure all the cupboards are shut in future. I can't have this palaver every morning.'

Cindy did not eat or drink that day either. But she did use the litter tray. She was a small cat despite all the fluffy fur and she could creep under almost anything. She hid under the music centre, squeezed herself between the desk and the wall, flattened herself under beds where only dust collected, burrowed her way into every cupboard. They spent the whole weekend hunting for a small, pathetic face and two baby blue eyes.

She then discovered a top shelf behind a barrage of plants. She sat there, eight feet high, safe and camouflaged, able to contemplate the people below.

For a while they fed her on the shelf, climbing up on the kitchen steps to leave saucers of milk and the odd Munchie.

The woman put the lead on Cindy's collar and took her to the garden door and sat down on the top steps. The cat stood beside her, astonished by the outside again.

'This is the garden, Cindy,' said the woman. 'You'll love it when you get used to it. You'll be able to play in the garden and climb trees. It won't hurt you.'

Cindy was persuaded to sit for a moment, calmed by the woman's voice, just beginning to be a mite curious about this strange new outside. Then suddenly something alarmed her, and she dashed back indoors, dragging the lead, straight upstairs and into the depths of the wardrobe.

'I won't rush her. One step a day until she gets used to it. We'll see if that works.'

They went one step further into the garden each day. Sometimes Cindy stayed only a few moments before something frightened her: a bird, an aeroplane, a rustling branch, a butterfly . . .

They walked a few yards together. It was a token walk. Then Cindy tugged at the lead to go back into the house. She was eating now at an allotted place, just a few mouthfuls before climbing up to her hideaway behind the plants.

One day the lead disappeared. Cindy found herself sitting on the top step with the woman, quite free. It was a heady moment. She took a few tentative steps alone and sniffed at a plant. An ant ran across her path. A leaf fluttered to the ground. She retreated back into the house, still unsure.

The door to the garden was left open. She peered round it, looking, sizing it up. The woman was always somewhere near, watching patiently.

She began to follow the woman when she went outside. She sat and watched her weeding the flowerbeds; picking beans, snipping dead-heads. There was a garden table and Cindy sat on that, absorbing this new green world, the sun warming her fur, and slowly her fears went away . . .

But one day she went outside into the garden and the shock tingled her spine right to the end of her tail. Confusion added to her distress. She bounced on the wet grass like a lamb. The ceiling was pouring water. Had they got taps up there? She peered through the wet leaves, expecting to see some gigantic gusher spraying the earth. But there was nothing, only moody grey clouds. She shook her paws fastidiously. She did not mind a bath now and again, but this amount of water was ridiculous.

'It's only raining,' the woman laughed, as Cindy sprang across the grass to come in. The cat shook out her fur and dried off on top of the boiler.

By now she had discovered the joys of the garden. There were games to play. The best was racing. Cindy would follow the woman to the far end of the garden, then the woman would turn and look at her expectantly.

'Race you to the house, Cindy!' she challenged. She set off running up the lawn towards the house, looking back at the still, indifferent cat. 'Come on, Cindy. Race you.'

When the woman was precisely three-quarters of the way up the lawn, the cat sprang into action. She flew through the air, light as wind, her long pale fur streaming, her paws bouncing off the soft turf. She shot between the woman's legs, the fur brushing her skin like thistledown. The cat leaped onto the steps and sank gracefully with a little humorous half-look, as if to say: 'Well, what took you so long?'

It was a game she played again and again, always winning.

In winter, the snow came; that was something else. It did not frighten her. She was losing her fear of strange things. Snow astonished her, then annoyed her. She shook her paws free with each long stride through the pesky stuff. When she found herself up to her chin in a drift, it was time to cut short her visit. They could keep snow, along with rain. They were only fit to be watched from the dry shelter of a window-sill.

She liked the car. 'Coming for a ride?' and she did not need asking a second time. She often made the round trip to Caterham, either sitting on the driver's knee or the woman's lap, or stretched out on the back shelf, her nose on her paws, her bright eyes taking in all the new sights.

Cindy's Siamese call was strong, but she only used it when she had something definite to say. The old cat got caught in the tiled space between the two front doors and it was Cindy's call that brought the woman into the hall to see what was the matter. Cindy had not moved from beside the door.

'That was very clever of you,' said the woman, freeing the old cat. 'Thank you.'

Another evening a loud miaowing came from the kitchen, which the woman heard even above the television programme. She hurried through and immediately saw the cause. The stock-pot was bubbling and rattling on the stove, its contents boiling over.

'Sometimes I wish you could talk,' she said, lowering the gas. 'I'm sure you have a lot to say.'

Cinnamon Rhama had definite airs and graces. If she was told off (mainly for sharpening her claws on the side of a chair), she retreated in a huff and sat in a corner with her back to the room. But her nature was sweet and the huff did not last long.

She also understood that her long tail was a hazard and quickly forgave any clumsy human who stepped on it.

She grew to trust the woman; allowed her to bath her, groom her, put ointment in her eyes, special oil in her ears. She sat on her lap while the woman typed or read the newspaper, or tried to sew or knit.

The morning began with no hint that it would be a different kind of day. Cindy had taken to waking the woman in the mornings. The moment the kitchen door opened, she sprang off the washing-machine and ran swiftly upstairs.

She jumped up onto the duvet, sat on the woman and began to pat the woman's face with a gentle brown paw. When this had no effect, her maternal feelings stirred and she began to clean the woman's chin, or fingers or cheek . . . any exposed skin got the treatment. The woman had become an expert at dodging the rough little tongue.

The third stage was the nips. The woman kept very still as Cindy nipped her chin for she had seen the size of those strong teeth. But Cindy never hurt and there was never a mark.

'All right, Cindy. I'll be up soon. I've got a lot to do today. We've got very special visitors.'

Reassured, Cindy tucked her nose under the woman's chin and joined her for another forty winks.

The woman was busy. She did a lot of cleaning and cooking cakes. Cindy was not perturbed. This did sometimes happen. She sat in the garden, enjoying the sunshine, her pale fur tipped with its radiance.

A car drew up and a woman and small boy got out. Cindy recognized the voice, though she did not move. The knowledge of Lisa's arrival erased her time in the country in a flash. She remembered the studio flat, the tall walls, the skylight and its fleeting glimpses of sky. The memories came back strongly.

The small boy went straight to Cindy and tried to lift the cat.

'Take Cindy home now,' he said firmly.

Cindy struggled out of the awkward grip and landed on her four paws. Her face was a mask.

'Come on, Cindy. Do your victory roll,' said the woman, encouraging Cindy to show off her floppy somersault. But Cindy did not move. 'Come on, you funny thing. It's Lisa . . . don't you recognize her?'

'I guess she's being a little off-hand at first,' said Lisa, laughing. 'Because I've been away. She'll come round.'

Cindy disappeared down the garden as the visitors went in for tea. She climbed to her favourite place and contemplated the sky.

The woman was disappointed. She wanted Cindy to be her usual sweet and engaging self, to show Lisa that Cindy had been happy living with her. But the cat was showing a stubbornly anti-social streak, and it was not like her.

Later, the woman fetched Cindy in from the garden, stroking her so that a reluctant purr started somewhere in her throat, but it soon stopped. She looked at the woman suspiciously.

'Come in and behave,' said the woman. 'I don't want Lisa to think you dislike it here.'

Cindy sat motionless in the middle of the room. Then she walked under the table and sat with her back to everyone in her huff position. She sat there for the whole of Lisa's visit, refusing to come out, refusing to be tempted by Munchies. The line of her back was one of disapproval and unco-operation. She would have nothing to do with anyone. The woman was at her wit's end.

'I simply don't know what's got into Cindy,' she said. 'She's not usually like this.'

At last the visitors rose to leave. The small boy crawled under the table and hauled Cindy out.

'Take Cindy home now,' he said.

'Oh no,' said Lisa. 'We can't take Cindy back to America with us. Besides, she has this lovely garden to play in.'

It was quite a few minutes before Cindy realized that they had gone. The car had driven away and the woman was clearing dishes into the kitchen.

Cindy went and sat at the garden door, waiting for it to be opened. The woman bent and touched the soft furry head.

'Did you think they had come to take you away?' she whispered. 'To tell you the truth, so did I.'

She opened the door and Cindy flew out, her fluffy tail like a plume. She sprang onto the grass, executed a few floppy somersaults, heady with the sense of freedom and joy under the blue ceiling of the sky. Then she looked back at the woman, expectantly. 'Race you,' said the woman, starting to run.

They ran down the lawn, woman and cat, exhilarated with the relief they felt. They were still together.

There was no need for words. The cat simply let the woman win.

Top Cat

There was such a lot of fuss about this thing called Christmas. Streamers he mustn't play with; presents he mustn't sit on; decorations he mustn't chew . . . Sammy was fed up with Christmas before it had even begun. He was used to being the focus of attention and now Christmas – whatever that was – was uppermost in everyone's thoughts. Was it another cat? If so, Sammy wasn't having it. There was only room for one cat in his household.

Sammy sat watching the driving rain from the comfort of a window-sill. The weather was appalling, even for December. He decided not to go out until it was a sheer necessity. If he was bored he would go and play with Danny's toys or stalk that spider that lurked on the landing. He might just have a little snooze.

It was dark when he awoke. Time for a stretch, a quick wash-and-brush-up of his long, elegant ginger and white fur, a flick of his long whiskers and he was ready for supper.

'I haven't had time to cook your coley,' said Christine. 'You'll have to make do with a tin. I've been so busy Christmas shopping.'

After his supper, Sammy wandered outside. The family were all preoccupied with what they were going to buy for Christmas, make for Christmas, do for Christmas. This Christmas person must be very important, Sammy thought.

His thoughts were still bobbing around when he noticed that he had wandered further afield than normal. The houses were all strange ones and the streets smelt different. He circled warily, trying to pick up a familiar scent.

Suddenly a pair of yellow eyes confronted him; then bared, snarling long teeth. Sammy leapt back, adrenalin pumping. Another deep growl from behind froze him in his tracks. Sammy hissed, fluffing out his fur to make himself look twice his size, tail thrashing.

But Sammy wasn't fooling anyone. He was still only cat-size, and the dogs were big, dirty and hungry. They knew they had him cornered and they crouched, ready to attack, sharp claws rasping on the slippery paving stones.

Sammy made an instant decision. He fled. He cleared the nearest dog with one bound and ran for his life. He did not know which direction to take. The terrifying chase took him further and further from home. It was alien country. The dogs yelped at his heels, getting closer as their longer strides narrowed the gap.

Sammy found himself in a big yard. He was panting and tiring rapidly. He knew he couldn't go on much longer; he must find some refuge, preferably a very tall tree. Something huge was ahead of him. He had never seen anything so tall and dark and menacing. It soared into the sky like a tree, but it was a giant, branchless tree, its tip lost in the rain-laden clouds. But there was not a leaf in sight.

There was no time to wonder what it was; the dogs were almost upon him. Sammy took a flying leap onto the lowest rung of a ladder which was bolted to the side of the tall structure. His claws slipped on the wet rungs, but with supercat strength born of sheer terror, he hauled himself up out of reach of the snapping jaws.

It was a narrow, slippery perch, even for a cat. He climbed a little higher, hoping for something rather more substantial. There seemed to be more than one ladder, each twice as long as a man, overlapping, and where they overlapped the double width of rung gave Sammy more of a pawhold. He settled on a double rung for the night, the rain pelting him from all angles, stinging his eyes. He tucked his nose miserably into his wet fur and wished he were at home. He felt the first pangs of hunger in his stomach.

The dogs were milling around below, sniffing, snarling, confident that their prey would have to come down. They barked noisily in the mill yard, intoxicated by all the new smells, eventually finding places to shelter from the cold and rain.

Sammy crouched, motionless, thinking about this massive, inhospitable, silent tree. No leaves, no frisky birds, no nice rustling sound; just an impassive giant planted in the ground by some super being from the sky.

He sniffed. He smelt soot and brickwork. Bricks meant a wall. It was a tall round wall. How strange. It was certainly not a house. He had never seen a house that had no windows or doors and reached up into the clouds. But at least the bricks accounted for the lack of branches and leaves. Soothed by that little bit of reasoning, Sammy closed his eyes again and tried to sleep.

It was a bitterly cold December night; when dawn eventually crept unwillingly into the frosty sky. Sammy's wet fur was stiff with ice-white crystals. His limbs ached with coldness. He stretched himself unsteadily, longing for a good leap and run across gardens, hedges and railings.

He saw the dark shapes below of the dogs lolling in sleep, yawning and scratching. There was nowhere to go but up.

Perhaps there might be somewhere, up there. His heart lightened and this encouraging thought spurred his climb. The round wall looked as if it went straight into the sky, but it might not. He passed a derelict bird's nest pathetically stuffed into a crevice. Nothing in it but a few old spiders. He didn't eat spiders; not yet anyway.

Some schoolchildren saw him first. They shouted and waved.

'Puss, puss, puss.'

'Poor thing.'

'C'mon, Superman.'

Sammy took no notice. He was not feeling sociable. He climbed a few rungs higher.

The mill yard was coming to life. Workers began to arrive by car, on motorbikes, bicycles, on foot. By now Sammy was a ginger blob half way up the chimney. He was very frightened by all the noise and commotion below. He was hungry. He licked some of the moisture off his fur, longing for a saucer of warm milk.

He peered down. It was a very long way. People were blurs of muddy colours, all heads. He couldn't see the dogs; perhaps he would take a chance and go down. He turned stiffly, each paw placed with care on the cold, rusty rung. It was breakfast time and he had missed a late-night supper.

It was then that Sammy discovered he couldn't go down. It was nothing like a tree, he couldn't leap from branch to branch in a zig-zag route downwards. He squinted at the rung below, trying to puzzle out how to reach it. The blood rushed to his head and his vision blurred. It was impossible. The rung was flat, almost non-existent. He was stuck.

Fear raced through him. What could he do? He leaped a few rungs higher in his panic, vaguely aware of a wave of sound from the ground.

'Look! That's a cat! Half way up the chimney.'

'Cripes. It's stuck all right.'

'Call the fire brigade.'

'How about the RSPCA? They'd know what to do.'

'What about the steeplejack. You know . . . ?'

'Fred.'

'That's him. The one that's on the telly. Fred Dibnah.'

Fred Dibnah was a television celebrity, made famous by his steeple-climbing programmes. Sammy knew nothing about all that; he knew nothing about the news cameras arriving, being flashed skywards and popping off photos of him; he knew nothing of the television lens being focused on the chimney and the commentator interviewing anyone who would say anything.

'It gave me a real fright,' said a girl, bright magenta hair gelled out to porcupine spikes. 'I looked up the chimney and I said to my friend: "Look, Grace, there's a cat up the chimney." That's what I said. I don't know how it got there."

'Have you any idea how it got up there?' asked the reporter, keeping to his basic line of questions. He whipped the microphone back to her glossy lips.

'No,' she said, shaking her head carefully. 'It climbed up there, I suppose.'

Luckily Fred Dibnah was already at the mill, preparing to start some scheduled chimney-repair work. He collected his tackle and strode through the crowd at the foot of the chimney. He could just make out a gingery blob about a hundred feet up the steel ladders, two thirds of its height.

'I hope it doesn't bite,' he said jovially, strapping on his harness.

By now Sammy was terrified out of his wits. He was not going to let anyone within scratching distance. Instinct made him take the only action left to him . . . to climb higher and higher, rung by rung. The wind combed fiercely through his fur; the ladder creaked and seemed to sway.

Suddenly there was no more ladder to climb. Sammy was amazed. He was at the top. It was another strange place. Cautiously he crawled onto a narrow ledge, stretching his stiff legs in their first real movement for hours. He inched himself slowly round the ledge, blinking against the gale that howled like banshees around the top of the chimney.

He was hardly able to appreciate the view of Greater Manchester stretching into the dim grey Lancashire distance. An endless vista of factories, power stations, housing estates, church spires and cooling towers became a blur. He peered tremulously over the inner edge . . . down, down into a black void that plummeted into the very core of the earth. Sammy shivered. It smelt acrid and stale. He knew its darkness was dangerous.

'Don't be frightened. There, there, there, puss, puss, puss,' called Fred encouragingly, peering up from the ladder below the top. 'Come along now, good pussy. Come to Fred.'

Sammy wasn't coming to Fred. He wasn't going to anyone. He was too terrified to move, crouched aloft, watching the man with fixed, staring eyes as if he was an alien creature from outer space.

'I've a nice bit of sardine for you,' Fred tempted. 'How about some sardines from the canteen? Come along, old boy. Come on, ginger.'

Sammy's stomach was gnawing with hunger, but his taste-buds acted on smell, not words. He could not tell what Fred was waving about. Fred had brought up a wire mesh basket, tied to his waist. Sammy did not like the look of it . . . baskets meant captivity and visits to the vet.

Fred proffered more tempting morsels from the canteen, wishing the cat would make up its mind. Conditions were very unpleasant, with driving rain and a fierce wind. Even with his skill and experience of high buildings, this was no picnic.

Sammy flattened his ears to cut down wind resistance and huddled into his fur. The day wore on; television crews came and went. Fred threw sardines around, most missing the ledge and dropping onto spectators' heads.

A cameraman removed a sardine from the peak of his cap. 'I know it rains cats and dogs in Manchester,' he said. 'But fish is ridiculous.'

As the light began to fade, Fred came down, shaking his head. It was too dangerous now to stay aloft, or even try another attempt that afternoon. Sammy was doomed to another night . . . if he didn't fall off.

While millions of television viewers watched the drama of the rescue attempts on the news in the comfort and central heating of their homes, Sammy was slowly freezing into a hump of abject misery. Only his long fur saved him, and the pockets of warm air still trapped in its wetness. He pushed his nose into what little warmth he could find and tried to concentrate on not being blown off his perch by the bitter wind.

He had found a tangle of rope securing some tackle to the brick-work, and dug his claws into the fibres. It was the only thing he could cling to. His frozen spirit put him onto automatic pilot as he hung on through the long night.

When dawn of the second day came, the weather had not abated. The driving rain still stung, the wind still howled and buffeted the top. Even Fred queried the wisdom of attempting another climb in such conditions, but the plight of Lofty – as Sammy had been christened by the media – had caught the imagination of the country. He was front-page news in most of the national newspapers.

Fred did not like the thought of the cat slowly starving to death 150 feet above Bolton. He would have one more try. He fastened on his cumbersome harness and started the climb.

'Come along, Lofty, now,' he coaxed, holding out a morsel of cold chicken saved by the canteen staff for their most reluctant customer. 'Nice puss. You don't want to stay up here in this nasty old place, do you? Don't you want to go home?'

Sammy did want to go home, but by now he was frozen, both with fright and cold. A second night aloft had reduced him to a shaking bundle of confusion. He defied Fred's entreaties without knowing why. He refused food despite his raging hunger and thirst. He clung relentlessly to the rope, only once forsaking it – to retreat further round the ledge when Fred got too close.

Fred jammed his cap firmly over his tingling ears and began the descent. It was time to knock off for a bite to eat and a pint of beer at the pub. His hands were frozen and it would need nimble fingers to catch that cat.

'I can't make him budge,' he said sadly.

A crowd of mill workers gathered below the chimney in their lunch-hour. It was drama on their doorstep. They craned their necks to catch sight of the tiny silhoutte of pointed ears just visible against the sky.

The weather was deteriorating even further. The whiplash rain soaked spectators in minutes. But they hung around, stamping their feet, waiting for something to happen. Gerry Rodgers stood silent among the crowd. It was his lunch-break from a nearby rubber factory. He liked cats. He hoped to see the ginger cat rescued.

He tipped his head back. The chimney was the tallest, blackest, most frightening thing he had ever seen. The ladders crawled up the outside, disappearing into infinity. It towered above him like a monster from some disaster movie.

Suddenly Gerry made up his mind. Steeling his nerves, he raced to the chimney and shot up the first ladder. He climbed quickly, allowing no time to think, no time to look down, keeping his eyes fixed only on the rung above. He climbed, hand over hand, with relentless determination.

Gasps went up from the crowd. Time and again his green wellies slipped on the wet rungs, but he clung on, using the strength in his wrists till he gained a surer foothold. Rain plastered his dark fringe to his forehead. His clothes were soaked. The howling wind filled his ears with unholy ferocity. All this, he thought wryly, for a scrap of ginger fur.

He caught his breath at the top, and heaved himself onto the ledge, panting. He was thirty years old, but at that moment he felt about ninety. He could see that cat, its fur flattened and sodden. It looked as terrified as Gerry felt.

'Puss, puss, puss,' he called gently, the wind whipping his words away to the distant grey hills. 'I won't hurt you.'

But Sammy was not moving for Gerry either.

'Come along . . . you can trust me. I'll get you down.'

For thirty minutes Gerry sweet-talked the cat to come near enough to grab him. But he was always just that bit out of reach. Gerry clung to the top ledge, so cold he could hardly think. He could not stay there much longer.

A sudden gust nudged Sammy along a few inches. It was a chance movement that brought him within reach of Gerry's long arms.

Sammy felt himself grabbed by the scruff of his neck. He was swung off his safe perch. He found himself struggling in mid-air, all four paws windmilling like fury. The rain lashed at his eyes and a blurred panorama of sky, brickwork and bearded man whirled before him. He went wild with terror. He was being carried down with an awkward, jerking movement. The man descended painstakingly, rung at a time, using only one hand to hang onto the side of the ladder, the weather-bitten steel rasping his skin.

The other hand held the cat in a vice-like grip. Sammy fought the hand and arm that held him, unable to realize what was happening. It was all part of the nightmare. His bedraggled tail waved in a furious question mark.

'Now, now, pussy. Don't struggle or you'll have us both off.'

They were forty feet from the ground when Fred came back from his beer break. He hurried to hoist the wire animal-basket up to Gerry on a rope. Gerry bundled the cat, head first and upside-down into the basket and slammed the lid. He leaned back onto the ladder with relief. His wrist was numbed and aching with pain; he could not have held on much longer.

Sammy huddled into the swaying cage as it was lowered gently towards the ground. He dug his claws into the wire mesh as he swung in the air. He felt horribly exposed. He saw crowds of people below; they were getting bigger . . . policemen, camera crews, reporters, factory workers. What were they all staring at?

A terrific cheer went up as the cage bumped onto the ground, then the crowd broke into spontaneous applause. Gerry felt his knees buckle as his green wellies stepped off the last rung and touched the firm yard beneath. He straightened himself, grinning, aware that he was shaking.

The police were waiting for Gerry – but not with congratulations. It was an offence to climb someone else's chimney, even to rescue a cat.

'We shan't charge you,' said the police officer. 'But you're an idiot. No insurance, no harness.'

'I saw the cat on the television last night,' said Gerry, as if that was reason enough.

'Were you scared?' asked a reporter.

Gerry looked back up at the 150–foot chimney and its dwindling rim in the mist.

'I tried not to look down,' he said with a shudder.

Sammy was taken to the RSPCA van parked nearby. Someone was rubbing him gently with a towel. They were pouring milk into a saucer. There was the delicious smell of food being unwrapped. Chicken, fish, liver . . . Sammy didn't care what it was.

As his tongue curled round the milk, he nearly choked in his eagerness. He lapped and lapped, knowing the delicious smells were all for him when he had slaked his thirst. He began to purr. He couldn't help it, because now he had his answer. Now he knew what Christmas was.

Xinia and the Witch

Xinia was small, fluffy, predominantly marmalade in colour and inclined to be overweight. She did not know this as she was completely colourblind and disinclined to face facts. She thought herself to be a sleek cat, black as a raven's wing and destined by Fate to ride forever on the back of a broomstick.

It was the broomstick fixation that led Xinia to wander. She had had four homes in three years. They were mostly on lonely, isolated hill farms where you might expect a witch to lurk. But each time Xinia's hopes of finding one were doomed to disappointment, and so she decided to move on once again.

She moved on to Tupminster, a small village tucked away in the Cotswolds, green and growing, but still full of charm. There was a row of old farm labourers' cottages by the road leading into the village which had been turned into trendy weekend homes. The end cottage had more garden than the rest, and on her knees in the middle of the front path was a gorgeous female creature.

She was slim, willowy, with skin like fresh cream, cheeks flushed with her exertions at gardening, and a cascade of glossy black hair hanging down her back. At least Xinia thought it was glossy black hair, but really it was amber-blonde, with red and gold streaks that were a photographer's delight.

The young woman put down a trowel and began to leaf through a clutch of seed packets. 'Virginia stock, Godetia, Candytuft, Gloxinias . . .' she began to chant in a low voice.

As soon as Xinia heard her name called she leapt into action. Hello, new home! She threw herself enthusiastically into the young woman's arms, purring, pawing and generally making a nuisance of herself.

'Hello, pussy. Where did you come from?' the woman asked, removing her gardening gloves in order to give Xinia a friendly stroke.

Between purrs and chin-licking with her small, rough tongue, Xinia noted this refinement with some satisfaction. This was obviously the very nicest kind of witch. Xinia trampled happily over the scattered seed packets and then threw herself back into the witch's arms. Home number five was settled.

'Heavens, keep still, you funny little thing,' the young woman laughed, trying to free her hair from Xinia's claws. 'I'm not a bed and I don't need a bath. But I do think it's coffee time, don't you?'

Coffee might have magical properties but any time was milk time, so Xinia followed the young woman indoors, carefully keeping her long fluffy tail out of the way of the girl's bare feet. Bare feet, thought Xinia, were quite an improvement. Most witches wore the most awful heavy black boots with sharp, painful heels.

Sally Jenkins put her percolator on the stove and then opened the refrigerator door to get out some milk.

Xinia's amber-flecked green eyes widened with astonishment. Inside the door the milk was actually standing up, all by itself, in tall round shapes! It was quite amazing. Xinia was used to watching milk squirting from those stupid brown animals and being slopped around in pails. But here it was actually standing up in regular shapes inside this cupboard. Xinia held her breath, expecting the milk to suddenly collapse and spill all over the floor.

Sally poured some milk into a saucer and put it down for the cat. 'There you are, pussy,' she murmured absentmindedly. She took a letter from her pocket and began reading it as she stirred her coffee. The letter looked as though it had been read many times. Sally gave a small quivering sigh. 'He says he's found somebody else and that it's all over,' she said. 'I can't believe it . . . everything was so wonderful . . .'

Xinia listened, but only to be polite. She began a swift inspection of the cottage, climbing over books, skidding along oak window-ledges, sniffing at pot plants and greatly admiring the soft patchwork bedspread in Sally's bedroom. She was not yet entirely certain that Sally was a witch, but she thought she would hang around for a few days to make sure.

There were many things about Sally that were very witch-like. She had only to touch a small black box and the room was instantly full of discordant music like banshees let loose. She had a strange kind of crystal ball, square shaped, which again she had only to touch and people were captured on it, much smaller in size but actually in the room. Xinia often sat with her nose only inches away from the screen, mesmerized by a round black blob that whizzed about like a flying insect. Sometimes she would shoot out a paw to catch it, but she couldn't penetrate the magic.

'What are you doing?' Sally would laugh. 'Playing goalie?'

Sally seemed to spend a lot of time talking down a long, flexible cord, which, although clever, appeared pretty pointless to Xinia. She did not have a cauldron, but there was a grey pot she often put on the cooker which hissed ferociously in the most alarming manner.

What almost convinced Xinia that Sally was a witch was the discovery that Sally sometimes took off her hair. Xinia nearly jumped out of her fur the first time she found Sally's hair sitting on a stand on the dressing-table with no Sally underneath it. She sniffed at the wig cautiously, patting it with a tentative paw. It was real all right. It was even curly, whereas Sally's other hair was straight. Xinia was most impressed.

Sally was pretty lonely, even for a witch. She never seemed to go to any covens to meet other witches. She did a lot of gardening and talking to herself and reading letters and experimenting with spells that she called cooking. But often she sat in the evening gloom of the little sitting room, not bothering to put on the lights.

'I'm going to be an old maid,' she said one night, hugging Xinia tightly. 'They'll call me Sally the Spinster.'

Xinia thought this a very odd remark to make, especially when there wasn't a single spinning wheel in the house. She made a quick reconnaissance of upstairs and downstairs to make sure that Sally hadn't sneaked one in, but there was nothing more mechanical than a bag of crochet which Sally wasn't making much headway with.

Sally didn't sleep much, but then witches don't need much sleep. She often wandered about the cottage in the small hours of the morning, coming into the kitchen to make herself some hot milk.

Xinia didn't really mind being woken up by the light being switched on. Any time was milk time. But she did think all that crying on the kitchen table was taking things a bit far. Witches didn't usually shed tears, but this one did and Xinia objected to being used as a superior sort of paper tissue to mop up the tears trickling down Sally's cheeks.

'I do miss him so. What am I going to do?' she sobbed into Xinia's fur. 'Whatever am I going to do? I can't go on like this . . . I can't work . . . I can't think . . . it's awful.'

Xinia did a quick lick to rearrange her damp fur and agreed whole-heartedly. It certainly couldn't go on like this. They were both losing their beauty sleep, and Sally hadn't cast a really good spell all the time she'd been there.

Xinia went for a long, thinking walk, snapping at dragonflies, chasing ants and terrorizing the stone dwarf who fished all day long in their neighbour's goldfish pond.

Of course, what Sally needed was another man so that she would stop missing this other one and start knowing what she was going to do. But she would never meet another man staying in the cottage all day reading sad books and trying to find out where she'd gone wrong in her crochet.

Xinia only knew one man. She'd met him at those four farms she had lived on. She remembered the nice polished smell of his boots and the gentleness in his voice as he tended a sick cow or a mare in labour. She even knew his name – Gavin Jones. But mostly people called him 'the vet', whatever that meant.

She knew where to find him, too. He had a rambling red-brick house where people brought all their sick animals – dogs with hot noses wrapped in blankets, and fractious cats in baskets, spitting straw. Xinia took to sitting in the middle of a flowerbed outside the surgery, waiting for Gavin Jones to come out.

'Hello, thing,' he said quite kindly several times as he got into his estate car to start on his rounds.

One morning he came out talking to a plump woman who was carrying a bandaged poodle.

'You'd better keep him warm, and make sure your husband's work-shop is locked in future. I think life is getting more and more dangerous for our pets,' said Gavin Jones. Then he spotted Xinia among the French marigolds. 'Hello, thing,' he said.

Xinia gave him a long, cool stare, flicked her tail haughtily and then deliberately scratched up a geranium.

But what she had overheard was food for thought. Obviously being the vet had something to do with looking after pets in danger. Perhaps if she did something dangerous, then Gavin Jones would arrive at the cottage, meet Sally, and before you could say 'Mary Poppins' they'd be speeding down the M1 on a broomstick.

So that night Xinia made her bed in a box of old jam jars that Sally had been saving for the blackberry season. She trampled energetically, sliding and clattering jars about, making a great fuss and being terribly dangerous.

Sally fished her out and held the marmalade cat at arm's length.

'You great goof,' she laughed, her pretty dimples showing for the first time in days. 'You can't go to sleep on jam jars! Let me find you a nice new piece of blanket.'

The next day Xinia climbed on to the roof of the cottage, then leapt on to the chimney stack and pretended that she couldn't get down.

'Dinner time!' Sally shouted from the garden, banging a fork on a tin of cat food. Xinia tried to look pathetic and frightened. Then she did a little bit of pretending to jump and being overcome with terror at the brink.

'Oh, come on,' said Sally, exasperated. 'It's getting cold out here. I won't let you watch any telly!' she threatened.

Xinia crouched down and prepared to sit it out, hurt that Sally could be so ungrateful. Still, witches were unpredictable. It wouldn't do to upset one. She didn't want to be turned into a toad.

About half-past ten, Xinia picked her way down in the dark and pushed open the kitchen door. Sally was mashing some sardines in a saucer.

'Did you enjoy the view?' Sally asked sweetly, putting the saucer down on the floor.

But she had been crying again, and although Xinia was starving, she could not help twining herself round Sally's ankles a few times.

'Oh, pussy,' Sally sighed. 'You don't know what being in love is like . . .' and she ran out of the room, forgetting to give Xinia any milk.

Xinia sat there, licking her paws, her mouth as dry as old fish bones. She couldn't open the cupboard where the milk stood up by itself. She jumped on to the draining-board but there wasn't a drip of water to be seen.

She wandered into the pantry and leapt up on to the marble shelf, jumping awkwardly because she was stiff from sitting on the roof all day. Normally she would never have knocked anything over, but something new was there – some contraption of tubes and funnels. Sally edited cookery books for a living and all sorts of strange things were always going on.

The contraption crashed to the ground, shattered, and a pale liquid spread all over the floor. Water, thought Xinia joyously. She leaped down and began to lap it up. Well, it wasn't quite water, but beggars couldn't be choosers. She drank her fill, but soon began to feel quite odd. Something was happening to the kitchen walls . . . perhaps Sally was doing a twirly spell?

Her head was muzzy and her legs felt as if they did not belong to her. Xinia looked down carefully and was relieved to see that they were still joined on. But what . . . on earth . . . was happening?

She staggered round the kitchen, suddenly quite merry and happy. Of course, being such a young witch, Sally couldn't be expected to get everything right the first time, but still she was trying and that was a hopeful sign.

She was vaguely aware of Sally coming into the kitchen, all floating and misty in a white nightgown. Really this was getting better all the time. Levitation now.

'Whatever's the matter?' she heard Sally exclaim. Then Sally was talking in the hall. 'Hello? Hello? This is Sally Jenkins, six Elm Cottages. I'm so sorry to call you out so late, but I'm terribly worried about my cat. She's staggering about in the most unnatural manner . . . thank you very much.'

Xinia was clambering unsteadily up the stairs – or was she coming down the stairs? – when Gavin Jones arrived at the cottage. Sally opened the door to him a large shawl wrapped round her shoulders, her amber hair clouding her pale face. He looked uncertainly at the vision of white and gold in the doorway, and coughed. 'Miss Jenkins?'

'I think she's drunk,' said Sally.

'You've got a sloshed cat?' he asked, wondering if he was dreaming.

'Please come in and have a look at her.'

'What was it? A drop of mother's ruin?' asked Gavin.

'No, my elderflower wine. It's been fermenting in the larder and she must have knocked it over and drunk some . . .'

'Ah . . . the raw stuff. Elderflower, eh? Can have quite a kick,' he said pleasantly.

Xinia saw two Gavin Joneses coming towards her. She didn't much mind which one picked her up. He held her very gently and stroked her in an understanding way.

'I think it might be best if we just let her go away and sleep it off somewhere safe,' he said a little later.

When Xinia eventually woke up around midday, Gavin Jones was in the kitchen having a cup of coffee with Sally.

'Hello, here comes the patient,' said Gavin, going down on to one knee. 'How are you feeling this morning? A bit groggy?'

'Will she have a hangover?' Sally asked anxiously.

'I've really no idea,' said Gavin, his eyes twinkling. 'Perhaps we ought to put her in touch with Alcoholics Anonymous before she gets a taste for elderflower wine. But first, a little warm milk . . .'

After that, the nice looking young vet was always at the cottage, whether Xinia was thinking up dangerous exploits or not. He either popped in on his way to somewhere, or on his way back from somewhere. Sometimes Sally grabbed a coat and went with him which was very promising. In fact, soon she had stopped crying, and the pile of letters on her dressing table were gathering quite a dust.

'The office phoned today to see how I was,' said Sally one evening as they were strolling in the garden. 'I only took a month's leave and it's nearly up. I shall have to go back to my editorial chair before they give my job to someone else.'

'I shall miss you,' said Gavin quietly.

'I'll be back most weekends,' said Sally, apparently pretending that she had not heard him. 'It's not really that far from London.'

Xinia sat in a tree half listening. She couldn't understand why Sally had to go . . . there were plenty of chairs in the cottage. What was so special about this editorial one? Perhaps it had some kind of magic.

Xinia stood on a branch and arched her back. She supposed, reluctantly, that it was time to move on. She'd never been absolutely sure that Sally was a witch, anyway.

Having decided, Xinia left without further ado. She walked straight down the road, across the fields and began to climb the hilly country. Before darkness fell it began to rain, lightly at first but soon it developed into a steady downpour. Then, after a low far-off rumbling, the sky suddenly burst with a clap of overhead thunder; lightning flashed across the dark clouds with crazy fingers. Xinia thought at first it was Sally's doing, making a spectacular fuss. But how could it be? All the time she had lived at the cottage, Sally had never once been angry. No, it must be some other lot.

Xinia tried to find a dry spot to shelter until the storm was over, but the hours of steady rain had soaked everything. Eventually she gave up the hills and found a road to walk on; the ditches were running with rain, and even the road was covered with deep, slopping puddles. Xinia stopped and shook the drops off her paws fastidiously.

Suddenly she was blinded by the headlights coming towards her along the road. Her wits vanished and she froze, petrified, convinced that it was a she-wolf, eyes flaring, jaws ready to crunch her into oblivion . . . The car screeched to a halt within yards of her. Both doors were flung open and a man and a woman got out, running through the torrential rain.

Xinia found herself being scooped up and crushed against a wet raincoat. Sally cradled the bedraggled cat like a baby.

'Whatever are you doing out here in the wilds?' she cried in amazement. 'You're miles from home and absolutely soaked. You'll get lost wandering off like this.'

'And run over . . . sitting in the middle of the road to tidy up,' said Gavin. 'Let's get back into the car. We were going out to dinner, but I suppose we can hardly take a drowned cat with us.'

Suddenly he put his arms round Sally and kissed her, standing in the middle of the road in the pouring rain.

'Don't you realize I love you?' he said, almost roughly. 'You've bewitched me and I'm utterly under your spell. You're beautiful . . . a beautiful witch.'

Xinia, squashed between two raincoats, forgot her discomfort. So Sally *was* a witch after all, quite definitely a witch. Gavin Jones couldn't be wrong. He knew everything.

'Let's take this scruffy thing home first,' he went on tenderly, 'and then we must have a talk . . . a proper talk.'

Sally nodded, smiling. 'That's a good name for her,' she agreed. 'Scruffy.'

Xinia went completely limp. She practically died with mortification. Scruffy! She would never get used to it . . . never, never.

She closed her eyes, nursing her wounded pride, as she was carried back to the car. Sally wrapped her in a warm knitted scarf and settled her comfortably on her lap.

'I hope she won't be frightened of the car,' said Sally. 'I don't suppose she's been in one before.'

But Xinia wasn't frightened. She wasn't frightened of anything. Soon she sat up and took an interest in her new surroundings, fascinated by the rivulets of rain and the windscreen-wipers chasing them, and the dark countryside flashing by.

'I'll put the heater on,' said Gavin. Then he touched another switch and the air was filled with soft, melodic sound.

Xinia was most impressed. This must be some sort of updated version of a broomstick, she thought. Well, it was certainly an improvement on the old type. . . .